F

This book may be returned to any Wiltshire
library. To renew this book phone your library
or visit the website: www.wiltshire.gov.uk

Wiltshire
COUNTY COUNCIL

LM6.108.5

FREDERICK NOLAN

THE GARRETT DOSSIER: DOSSIER: ALERT STATE BLACK

Complete and Unabridged

LINFORD
Leicester

First published in Great Britain

First Linford Edition
published 2008

Copyright © 1989 by Frederick Nolan
All rights reserved

British Library CIP Data

Nolan, Frederick W., *1931 –*
    Alert state black.—Large print ed.—
(The Garrett dossier)
Linford mystery library
1. Police—Great Britain—Fiction
2. Terrorism—Prevention—Fiction
3. Suspense fiction 4. Large type books
I. Title
823.9'14 [F]

ISBN 978–1–84782–188–1

Published by
F. A. Thorpe (Publishing)
Anstey, Leicestershire

Set by Words & Graphics Ltd.
Anstey, Leicestershire
Printed and bound in Great Britain by
T. J. International Ltd., Padstow, Cornwall

This book is printed on acid-free paper

THE GARRETT DOSSIER:
ALERT STATE BLACK

Charles Garrett, Special Branch's expert in terrorism, is also a victim of its effects: in an aborted assassination attempt, his wife was murdered. Now on a mission to Northern Germany to neutralize a terrorist cell led by the man who murdered his wife, his every move is blocked, and his German undercover ally assassinated. And it gets worse when he discovers a secret project that threatens the future of humanity — for he becomes the one they want to neutralize . . .

For Jacky: especially the naughty bits.

1

His name was Sean Hennessy. He was a good-looking fellow in his mid-thirties with bright blue eyes and carroty hair, dressed in an open-necked sport shirt, yellow leather bomber jacket, dark slacks, and scuffed suede shoes with sponge rubber soles. He could have been anything: a farm worker, a taxi driver, a mechanic. Indeed, at one time or another, he had been all of those things, but in fact, he was none of them. Sean Hennessy was what they referred to in Ireland as a 'hard man,' a staff officer of the IRA, head of its terrorist operations in northern Europe.

He decided to launch his third campaign, following successful ones carried out during the preceding two years, in May. Like everything he did, it was meticulously planned. There were to be two teams. The first, consisting of Vic Briggs and Bob Tanner, was given the code name 'Maynooth.' Jeff Hughes and Nick Barrett made up the second, 'Wicklow.' Their briefing was short, their task simple: find a 'target of opportunity,' strike, and disperse.

The two strike teams left Düsseldorf together on Saturday, April 30, and drove the thirty kilometers to Mönchengladback in a Mercedes 280SEL rented from Hertz. At the entrance to the long-term parking lot near the Hauptbahnhof, Jeff Hughes took a ticket from the machine, reversed the car, and drove up to the barrier again, whereupon the machine obligingly delivered a second ticket. Nick Barrett took about thirteen seconds to open up a metallic gold 3-series BMW, and another ten to get it running.

Jeff Hughes piled into the passenger seat, and Barrett drove out of the car park, using the second ticket to get past the exit barrier. Then, as Briggs and Tanner headed north in the Mercedes, the team Hennessy had code-named Wicklow drove west on Highway 230 in the stolen BMW arriving at the little town of Roermond at about nine.

In common with towns all over the country, Roermond celebrated the birthday of Queen Juliana on April 30 with fireworks and a fair that spilled down the narrow old streets radiating from the town hall. Many downtown cafés and bars stayed open all night, crowded with young people. One of the most popular places in town, which claimed to serve thirty-eight different brands of beer, was called Die Bijenkorf, the Beehive. The men from Düsseldorf pushed their way in through the crowd to the bar. Hughes ordered two bottles of Amstel and looked around. To his right along the bar, he saw three very young Royal Air Force squaddies drinking beer.

He moved along the bar until he was next to them.

'Packed in here, isn't it?' he said to the nearest one.

'Yeah.' The young airman looked as if he was relieved to hear the sound of a friendly voice. 'You English, then?'

'Yeah,' Hughes said. 'What are you lads drinking?'

'Lager,' the youngster said. He was tall

and thin, with a bad case of acne.

'Here for the weekend, are you?' Hughes said, signaling to the barmaid.

'Right.'

'*Juffrouw, geeft u ons vijf biers, alstublieft*,' Hughes told the waiting woman. She smiled mechanically and worked her levers, unimpressed by his schoolboy Dutch.

'My name's Jeff,' Hughes said. 'This is my mate Nick Barrett.'

The air-force lads introduced themselves. Billy Conlan was from Bridgnorth in Shropshire; Tommy Rath was from Liverpool. The third member of the trio, the one with the acne, said his name was Pete Russell, from Penge, in south London.

'What's your line, Jeff?' Conlan asked. 'You workin' in Holland?'

'On the building,' Barrett said. 'Moving around. Germany, Holland, Belgium. Wherever. Who wants another?'

The RAF boys needed no second invitation. Barrett ordered more beer. They talked about soccer. Pretty soon they were all good pals.

'Where's all the girls in this place, anyway?' Pete Russell said loudly.

'Probably all at that disco we saw,' Hughes told him. 'On the way in. What was it called?'

'The Bebop,' Barrett said, watching the three RAF boys.

'How do we get there?'

'You know where the Hornerweg is?'

'Never been here before,' Rath said.

'You got wheels?'

'Yer, outside.'

'Right. Follow us,' Barrett said. 'Cross over the bridge. Follow the main road. We'll lead the way.'

'Come on, then.'

The English boys were driving a Peugeot 205 convertible with the top down. They piled in and waited until Barrett turned the BMW around and led the way over the Maas bridge and onto the divided highway leading west. The road was brightly lit by orange sodium lamps that cast an eerie glow on the gray-white concrete. An overhead sign indicated that the village of Horn was six kilometers ahead.

In the BMW, Barrett gave terse orders. Jeff Hughes ran the rear-side window down and readied the Heckler & Koch submachine gun that Hennessy had given them, slapping a fifteen-round magazine of 9mm ammunition into the clamping sleeve. He rested the barrel of the submachine gun on the door as Barrett eased off the accelerator.

The lights of the following Peugeot grew brighter, came closer. Hughes waved an arm, signaling the Englishmen to overtake them. They saw the Peugeot's indicator blink, and the little white car swung out into the center lane. As it drew alongside, Hughes opened up with the submachine gun. Firing at a rate of nine hundred rounds a minute, it took only one second to empty the fifteen-round magazine. The effect was shocking. The little white Peugeot swerved violently to the left, smashing into the central crash barrier with a tearing scream of tortured metal and a showering cascade of orange-yellow sparks. Hughes neatly slid the BMW off onto an exit road as the doomed Peugeot lifted upward and over, flying sixteen feet into the air before landing upside down in the middle of the highway. Chunks of body work flew off it like misshapen Frisbees as the vehicle skated wrong side up across the entire width of the highway, ending up with a huge metallic crunch against the concrete ramping that bordered the exit road. A brief *whoomph*! of sound signaled the ignition of the gas in the tank, and in another moment blue flames began flickering around the torn body work. There was an enormous silence; nothing moved.

★ ★ ★

Twenty five miles upriver at Venray, in the heart of the fenland and forest country known as the *peel*, the disco on the Stationweg was emptying out. Here, as in Roermond, everyone was celebrating the queen's birthday: the streetlights were festooned with orange balloons, colored lights, and red, white, and blue bunting.

Outside the disco, a group of servicemen from RAF Laarbruch were chatting up a couple of Dutch girls. The young men were persistent but unsuccessful, and the girls drifted off, trailing promises they would never keep. The three uniformed boys dawdled back to the side street in which they had parked their car, a Volkswagen Passat. They got in and the driver, an aircraftman named Derek Warden, moved slowly out onto the main street.

In theory, the bomb that Bob Tanner had clamped under the Volkswagen should have gone off immediately. Instead, the mercury trembler remained in position as the car edged slowly along the crowded street, moving faster as it left the village behind. At the T-junction that would take it onto the Nijmegen road, Warden hit the brakes. The jolt tripped the mercury fuse, and the car exploded in a ball of flame, the force of the explosion so great that the windshield frame was later found more than a hundred yards away. The three young airmen in the car died instantly, their bodies burning like plastic dolls inside the searing metal chassis.

* * *

At precisely five A.M., the two killer squads rendezvoused at Venlo, halfway between Roermond and Nieuw Bergen. The stolen BMW was abandoned outside the museum on Goltziusstraat. Then all four men piled into the rented Mercedes and reached Düsseldorf as news of the killings made the morning TV. An hour later, a man from Hennessy's unit dropped Briggs and Tanner at the main downtown railway station, took the other two to Düsseldorf's Lohausen Airport, turned in the rental car to Hertz, then took a taxi back to town. On the way back to the safe house, he picked up the daily papers. The assassinations had been given major headline coverage in the Dutch and German papers. Hennessy smiled as he read them.

Although the operation had been a complete success, the Roermond and Venray hits were just the beginning. He got out the map and stared at it. There, he thought. And there. They would strike at the defenseless British army again and again, all through the summer. And then, the grand finale, the pièce de résistance. His farewell performance. He smiled at the thought. The name of the little town stared back at him.

Lauenburg.

2

'These damned madmen have got to be stopped. Once and for all!'

Short, stockily built, Nicholas Bleke looked more like a successful lawyer, or perhaps a high-flying business tycoon, than anything else. His gray-white hair was cut very close to the scalp. His eyes were shrewd and alert. He was the kind of man who would remain inconspicuous in a crowd until one noted the uncommon something in his mien, the invisible mantle of command.

'Look at this!' Bleke said, tossing a newspaper over so that Garrett could read the headline: SECURITY LAPSES THAT GIVE IRA A CHOICE OF SOFT TARGETS. He did not need to read the editorial; it was just another in an all-too-familiar litany that had filled the newspapers since the beginning of the latest IRA terror campaign, or rather, the renewal of the terror campaign.

'I've managed to keep PACT out of it up to now,' Bleke said. 'Century House kept insisting they were on top of things, that they'd break it wide open. But dammit, they're no nearer now than they were when the first bomb went off.' Century House was the steel and glass block that housed the 'Research Department' of the Foreign and Commonwealth Office, better known as DI6, or the Secret Intelligence Service. PACT was the special antiterrorist branch, of which Bleke was the head.

'They did pick up two of Hennessy's team, sir,' Garrett pointed out.

'Nothing but damned luck!' Bleke snapped. 'It was the Germans who got them. No credit to Six there!'

Toward the end of the summer of 1988, German customs officers had arrested two men trying to cross into Germany from Holland along a remote farm track. It was first believed that the duo were drug smugglers, but when the police found two Heckler & Koch submachine guns in the trunk of the car, and an H&K pistol jammed between the two front seats, they knew they had bagged bigger game. The men were carrying British passports, one in the name of Alan Gregory, the other Colin Rickards. It was quickly established that the man claiming to be Gregory was in fact Seamus McQueen, and that Rickards was really Peter Egan, both well-known members of the IRA's East Tyrone Brigade.

Egan and McQueen were handed over to a special interrogation unit from DI6 flown in from London. These skillful questioners, known as 'dredgers,' carefully but relentlessly dismantled their defenses and demolished their legends, the cover identities they had been using.

Egan was the first to break, and as is often the case, once he started talking it was as if he could not stop. He confirmed that the leader of the European assassination squad was Sean Hennessy, his lieutenant a Derry man, twenty-nine-year-old Tony Gallagher. There were six men in the unit, four now that McQueen and Egan were down. The other two members of the team were Davy McGinnis and Pat Mullan. They were operating out of a safe house in Düsseldorf's northern suburbs, picking up casual work as *gastarbeitern* — dishwashers, waiters, building site laborers. As soon as they had this information, BSSO — British Security Services Overseas — closed in to shut the operation down. They were too late: the arrest of Egan and McQueen had been frontpage news in the German papers, and by the time the Düsseldorf address was checked, the hide had been abandoned.

Hennessy and his cohorts had gone to ground, but where? There was no way of knowing. As in all intelligence work, all the hunters could do was wait until the enemy made another overt move. And that did not come until the following spring.

By that time, the stringent security checks that had been instituted following the attacks during the summer of '88 had been bit by bit relaxed, and life on the Rhine army and air-force bases had returned to normal. The findings of the Dutch police, reports from army intelligence and British Security Services

Overseas were fed into the data banks of TREVI, the international police network set up to counter terrorism in Europe. The results indicated that the attacks were probably all mounted by the same terrorist cell — Hennessy's unit. Knowing that, however, was not at all the same as isolating it and neutralizing it.

'You think there's anything to these reports about German terrorists giving these people aid and comfort, Charles?' Bleke said, as if reading Garrett's mind.

'Anything is possible,' Garrett said. 'Up to comparatively recently, we thought that the IRA had no links with European terrorism. Now I'm not so sure. There was a feud among the leaders of the INLA. Some of their people may have defected to the Irish. That would have given the IRA access to the West European Anti-Imperialist Front. God knows, they aren't choosy who they work through.'

The West European Anti-Imperialist Front was a loose affiliation of the more radical European terrorist organizations — Italy's Red Brigade, France's Action

15

Directe, Germany's Red Army Faction, and revolutionary communist cells in the Netherlands and Belgium. BSSO had done what it could to locate the nerve center of this organization, but without success. The current thinking was that the West German terrorists might well be providing safe houses for the IRA unit to operate out of.

'What do you think, Charles? Is it Hennessy?' Bleke said.

'It has to be,' Garrett said. 'Quite apart from anything else, the IRA just hasn't got that many active service units. On top of that, I talked to Klaus Prachner in Cologne. He says their people got an almost positive ID of Hennessy from a hotel clerk in Düsseldorf. The question is, do we want to get involved?'

'I've got news for you,' Bleke said grimly. 'We've been instructed to get involved. Orders direct from Herself.'

Garrett shook his head. Direct intervention in the field was always difficult, and there were a lot of people hacking about in the undergrowth already. DI6, or the Special Intelligence Service, as they preferred to be called, were active through their European subsidiary, British Security Services Overseas (BSSO), based at Rhine army HQ with outstations in Cologne and Berlin. Germany's Office for the Protection of the Constitution, the *Bundesamt für Verfassungschutz* (BFV), and even the Americans were all taking a direct interest in the activities of the terrorist groups. Committing PACT to the field would put a number of highly sensitive noses out of joint, but if the Iron Lady wished it so, then so it must be.

PACT was, in many ways, her baby, and although the organization was only a few years old, it already had a number of significant successes under its belt.

The organization was born immediately after the bombing of the Grand Hotel in Brighton, in October of 1984, when the IRA nearly succeeded in assassinating Margaret Thatcher and most of her cabinet ministers. A high-level secret meeting to review the government's security and counterterrorism capabilities had been called at Chequers, the official

17

country home of the prime minister in Buckinghamshire.

Among those present were the home secretary; the heads of the security services, D15 and D16; the coordinator of intelligence and security at the Foreign Office; a representative of the joint intelligence chiefs; the deputy assistant commissioner in charge of Special Branch; the commissioner of metropolitan police; the president of the Association of Chief Police Officers; and the colonel commandant of the Special Air Services Regiment.

The result of their weekend deliberations was the establishment of a new executive, designated PACT — Punitive Actions, Counter Terrorism. Working in close cooperation not only with British law enforcement and security agencies, but also the Europolice network TREVI, its special mission was to detect, counter, and neutralize, using any means at its disposal, the planners and perpetrators of terrorist strikes and political assassinations. It was implicit that the phrase 'by any means' meant quite literally what it said.

In January of 1985 a front company, Diversified Corporate Facilities, was established; its offices were in Lonsdale House, Berkeley Square, a Ministry of Defense building situated within walking distance of D15 headquarters on Curzon Street. Early in February, Brigadier Nicholas Bleke, a senior officer in K-7, the counterespionage arm of D15, was appointed its chief executive officer.

The prime minister let it be known that it was her wish — which was the same as a directive — that Bleke be given carte blanche in his selection of personnel; she had the highest regard for this dedicated and ruthless spycatcher. Bleke knew exactly what was wanted and exactly the kind of men he would need. He began by calling in from registry the service jackets of the men who would become his executive officers: Harry Loeb, the best financial man at Curzon Street House; and Tom Ashley, a computer genius at the Royal Armaments R&D Establishment in Chertsey whose job it would be to set up the links between PACT, D15's R2 complex in Euston Tower, GCHQ in

Cheltenham, and the TREVI computers in West Germany. There were others, but the most important of them all was a man Bleke had himself recruited into the Service a decade earlier, and whose career he had discreetly promulgated: Charles Garrett. If PACT was going to succeed, it was going to need men who knew how to play as rough and as dirty as the terrorists themselves, and nobody Bleke knew played rougher when he had to than Charles Garrett.

'How do you feel about going after Hennessy?' he asked Garrett now. It was not an idle question. He knew Garrett had a score to settle with Hennessy that went back to a time before PACT had been set up. Garrett had been on what were euphemistically called 'special duties' in Northern Ireland. This involved running E4 — operations — teams from the Lisburn headquarters of the D16 liaison officer, known to every Irish terrorist as 'the Rathole.' Somehow — no one ever knew how — the IRA had identified Garrett and kidnapped his wife, Diana, with a view to exchanging her for an interned IRA supremo, Patrick McCaffery. The kidnap team was led by Sean Hennessy, hardly a new name to British intelligence. Garrett was encouraged to set up the exchange, but nobody told him that it was going to be used for an ambush. The moment Diana Garrett was safe, an SAS unit was to take both McCaffery and Hennessy out of circulation. It should have worked like a charm, but one of the SAS snipers got buck fever and shot McCaffery before the woman was under cover. In a three-second burst of murderous gunfire, Hennessy had killed Diana Garrett and escaped.

'Hennessy isn't that important anymore. One day we'll take him out. Sooner or later. I can wait.'

'I'm glad to hear you say that, Charles,' Bleke said brusquely. 'I don't think it's healthy for these things to be personal.'

Garrett made no reply. There were some things you could not tell anyone, and especially not to a man who in some ways was more a father to you than your own father.

21

'The BFV sighting was in Düsseldorf, you said?'

'That's right.'

'Do a clean job,' Bleke replied.

★ ★ ★

Sean Hennessy.

He could quote most of what was known about the man without even looking at the dossier. Born March 7, 1953, educated at Dungannon Grammar School, a car thief at twelve, a lookout at fourteen, a member of the East Tyrone Brigade by the time he was eighteen. The psychological profile compiled by the mind hunters at Kelvin House indicated why Hennessy was such a hard fish to catch. He was a man who rarely took chances, figuring the odds for and against himself as efficiently as a calculator, a paradox who could talk of becoming a priest one moment, and the next carry out a ruthless sectarian killing. In security service parlance he was classified as Most Sought and Highly Dangerous. Anyone who lasted as long as he had in the terrorist business had to be as good as the best of the men who were up against him.

After the death of Diana Garrett, he had gone underground. It was suspected he had been a part of the team that had bombed the Grand Hotel in Brighton in October 1984, but the security services had never been able to come up with hard evidence. If BFV was right, it looked very much as if Hennessy had taken command of an active service squad in Europe and was still there.

After the capture of Egan and McQueen, the German security police had launched a nationwide dragnet. There had been numerous sightings of a man, or men, who might have been Sean Hennessy and his fellow terrorists. Subsequent investigation had narrowed the leads down to three: two in the Düsseldorf area, one in Cologne, and another in the Rhine Valley, south of Bonn. The last of these seemed the best bet: the suspect was a man who had worked for a month on an estate called Schwarzenberg, about twenty-five kilometers south of Linz. He had papers in the name of Jim Kitson, born in Newport, Wales. Short, sturdy, red-haired, and blue-eyed, he certainly fit the descriptions of the Irish terrorist, and he had been seen in the company of a young, dark-haired man with blue eyes and a beard who fit the general description of Tony Gallagher.

There were some others, notable among them one in Bad Godesberg, the other farther south in Koblenz; the leads were less specific, but no less likely. Hennessy might be operating from anywhere in northeastern Europe. It was more than his life was worth to stay in any place longer than a few weeks, and by the time any law enforcement agency tracked him down, Hennessy would already be on his way to another hideout. No, the answers, if they were anywhere, were on the ground in Germany.

He picked up the phone and called Arthur Cotton, head of transportation at Lonsdale House.

'Arthur, I want to go to Cologne tomorrow.'

'Early or late?'

'Morning, anyway.'

'First flight is British Airways at nine o'clock. Gets in around eleven-fifteen. If you go to Düsseldorf, there's a plane at eight-thirty-five that gets in half an hour earlier.'

'Cologne'll do. I'd only lose the time in traffic anyway. And Arthur, I'd like a decent car when I get there: a Merc or a BMW. Car phone, Fax, all the toys.'

'Okay, will do. I'll check back with you later.'

Garrett hung up and dialed the unlisted number that would connect him directly with Jessica Goldman.

'Take these chains from my heart and set me free,' he said when she answered.

'Ray Charles, how nice of you to call.'

'I have to go to Germany tomorrow. Can we have dinner tonight instead?'

'I was going to have an early night.'

'I see no problem.'

'Chauvinist pig!' she said, and he could imagine her smiling. 'About eight?'

'See you then.'

He hung up and returned to the dossier

on Sean Hennessy, studying the photograph intently, as if it could speak. He could almost hear Hennessy's voice: *I'll find you one day, you bastard! One day we'll settle this, Garrett!*

Diana had hated Northern Ireland. It always rained, she said.

'I wish we were back in Berlin,' she had said. 'I wish we were any damned place except here.'

He met Diana Page at a private viewing, Treasures from the Thyssen Collection or something like that, at the museum of the Charlottenburg. She was with a couple he knew from his earlier tour of duty, Karl and Penny Barth.

Diana Page was not a beautiful woman, but she was striking, certainly, with dramatic dark eyes and an abundant cascade of jet black hair that made her naturally fair skin seem even paler. She was quite small, but there was nothing frail about her.

They saw each other all through that summer. He had the use of a small sailboat on the Wannsee, and they spent their weekends on board, sometimes with friends, sometimes just the two of them. They were married the following September, just a month after Diana's twenty-fifth birthday. Two months later, Garrett was assigned to 'special duties' in Northern Ireland.

'I won't go,' Diana said.

'We have to go, Diana. You know that. I have to go wherever they send me. You knew it when we got married.'

She was immediately penitent, understanding. Of course she knew that he had no choice. She was the daughter of a career diplomat, and she knew that it was part of the job, going wherever they sent you, whether you liked the idea or not.

He did not realize that she hoped, prayed, expected him to fight the posting, to do anything he could to get out of being sent to Belfast. Maybe if he had done as Diana had hoped, both their lives would have been different. Maybe if what had happened between them had never happened, what happened between her and Hennessy would never have happened. How could you know? You did what you thought was the right thing, and you only found out you were wrong when it was too late.

He still wondered if she had blamed him as she died.

3

Garrett browned two small portions of goat's cheese under the grill and served them on a bed of salad and slivers of fresh fruit.

'Ta-daah,' he said.

'Ooh,' Jessica said. 'Yum yum.'

They ate without talking; it was as if she had sensed his mood and was content to let him decide when to break the silence. When they finished eating, they stacked the dishes in the dishwasher and sat on the long sofa in front of the fire. Above the fireplace was a seaside painting by Sir John Lavery that had been a twenty-first-birthday present to Garrett from his father. Jessica gazed at it, admiring as always the simplicity of the scene, the impressionistic way the artist used light.

'You're very quiet tonight,' she said, pouring the coffee. 'What's bothering you?'

'I don't know,' he said. He shrugged. 'Yes, I do.'

She touched his cheek. 'Do you want to talk about it?'

He shook his head. 'It wouldn't help.'

'It's that Irishman. Hennessy.'

'Yes,' he said. 'I hadn't thought about him for a long time. Then today . . . it all came rushing back, every detail of it pin sharp. I could hear the leaves rustling in the trees, smell the cut hay in the field.'

'You've never really talked about Diana.'

'I know,' he said.

'Why?'

He shrugged again.

'You think it would be painful?'

He turned toward her, making an effort to grin.

'It was my impression that psychiatric treatment was for people who found their particular stresses unbearable.'

'Sometimes,' she said. 'You didn't answer the first question. Do you think it would be painful to talk to me about Diana?'

'Yes,' he said, his smile disappearing.

'And you'd rather me have the pain than you.'

'Now what the hell does that mean, Jess?'

'Charles, I told you right at the outset that I wasn't going to be your R&R lady. If you need someone to stroke your fevered brow and tell you how wonderful you are, I'm sure there's a bimbo somewhere made especially for you. With me, you've got to go all the way down the line. No secrets, no locked doors.'

'You've got a few of your own.'

'I know.'

They were silent for a moment. Jessica sat with her hands folded in her lap. She had dark, lustrous eyes, and her thin, high-cheekboned face was framed by a tumbling mane of dark hair. She was not film-star beautiful, but he never ceased to find beauty in her.

'You've never talked about Ireland,' she said. 'I'm not even sure when all this happened.'

'Eighty-three. A long time ago.'

'What were you doing then?'

'I ran a special intelligence unit in

Lisburn. That's a town about eight miles south of Belfast. Security Services Liaison Office. They called it the Rathole.'

'Go on.'

'Our job was to infiltrate IRA cells. I had a man inside one, an arms-buying unit. His name was Tom Flynn.'

'And this man Flynn infiltrated the IRA?'

'It took another six or eight months. They're not fools. They can spot a plant a mile off. Every newcomer goes through it; it's a sort of test, of your manhood and your sympathies. And Tom passed with flying colors. The IRA has no trouble enlisting muscle, but brains are harder to come by. Someone like Tom, someone as clean as a whistle, who could travel between Northern Ireland and England without difficulty, was an absolute godsend. So he was enlisted as a courier.'

'What do couriers do?'

'They carry messages, or money. Set up meetings. Establish drops and hire cutouts — I'm sorry, I'm talking jargon again.'

'I know what drops and cutouts are.'

'Of course,' he said. Jessica was a psychotherapeutic counselor at the ministry of Defense Medical Establishment on London's Cleveland Street. Her day-to-day work involved untangling the psyches of burnt-out cases who had been brought in from the cold gray world of fieldwork in enemy country. Destressing, they called it. It was as good a phrase as any.

'Flynn was worth his weight in gold,' he went on. 'He was seconded to a unit in County Tyrone led by an IRA staff officer named Pat McCaffery. It got so McCaffery couldn't belch without us knowing about it. Every time the unit got an operation together, Tom would feed us the information and we'd go in and bust it wide open. The bandits couldn't work out how we were outguessing them all the time. What we really wanted, of course, was to catch Paddy McCaffery red-handed in the middle of an arms deal, and finally, with Flynn setting it up, we did just that.'

'How?'

Acting on Flynn's information, I put together a proposition by means of which

McCaffery was able to buy a consignment of weapons in America; of course, the whole shipment was under surveillance from the moment it went aboard. The idea was that the guns would be smuggled ashore at Portnoo in County Donegal, and McCaffery would pick them up there. The army was waiting. There was a gunfight. Four of McCaffery's men were killed, the others — including McCaffery — taken prisoner.'

'How does all this — '

'You'll see,' he said, and his voice was harsher now. 'You'll see. All right, we had McCaffery. The next thing we needed to do was turn him inside out, put him through deep interrogation, and pump him dry. His people knew that if we did, they would be in deep trouble; McCaffery was a keeper of secrets. So one of their best assault units was assigned to getting him out of prison. The leader of the unit was — '

'Hennessy.'

'Sean Hennessy. What I didn't know was that while I was setting up the scam that netted McCaffery, one of their people who had known me in Germany had identified me as the middleman. I was blown and that gave Hennessy the lever he was looking for. Somehow or other he found out the name I was using in Lisburn, and a week later he ambushed my wife's car as she was driving home from visiting a friend. Lifted her out. Kidnapped her.'

'Go on.'

'I moved heaven and earth to find her, but it was no use. She could have been in any one of half a million little white cottages in any one of a thousand sleepy little villages where a stranger would be spotted the minute he showed his face. We had to wait for Hennessy to make his move. It wasn't too long. Ten days, a fortnight. He offered us a deal — Diana in exchange for McCaffery. My people told me to go ahead. It was no deal at all but we had no choice. Hennessy stipulated that I come alone to make the exchange. It was to take place at an isolated crossroads, near a place called Fintona. I . . . it was then . . . '

35

'Tell me,' Jessica said softly. 'Tell me the rest of it.'

'My own people used me,' he said, without emphasis. 'As a Judas goat. They had already broken McCaffery; he was no use to them anymore. But they weren't going to let him go back into business. The plan was to ... dispose of McCaffery and, if possible, lift Hennessy — he was on the Most Wanted list even then — so they let me deal with him to get Diana back. Any other time I would have realized what was happening, but all I could think of was getting her out of it.'

Hennessy had chosen his spot well. The rendezvous was out in open countryside, at a junction of minor roads at a place called Vinegar Hill, where one of the roads ran more or less east-west from Fintona in the general direction of Irvinestown, another joined it from Rakeeranbeg to the north, and a third joined at right angles from Drummallard to the northwest, where it eventually met the main road from Fintona to Dromore. The junction stood amid hummocky hills speckled with sheep.

Hennessy's instructions were explicit: drive up to the junction from the direction of Rakeeranbeg Bridge and wait on the northern side by the black-and-white signpost. Garrett pulled the Land Rover to a stop and got out. McCaffery was inside, handcuffed to the grab handle. He walked around the vehicle, checking the road. It was as empty as a desert. The hills on both sides of the road were maybe three hundred feet high. On the far side of the Drummallard road, about two hundred yards away, was a pile of stones that had once been a cottage. He looked at his watch: two minutes.

Now he saw a vehicle turning into the road south of where he stood. As it drew nearer he saw it was a pillarbox red Ford Escort van. The van eased to a stop on the far side of the junction and Hennessy got out. He was wearing a leather jacket and blue jeans.

'Is it yourself, Garrett?' he called.

'You know it,' Garrett said. 'Where's my wife?'

'In the van,' Hennessy said. There was a strange, strained timbre in his voice.

What was it? Amusement? Contempt? 'Let's see Paddy, then.'

Garrett reached inside the Land Rover and unlocked McCaffery's cuffs.

'Get out,' he said quietly. 'And stand perfectly still. Don't make any mistakes, Paddy. I'll kill you if you do.'

He raised his voice so that Hennessy could hear him.

'Here he is, Hennessy! Let me see Diana.'

Diana got out of the van. She was wearing a white blouse, blue jeans, Dunlop Green Flash tennis shoes. They were not her own clothes. Hennessy was behind her, holding her upper arms, using her as a shield.

'He told me to start McCaffery across,' Garrett said, his voice so quiet that Jessica had to strain to hear it. 'I told him I'd count to three and they could both start walking simultaneously. I saw Hennessy let go of Diana's arms. She turned around to look at him once, and then started walking across toward me. I gave McCaffery a push. They had about twenty yards to go. And I . . . the air

38

smelled. I can't explain what I mean. But I knew something was wrong.'

'What happened?'

'I . . . she looked at me, Jess. I don't know to this day if I felt it or knew it or imagined it, but she seemed to be saying, *I'm not ashamed.* And I felt something turn inside me, and I looked at Hennessy. He has blue eyes, pale blue eyes. I could see him as clearly as I can see you now. *Yes,* they said. *Yes, it's true. I had her.* And I looked at Diana and she was still walking toward me and then . . . and then . . . '

He got up and walked over to the window. A tug was chugging up the river toward Westminster Bridge, trailing a long low line of barges in its wake. Inside his head, like a movie he had seen a hundred times, he saw McCaffery walking toward Hennessy. Then just as McCaffery crossed the road, he lurched strangely and Garrett heard the sudden whiplash crack of the sniper rifle from the ruins of the cottage on the hillside.

Did he actually shout, or did he just think he had shouted 'No! No! No!' as he ran toward Diana, and saw Sean Hennessy skitter out from behind the Ford van, an AK47 in his hands. It made a strangely insignificant sound, *braaaaap*. Diana was running across the road as Hennessy fired. She slewed sideways and went down and Garrett heard the flat whip of the slugs going past him. Instinctively he dropped to one knee, his own pistol in his hand as Hennessy scrambled into the van and rammed it into gear. Garrett laid down a steady line of fire as Hennessy skidded around the corner, the rear end of the Ford fishtailing on the muddy bank, its wheels hurling huge clods of earth into the air.

'And then it was all over. McCaffery was lying dead on one side of the road, Diana on the other.'

'She never spoke?'

He shook his head.

'What about Hennessy?'

'The helicopters were in the air almost before the shooting stopped, but he had a bolt hole somewhere close by. They lost him.'

'Who was responsible for the ambush?'

'It had been planned at Stormont. Belfast. That's where the security services headquarters are.'

'But . . . they must have known — '

'Yes,' Garrett said harshly. 'They did. That didn't stop them, though. They wanted Hennessy. Diana was . . . a reasonable exchange.'

'And yet . . . you stayed in the security service? Even when it has cost you . . . so much?'

'No,' he said. 'I got out. I told them all to go to hell. I went over the hill, hid out in a little cottage I rented in Wicklow, tried to drown myself in Jameson's, but I kept floating to the top. After a while I came to terms with myself. With what had happened. I began to be able to think of Diana as a casualty. Once I was able to do that, I could channel the anger where it belonged: into fighting the bastards.'

She let the silence lengthen. This time it was not uncomfortable.

'One more question, then I'll stop. Do you really believe she slept with Hennessy?'

'Yes.'

'How do you feel about it?'

'Not great. But I can live with it. They told me how things like that can happen, the strange symbiosis that sometimes develops between hostages and their captors. Perfectly respectable people make violent love to utter strangers in the toilets of hijacked planes. It's as if the power of life and death is an aphrodisiac.'

'Sometimes,' Jessica said.

'Jess, this is hard for me to do. Talking about her to you.'

'Why?'

'I don't want her to come between us, Jess.'

'Then let her go,' Jessica said. 'Let her go, Charles!'

'I'm trying to,' he said. 'It isn't easy to do.'

'Why?'

He was silent for a long moment. 'I suppose I . . . I feel it was my fault she was killed,' he said very quietly.

'Would anything you did have changed what happened?'

'I don't suppose so. I just can't help wondering . . . '

'Yes?'

'I can see her going down, Jess. I can see the life going out of her eyes. That terrible moment. She knew. She must have known. And I keep wondering, as she died, whether she blamed me for that, too.'

'What else did she blame you for?'

'What?'

'You said, 'that, too.''

He shook his head. 'I don't know. Maybe if I'd never gone to Ireland in the first place . . . '

'Diana didn't want to go?'

'She wanted to stay in Berlin. She loved it there. The parties, the gossip, the whole social scene. She thought Belfast was a shithole, and said so very forcefully.'

'Get us out of here, Garrett. Get us out of this hellhole before I go stark staring raving mad.'

'Maybe I could get a couple of weeks leave. We could rent a car, drive down to Killarney.'

'You're not listening, are you? Get me out of here. Watch my lips: Get. Me. Out. Of. Here.'

'Why do you think she wanted you to know?'

'What?'

'Why did she want you to know she had slept with Hennessy? You said she looked at you and you knew. What was it, something in her eyes, the way she walked?'

'I don't know.'

'Yes you do.'

'It was her way of saying it wasn't her fault, it was mine.'

'She blamed you for making her do what she had done.'

'I suppose so.'

'And do you think it was your fault?'

'Maybe. No. Not that.'

'What, then?'

'I told you. The fact that she was there at all, dammit!'

'Why are you angry?' she said. 'It wasn't your fault. Why do you want it to be?'

'You think that's what I want?' He looked into her eyes and took her hands in his. 'You think that's what I want, Jess?'

Jessica was silent, holding his gaze, waiting.

'You think I'm holding on to the guilt because it gives me an out? An excuse not to make another commitment?'

Again she said nothing.

'I love you, Jess,' he said.

'Then let go, Charles. Let go of the past.'

'I'm trying,' he said. 'I really am. But letting go of the past is so damned hard to do.'

'I know, my darling, I know,' she said softly. She got up from her chair and walked across to the sideboard. She poured whiskey from a decanter into a crystal glass and took it to him by the window. He sipped it and smiled.

'God knows what it does to your liver,' she said. 'But I think you've earned it.'

'I'm glad I got it all said,' he said. 'I wanted you to know how it was. How I felt.'

'I know.'

'You're very good at this, aren't you?'

'I try to be.'

'I envy some of those burnt-out cases they send up to you.'

'They don't get quite the same

personal treatment you do.'

'Is there more personal treatment to come?'

'What did you have in mind?'

He drew her close, feeling the strength in the long lissome lines of her back. 'Jess, Jess,' he said. 'I want everything to be good for us.'

'It will,' she said. She took his face in her hands and kissed him on the lips, a devil dancing in her dark eyes. 'Especially if we both take our clothes off.'

4

When Garrett arrived at Köln-Bonn Airport, he found a message to tell him that a Mercedes 190 was waiting for him in the parking lot. He picked up the keys at the British Airways desk and drove into Cologne at a leisurely pace, detouring so that he could cross the old Deutzer Bridge with its fabulous view of the great Gothic spires of the cathedral. It was also the simplest way to reach the center of the city and the British Security Services Overseas outstation, a faceless concrete block near the Heumarkt.

Garrett used his key card to open the bullet-resistant glass doors, picked up the handset on the wall outside the door in the hallway, and spoke his name into it. He was asked to place his identification against the square of glass beside the door, and heard the discreet zip of the computer wipe. A moment later, the security lock clunked open, and a young woman in a white blouse and dark skirt held the door for him to enter the office.

'This way, Mr. Garrett,' she said, smiling brightly. 'Mr. Fritz has been expecting you.'

She led the way along a corridor, gray-carpeted, brightly lit. They took the elevator to the fourth floor and emerged into a corridor exactly the same as the one below. Each office had a nameplate on the wall outside of it, the names posted in bold Helvetica type. Emil Fritz's office was at the far end, a neat, uncluttered room with one-way windows that looked out onto what had once been the old town marketplace. He stood up as Garrett came in, a thin, bearded man with a prominent nose and washed-out pale blue eyes.

'Emil!' Garrett said, grasping the German's bony hand. 'It's good to see you again!'

'You too, Charles,' Fritz said. 'It's been a long time since Berlin.'

'You haven't changed a bit,' Garrett lied. When he had known Fritz in Berlin, fifteen, sixteen years earlier, the German had been a man well on his way up the ladder, one of the best of the counterintelligence people based there. Although only in his middle fifties, Fritz looked like a man who knew he had gone as far as he was going to go. Garrett wondered what had happened to him.

'I've changed,' Fritz said harshly. 'You don't need to pretend.'

'How long have you been here in Cologne?'

'Six years.'

'So you were here in Dickie Boyd's time?'

A smile briefly touched the German's face, as if he had recalled a fond memory. 'Those were the good days,' he said.

'And now it's not so good?'

Fritz shook his head. 'The last few years . . . ' He looked up, clamping his lips shut as the young woman who had shown Garrett in tapped on the glass window at the door. 'What is it, Gisele?'

'Did you want something, Herr Fritz? Tea, coffee?'

'No,' he told her. 'We're going out. Come, Charles. There's a nice little place across the street. *Gemütlich*.'

Garrett started to say he didn't want anything but bit the words back when he caught Fritz's meaningful glance. They went out of the office and across the busy square to a small café called the Tessiner Stubchen. Fritz headed for a table in a corner at the back of the place and sat where he could watch the doorway. Old habits die hard, Garrett thought. The waitress came and they ordered coffee.

'What's all this about, Emil?' Garrett asked as she left.

'Can't talk back there,' Emil replied, with a jerk of his head toward the office they had just left. '*Die Kanone* has too many spies.' He used the word in its slang sense, meaning not a cannon but a big shot.

'Shupe? That's what you call him?'

Colonel Paul Shupe was head of military intelligence, Rhine army, based at Rheindahlen, about forty-five miles northwest of where they were sitting. By virtue of his rank, he was also senior UKUSA liaison officer, responsible for joint intelligence with the American army.

50

'They call him a lot of things, Charles. They call him *Der Schupo*, the cop. Or *Herr Schuppe*, Mr. Dandruff. Those are the polite names.'

'I take it he's not popular.'

Fritz made a signal with his hand; the waitress was bringing their coffee. Did he think the girl was one of Schupe's spies, too? Paranoia was never far away in the spying business.

'Not popular,' the German said when the girl had gone away. 'A masterpiece of understatement. Everybody hates his guts.'

'You included?'

'Me especially,' Fritz said. 'You know how he got his job?'

'I've read his dossier. He took over after General Waverly died, didn't he?'

Garrett mentally reviewed what he knew about Colonel Paul Oliver Shupe. Forty-six years old. Born in York, a graduate in modern languages of the university there, Shupe joined the army as a commissioned officer; he transferred to army intelligence in 1980 and was posted to Prague as an attaché. He compromised

51

his position there with disastrously clumsy 'operations' and was moved out of harm's way before he did irreparable damage.

The standard procedure with intelligence personnel who fouled the nest was to put them somewhere they couldn't do it again. Shupe was stuck into the system at Rheindahlen as UKUSA liaison officer, responsible for maintaining communication links with United States Forces, European Theater, USFET for short. According to his dossier, he had been at Rheindahlen only two years when the officer commanding, General Lawrence Waverly, died suddenly.

'The way I read it, Shupe was made acting officer in command and then confirmed sometime later. Isn't that how it happened?'

'Not quite,' Fritz told him. 'Waverly was a good man. He knew how to delegate. He paid us the compliment of assuming we were professionals and let us get on with what we were paid to do. Then we had Shupe foisted on us.

'Bit by bit he took control. Two years

later, the old man died, and Shupe made his move. He just wrote me — and everybody else — out of the scenario by getting himself appointed acting CO.'

'They gave him the command.'

'He'd made it almost impossible for them to appoint anyone else,' Emil said. 'And once he had command, he started paying off old scores. Anybody who'd shown the slightest opposition got it in the neck.'

'Like you.'

'Like me. I was the senior intelligence officer in Rhine army, but he called me in and told me I was off field duties. Permanently. What he meant was, he was making me a damned clerk. And so — ' He spread his hands, palms upward, *you see?*

'You got a rough deal,' Garrett said.

'Ach, it's not important anymore,' Emil said. 'I'm fifty-two. I'll take early retirement in a few years.'

'Tell me what you've been doing about these bombings,' Garrett said, changing the subject in order to dissipate the bitterness that hung in the air like a curtain. 'Has there been any progress?'

'With Dandruff in charge?' Emil gave a short, sharp bark that might have been a contemptuous laugh. 'Our official line is that they are minor, and isolated incidents. Classification MCR.'

Minimum Commitment of Resources. Garrett shook his head. Somewhere within a couple of hundred miles Sean Hennessy and his team were biding their time, waiting to strike, and Shupe's reaction was to commit minimum resources to the task of detecting, countering, and neutralizing that threat. No wonder the Irishmen felt able to strike at will, go wherever they felt like going.

'What about the Americans?' he asked.

Emil gave another of his contemptuous snorts. 'They take their line from us. If we're dragging our feet, why should they get steamed up? Nobody's shooting their personnel or bombing their bases.'

'Tell me about Shupe's private life.'

'I don't think he has one.'

'Come on, Emil. He's married. It's in his jacket.'

'Ah, Betty. My wife Erica calls her the

mouse with teeth. Very English, you know what I mean? All that class business. If she thinks someone's a rung below her, she treats them like dirt.'

'How about other women?'

Emil shook his head vehemently. 'Not Shupe. To begin with, he's not the type at all. You know what I mean? He tries to be one of the boys, but you always feel it's an act; he isn't really and he doesn't want to be. He's like one of the people in that film, what was it called, you know, the one where the pods came down on the little town.'

'*Invasion* — '

' — *of the Body Snatchers*, that's the one! You know the way the clones acted like people, but they could only fake emotion?'

'There are people like that, Emil. They just aren't able to let themselves go as easily as the rest of us.'

'I know, I know, I can hear myself, bitching and backbiting and sounding like a querulous old man who's been passed over for promotion. It's just that I get so mad whenever I think about how the bastard got where he is.' He made an angry gesture. 'Ah, the hell with him. You want some more coffee?'

'Let's get back to the office,' Garrett said. 'I need to make a few calls. Unless there's anything else you want to tell me?'

'I shouldn't have said this much.'

Garrett put his hand on Fritz's shoulder. 'It won't go any further, Emil,' he promised.

Emil Fritz looked indignant. 'I never thought for a second that it would,' he said.

* * *

After he left the BSSO outstation, Garrett walked through the narrow streets to the Ratskeller, a restaurant in the ancient town hall. He found a table on the terrace. The sun was warm. It was hard to believe it was October. He stood up as he saw Klaus Prachner coming up the steps off the street. Klaus was an old friend who worked for BFV, the German equivalent of D15, a tall, spare man with pale blue eyes and lank blond hair. They greeted each other with bear hugs and backslaps.

'You look fine, Garrett,' Klaus said. 'It's good to see you.'

'You too, Klaus,' Garrett said. 'How's Heidi?'

Prachner shrugged. 'That's over,' he said.

'Sorry. I didn't know.' One of the curses of intelligence work was that the stress factors were so high, interpersonal relationships invariably suffered. A lot of operatives were either divorced, or drunks, or both. You could only hope the opposition had the same problems.

'You know why I'm here,' Garrett said.

'Come to show us how to do our jobs, I understand.' Klaus grinned. 'Help us catch the mad Irishmen.'

'We want them, Klaus,' Garrett said. 'Rather badly.'

'You, especially,' the German observed.

'You know about that?'

Klaus grinned. 'I'm an intelligence officer, man!'

'What's BFV's priority rating on the Irishmen, Klaus? On a scale of one to ten?'

'About four. We're leaving the legwork to British military intelligence.'

'Ah, Colonel Shupe. Tell me about him.'

'You want me to tell you, when you've got his dossier?'

'His dossier doesn't tell me what I want to know,' Garrett said.

'Is it too early for a proper drink? I'm coffee-logged, if there is such an expression.'

'If there isn't, there ought to be.' Garrett signaled the waiter. 'What do you want?'

'*Korn and Kölsch*,' Klaus told the man, who looked at Garrett and raised a haughty eyebrow.

'*Zweimal*,' he confirmed. Corn liquor with a beer chaser wasn't the ideal afternoon drink, but he knew better than to expect Klaus to talk without a couple of glasses of something inside him. They remained silent until the waiter brought back the drinks, serving them with a flourish and a '*Zum wohl!*'

'Clown,' Prachner muttered. He lifted his glass and clinked it against Garrett's, then tossed down the schnapps in one swallow. Garrett followed suit. He didn't care for German liquor much; it didn't taste of anything.

'Shupe,' he reminded Klaus.

'Okay, okay. He's one of those Englishmen who give the English a bad name. Like the football hooligans, you know? And worst of all, a racist. Calls us Jerries. He even tells Hitler jokes, for Christ sake! Can you imagine it?'

'So he's a boor. There are a lot of them in the army. There are a lot of them in intelligence, too. The question is, is he effective?'

'My opinion? He couldn't catch a terrorist if the guy shot himself on his office doorstep.'

'How about his people?'

'Nobody has a good word to say for him, but they put up with him. From what I hear, it's just as well, otherwise he'd be running MI alone.'

'How about your office?'

'We avoid him whenever possible.'

'How about Pullach and the Abwehr?'

The German foreign intelligence service, BND — the acronym stood for

Bundesnachrichtendienst, Federal Information Service — worked out of a complex at Pullach, south of Munich.

'Same thing,' Klaus replied. 'The minute anyone finds out that Shupe is involved, it's sorry, we're busy.'

Garrett sighed. 'I was afraid you were going to say that.'

'You mean . . . ?'

'I've been sent out here to stop these bombings, Klaus. These people have had their own way long enough.'

'Shupe isn't going to like that much.'

Garrett shrugged. 'I'll have to sweet-talk him.'

'I don't envy you,' Prachner said with a sardonic grin. 'You poor sad bastard! You'd better have another drink.'

While Klaus ordered more drinks, Garrett looked around. The place was full of well-dressed, prosperous-looking people. He wondered whether any of them ever gave a thought to men like Prachner, who regularly put his life on the line to protect their fragile world. Not hardly, as John Wayne used to say.

'Who's the UKUSA officer on the

American side?' he asked his friend.

Klaus frowned in concentration. 'A Major Barton,' he said. 'Paul Barton. He's based at Wiesbaden, I think. Or is it Frankfurt? I'll check it out when you come to the office. We don't have much to do with the Amis.'

Garrett grinned at his friend's use of the German World War II nickname for the Americans. He looked at his watch.

'Come on,' he said to Prachner. 'Let's go for a drive.'

'Where to?'

'Down the river. Linz.'

'Waste of time. We checked all that, Charles. It's all on the computer.'

'I know that. I just want to see the place. Get the feel of it. Tell you what, I'll even buy you dinner. We can eat on the river. Or at that place in the Mittelstrasse. What was it called? Alt Linz, wasn't it?'

Klaus shook his head. 'Do you ever forget anything, Charles?'

'Yes.' Garrett grinned, getting up. 'I often forget I said I'd pay.'

★ ★ ★

Figuring they'd want to get away fast once they planted the banger, McGinnis picked out a locally registered Volkswagen Golf GTI 16 valve job in dark blue, drove it out of the *parkhaus* on Dreikonigenstrasse, and tooled it around to the front of the Hauptbahnhof, where Mullan was waiting on the steps, two small attaché cases in his hands. He put the cases on the backseat of the car and got in.

'Any problems?' he said.

'You kiddin'?' Davy McGinnis grinned. 'Like taking the pennies off a dead man's eyes.' He accelerated, turning onto the Gladbacherstrasse and under the railway bridge out of Krefeld.

'Good-bye, Krefeld,' Mullan muttered, giving a little salute with his forefinger to his temple as they passed the yellow sign with its black diagonal telling them they were leaving the city limits. 'What a bloody boring town.'

McGinnis laughed. He liked working with Pat. Good sense of humor, Pat had. He took the autobahn south, turned east on E59. The disc jockey was playing something Latin by Peggy Lee, and Davy boop-booped tunelessly along. When he saw the NATO sign, he took the Wegburg exit ramp and headed south. It was growing dark; he put on the car lights.

'Be there soon,' he said.

Mullan grunted acknowledgment.

'What time you want to do it?' Davy asked.

'Anytime you like.'

'What are we using?'

'Semtex, same as always.'

'My dad told me they used to use ammonium nitrate in the old days. Mixed it up with fuel oil. ANFO, they called it.'

'Easier now, eh?' Pat Mullan said. 'Ten quid a pound and you can blow up the entire bloody world if you want to.'

'Twice as powerful as nitro,' Davy mused. 'You'd wonder how it could be that powerful and yet be so safe.'

'Miracles of science.' Mullan grinned. 'They're all around us.'

'There it is,' Davy said. The main entrance to NATO headquarters, Rheindahlen, with its white-painted curbs and neat-grass turning circle, was on their right. He eased off the accelerator so that they were only doing about fifty kph, and Pat Mullan stared brazenly at the guards at the gate as they went by.

'More like a bloody housing estate than an army camp,' he muttered, spreading the Landesvermessung topographical survey map across his knees. 'Take the next right, Davy.'

About seven hundred yards farther on, McGinnis eased the car into the right-hand lane, then onto a minor road connecting the major road they were on with another that ran diagonally across the far side of the base. All along the road on their right was an eight-foot-high wire fence with solid concrete uprights that angled inward. Coils of the razorsharp security wire called S-wire were looped along the top. Beyond the fence, ten or fifteen yards across neatly mown grass plots, were the enlisted men's barracks buildings, angled to the road and parallel to each other, graceless brick boxes with white wooden windows and red-tiled roofs. Concrete walkways bisected the spaces between them. Each building bore the name of an English county.

'Which is your least favorite county, Pat?' Davy said.

'Essex,' Mullan said. 'I was there once. Boring. Flat as a bloody pancake.'

'All right,' Davy said. 'We'll do Essex.'

He turned the car off the road, did a three-point turn, and headed back the way they had come. There were lights on in some of the barracks buildings across the way.

'Ten pounds should do it,' Mullan said. 'Pull over.'

McGinnis stopped the car. Mullan put on the courtesy light and reached back for one of the attaché cases. He took out an Icom IC2 transceiver and laid it to one side. Then he took out two slabs of Semtex and kneaded them like dough until they were long, sausage-shaped rolls. Into each of these rolls he stuck a glass vial containing pure gunpowder, with a relay and an Ultralife 1.5-volt battery wired to it.

'How do those things work?' McGinnis said.

'It's dead simple,' Mullan replied. 'When you talk into a transceiver, the changes in air pressure are converted to electrical impulses and transmitted through the aerial to the receiver. The receiving set reconverts the signal to pulses that vibrate the loudspeaker and replicate the message.'

'So?' McGinnis said dubiously.

'What I've done is stick a relay switch on the loudspeaker circuit in the receiver. When I press the send button on this one, it will convert the signal into a spark. The spark sets off the detonator, and up she goes.'

They got out of the car and checked the road. It was empty; no traffic in either direction. They ran across and crouched at the foot of the wire-mesh fence. Using heavy-duty wire cutters, McGinnis made short work of the 2mm-thick wire strands. He cut in an inverted L shape and then peeled the wire back so that it made a triangular entrance. Pat Mullan ran across the grass strip between the fence and the rear of the barracks building; McGinnis could not see him anymore in the darkness. He scanned the road anxiously for any sign of a car;

nothing in sight. He felt relief flood through him as Mullan's solid shape materialized in the darkness. Jeez, he needs a bath, he thought irrelevantly.

'All right,' Mullan said. 'Let's get the fuck out of here!'

As Davy McGinnis gunned the VW down the highway, Mullan fumbled on the floor until he found the walkie-talkie he had put there earlier.

'One to be ready,' he intoned. 'Two to be steady. And three to go.' He pressed the send button.

★　★　★

It was getting dark when Garrett parked the Mercedes in the cobbled marketplace with its Gothic town hall and higgledy-piggledy medieval houses, and they walked across to the Alt Linz, a low-arched restaurant with white walls and stone floors. The tables and chairs were solid and heavy, made in the old rustic style.

The owner's wife, a plump, smiling woman with rosy cheeks and dark blond hair, showed them to a table. There were only a few people in the place. They drank Rudesheimer while they waited for their food: *wildschweinbraten* with mushrooms, fried potatoes, and kraut. It was the game season in Germany. From the Baltic Sea to the Alps, every red-blooded German was either out hunting deer and boar, or in a restaurant eating it.

'Where was that sighting, Klaus?' Garrett asked.

'Up in the hills, not far from here. An old *Schloss* called Schwarzenberg. There are still one or two in private hands.' He pushed his chair back. 'Listen, I have to call in. Let them know where I am.'

He disappeared into the rear of the restaurant and Garrett heard him asking for the telephone. He looked around; the place was filling up with couples and foursomes. Not for the first time he noticed that young German girls seemed to like older men a lot more than their counterparts in Britain and the States.

It was no great stretch of the imagination to picture Hennessy eating here, a pot of beer in front of him, his face red from the sun, swapping jokes with the locals, blue eyes merry.

He saw him, as he always saw him in memory, half crouched behind the car on the other side of the crossroads. *I'll find you one day, you bastard!* Hennessy had shouted. *One day we'll settle this, Garrett!*

Over in the corner, three old men sat at the *stammtisch* with their beer and schnapps. At the head of the table sat a big, fat, red-faced man in a woolen jacket, his pale eyes watchful; next to him was an older man with a hook nose and a downturned mouth who wore an open-necked check shirt and heavy moleskin trousers; another had his back to Garrett. As he watched, an old man with a stick came in, joined them at their table, and ordered beer and a pack of cigarettes, although he had a cough like a dying horse. A few minutes later, an even older one came in, unshaven, his clothes creased and stained, walking with the aid of two sticks.

'Here comes the King,' one of the men at the table said. The old man sat down, and without being asked, the young waitress brought him a Hellbier in his own stein. He neither looked up nor thanked her.

'Well,' he said to the others. 'It'll rain before long.'

He made it sound as if he held them responsible. His advent seemed to have lightened their mood; they smiled. One of them started shuffling a pack of greasy cards. Old comrades, Garrett thought. It was not difficult to imagine them sitting here as young men, wearing the uniform of Hitler's army, with Lale Anderson coming through the loudspeakers instead of James Last. He signaled the waitress and told her to give the old men a drink. He lifted his glass when she served them.

The old boy with the two sticks leaned across. 'You're not from around here,' he said, with hesitant certainty.

'English,' Garrett replied. 'Looking for work.'

'You speak good German. What's your line?'

'Casual. Can't be picky these days.' He saw the old man looking at his hands. Caught out, he thought disgustedly; maybe the oldster had been in the police, not the army.

'You'll excuse me,' the old man said pointedly. 'You don't look the type.'

Garrett avoided answering by asking another question. 'I hear there's a big *hof* around here. You think there might be anything going on up there?'

'Schwarzenberg, you mean,' the one with the down-turned mouth said. 'You could try.'

'Do they hire a lot of casuals?'

The man shrugged and looked at the one they called the King. He regarded Garrett levelly.

'What do you really want up there, young fellow?'

Garrett shook his head. 'You're too wise an old owl for me,' he said, trying to look gauche. 'I'll tell you the truth. I'm after a fellow I know. Owes me a lot of money.'

'Ah,' the old man said, with a triumphant look at the others. 'I thought it might be something like that.'

'He's Irish,' Garrett said. 'Name of Jim Kitson. Bright blue eyes, carrot-colored hair. Stocky build, about thirty-five.'

'Kitson,' the old man said, rolling the name around his mouth as if he were tasting it. 'Kitson. Speaks German, does he?'

'Yes,' Garrett said. It was a fair bet Hennessy had learned enough to get by. 'Bit of an accent, though.'

'He would have,' the old man said. After a moment he shook his head. 'No. I don't remember him.'

'Many Irish in these parts, are there?'

'Not that many speaking German,' said one of the men.

'You go to Schwarzenberg,' the old man said. 'Ask for Hans Kupfer. Say Old Peter sent you.'

'I'm grateful,' Garrett said. 'Will you have another?'

'No more!' Old Peter said, holding up a shaky hand. 'I'll be up all night.'

They turned back to their own concerns and began playing cards. Garrett looked out across the cobbled square outside. It had begun to rain and the street shone black.

Prachner came hurrying back, his face

grave. He made a gesture: *outside*. They went out into the tiled hallway and stood by the cigarette machine.

'We've got to get back right away,' Klaus said urgently. 'They've had a bomb at Rheindahlen.'

'How bad?'

'I don't know. It only just happened.'

'IRA?'

'That's the funny thing. It's not the Irish. Somebody claiming to represent the Red German Army telephoned. Said they were responsible.'

Garrett frowned. 'Red German Army? Who the hell are they?'

'We're not going to find out sitting here,' Prachner said.

5

Rheindahlen was the largest of the many sprawling military complexes scattered all over what had once been, after the German surrender in 1945, the British zone of occupation.

As he approached the entrance to the base, Garrett saw that it was guarded by an armored car. Shutting the stable door, he thought. He presented his identification to the burly soldier at the gatehouse at one side of the heavy metal security gate. The soldier touched his beret with a forefinger and went into the hut, where he picked up a phone and made a call, watching Garrett the whole time. Garrett knew that look. *So you're the one.* Obviously his arrival was no secret; so much for internal security.

There were one or two small, but significant, signs of sloppiness about the area: cigarette butts on the tarmac, letters missing from the sign on the gate.

The young soldier came back, handed Garrett his ID, and waved the gate open. 'Straight ahead, sir,' he said. 'About four hundred yards. You'll see the headquarters building on your right. Adjutant's office on the left of the door as you go in. Captain Cameron is expecting you.'

In many ways Rheindahlen was more like a small town than a military post, the main difference being the security fence that surrounded the entire area, made of eight-foot-high concrete uprights supporting wire mesh topped with German S-wire. As a security screen it left a lot to be desired, Garrett thought. A fence like that only kept out people who didn't want to get in anyway. It wouldn't delay a determined schoolkid with a pair of pliers for ten minutes, much less a terrorist, even if it was fitted — which he doubted — with electronic detection devices and floodlighting.

He drove slowly down the company road, pulled into the parking bay in front of the headquarters building and went up the semicircular stone steps to the swing doors. Inside, a couple of MPs with blanco'd belts and holsters stood guard, their faces blank with boredom. Garrett reported to the adjutant's office and was asked to wait. After a few moments, a tall, thin, supercilious-looking officer came through a door on his right.

'You're Garrett? I'm Cameron, Colonel Shupe's aide. I'm afraid he's in a meeting at the moment.'

He made no attempt to be cordial, or to shake hands. It was not unexpected. According to Emil Fritz, Major George Cameron was known universally as 'Carbolic' because he was such a stinker. He was about fifty, his sparse blond hair receding, cheek and jawbones angular and prominent, the thin-lipped mouth beneath the blond toothbrush mustache twisted with condescension. A disillusioned face, Garrett decided, but there was no mistaking the hostility in the washed-out blue eyes.

'I can wait,' Garrett said.

They went into a small room with a frosted window, a desk, a couple of chairs. On one wall there was a small sink with a square mirror above it; beside that was another door. An interrogation room, Garrett thought, wondering why Cameron had brought him in here as he sat down opposite the desk. Cameron went around the desk and sat facing him, elbows together on the desk, fingers interlocked with his chin resting on them.

'How long do you think Colonel Shupe will be?' Garrett asked.

Cameron drew in his breath sharply through his teeth, as though he had been asked to forecast the Second Coming. 'I really couldn't say,' he replied. 'The colonel is a very busy man.'

'He got my message?'

'Oh, he knew you were coming,' Cameron said disdainfully. 'He has to get his priorities right, you know.'

'How lucky for him to have someone like you to sort them out for him,' Garrett said.

Cameron looked up sharply, but his visitor's face was expressionless. He cleared his throat with an irritated cough presumably intended to show displeasure and opened a manila file that was lying on the desk. 'Now then. You arrived on

British Airways flight 742 on Wednesday morning. You checked into the Dom Hotel — you have expensive tastes, I see — then had a meeting with Mr. Fritz at BSSO. Later you met a BFV operative named Prachner at the Ratskeller. You — '

'You had me under surveillance?'

Cameron raised his eyebrows, as if in surprise. 'It's nothing personal, Garrett. Colonel Shupe's orders. We keep an eye on everyone, you know. What were you doing in Linz, by the way?'

'I had dinner with Klaus Prachner.'

'Would you care to tell me the purpose of your meeting?'

'Not especially,' Garrett said.

'Don't think that because I phrased my question politely, I don't want it answered,' Cameron said, his voice hardening.

'And don't think because you're acting tough that I'm going to have a nervous breakdown,' Garrett replied. 'What the hell is all this about, Captain?'

'I'll spell it out for you. You are on a top-security army base. It's like a little island. You play the game by our rules or you don't play at all. You understand me?'

'I understand you,' Garrett said. 'It's making myself believe you're serious I'm having trouble with.'

Cameron made an impatient sound. He got up and went to the window, looking out. He spoke without turning around.

'You can work inside the system, or outside it,' he said: 'That's entirely up to you, of course. I would recommend the former. You will find life . . . difficult, otherwise.'

Garrett looked at him for a long moment, then shook his head in disbelief. He turned toward the mirror on the wall. Did they think he was so stupid he didn't know what it was?

'Am I suppose to take this charade seriously, Colonel Shupe?' he asked. 'Don't you people know who I work for?'

The door beside the mirror opened. Colonel Paul Shupe was a big man, well over six feet, a good two hundred and forty pounds. His hair was Italian black, greasy and limp. He had a florid, beefy face, with close-set eyes beneath heavy brows, thick lips, a heavy, square jaw. Behind him was a short, thickset, capable-looking man wearing the uniform of a sergeant.

'You're just another of those damned Ministry of Defense snoopers,' Shupe said, hitching his plump haunch onto the corner of the desk. He stuck a cigar in his fleshy mouth and lit it, blowing smoke down at Garrett. 'Isn't that right?'

'Push me around and see,' Garrett said.

Cameron made an angry sound. Shupe stilled it with an upraised hand. He looked at Garrett curiously, as though seeing him for the first time.

'PACT,' Shupe said, making no attempt to conceal the sneer in his reedy voice. 'Somebody in London says we've got a terrorist problem. I say what we've got is a bunch of crazies who want us all to go home.'

'That's not our judgment, Colonel.'

'Well, I have to tell you something frankly, Garrett,' Shupe said, leaning back in his chair and pulling on the wet-ended cigar. 'I can't honestly say I give much of a fuck what your judgment is.'

Garrett shrugged. 'Then I pass my assessment to London and let them make the decisions.'

Shupe's eyes narrowed. 'And what, may I ask, is your assessment?'

'You're in trouble, Colonel,' Garrett said. 'Terrorists are bombing army installations and killing military personnel and you don't appear to have the slightest idea what to do about it. On top of that you can't get any help from the Germans or the Dutch because your reputation stinks so badly nobody wants to do business with you. Discipline is lousy and morale even worse. In short, Colonel, your operation sucks. How am I doing so far?'

Shupe stared at him, the piggy eyes smoldering with contempt. In his peripheral vision, Garrett thought he saw a message pass in a look between the big man and Cameron. The tension went out of the burly body, and cunning replaced the aversion in the close-set eyes. Here comes the bullshit, he told himself.

'Well,' Shupe said, his reedy voice just too hearty to be convincing. 'You don't beat about the bush, do you, Garrett?'

'Not if I can help it.'

'You know what, George?' Shupe said, addressing the words to Cameron. 'I like this man.'

Cameron said nothing. Shupe clapped Garrett on the shoulder.

'I like you, Garrett,' he said expansively. 'I like a man who says what he thinks and stands up for what he believes. I think you and I are going to get along like a house on fire.'

Not the analogy I'd have chosen, Garrett thought. He said nothing, waiting.

Shupe cleared his throat uncomfortably and lit another cigar. 'See here, old fellow,' he said. 'I'll be straight with you. We've had our problems, perhaps more than our share. I'd be a liar if I said we hadn't. But you've got to understand, we tend to get a bit prickly when Whitehall keeps poking its nose into everything.'

'Sure.' Garrett put absolutely no inflexion in the word. Once again he sensed the messages passing back and forth between the two men, Shupe's eyes widening fractionally, Cameron's equally silent signal to his superior. *Let me handle this.* Tweedledum and Tweedle-dee, Garrett thought. What a pair.

'What the colonel is saying is, we rather prefer to clean out our own stables,' Cameron said. 'But perhaps some fresh insights would be helpful.'

'Let's start with the bombing,' Garrett said. 'What exactly happened?'

'Two explosive devices — PE, we think — were placed outside one of our barracks buildings,' Cameron said briskly. 'The incident report is being prepared right now.'

'Casualties?'

'Four dead. Eighteen injured.' He repeated the words like an automaton.

'I understand the local paper got a call from someone called the Red German Army,' Garrett said. 'Any idea who they are?'

'God knows,' Shupe said. 'If you want my opinion, it's another of those weirdo communist fringe groups trying to get its name in the papers.'

'Or somebody who wants you to think it's a weirdo communist fringe group trying to get its name in the papers,' Garrett said. 'I take it you requested a police forensic team?'

'They're on site now. We've had a preliminary analysis. The bomb was made of Semtex, and detonated with gunpowder. Probably remote control.'

'Semtex detonated with gunpowder?' Garrett stood up. 'That's classic IRA technique.'

Cameron shrugged. 'I can only tell you what we know.'

'I'd like to see where the bomb went off.'

'Sergeant,' Shupe said to the burly NCO who had come into the room with him. 'Get Mr. Garrett an ID card and take him wherever he wants to go.'

'Sir!'

'While I'm doing that, get me cleared to use your computers,' Garrett said. 'I want to look at every incident you've had, back to 1987.'

Shupe pulled a face. 'That might take a while.'

'What's a while?'

Shupe looked at Cameron. Cameron

shrugged. 'An hour. Two, perhaps.'

'Make it thirty minutes,' Garrett said, noting Cameron's poisonous grimace. 'Lead on, Sergeant.'

They went out of the headquarters building by the rear entrance and got into a Ford Taunus parked in a slot to one side of the doors. The sergeant turned right on a tree-lined road that looked like a suburban avenue. Neat villas with pretty gardens peeped through well-tended shrubbery.

'Officers' quarters,' the sergeant explained, his voice without inflexion. 'My name's Wood, by the way, sir. George Wood.

'Got a few years in?'

'This is my twelfth.'

'All in Germany?'

'Yeah.' The soldier nodded. He stopped the car and made a gesture with his chin. 'There it is.'

The two-story barracks buildings stood in parallel rows down the western edge of the base. Each building was named after a county in England: Cumbria, Berkshire, Avon, Dorset, and so on. Floodlighting had been set up around the damaged building. Beyond the perimeter fence, about fifteen yards from the barracks, was a minor road, now closed and littered with debris.

Garrett got out of the car and walked across to the site of the explosion. A uniformed German policeman started toward him, saw the sergeant, and stopped. Two men in civilian clothes were poking around in the debris. It was easy to see what had happened. The bombers had stopped at the roadside and cut a gateway into the wire mesh. Then they had simply walked across to the wall of the building, laid their bombs against it, and driven away.

'Exactly what time did this happen, Sergeant?' Garrett asked.

'Seven-thirty-eight P.M., sir,' Wood replied. 'Bit of luck really. There were only a few men in the building. If it had gone off during the night, now . . . '

Garrett looked at the barracks. There had been two separate explosions, one near the basement entrance and another below a ground-floor window. The concrete ceiling had collapsed, and furniture and window frames had been blown outward across the road. On the far side of the road, hundreds of windows in a furniture showroom and a paint factory had been shattered by the blast, which had ripped great gaping holes in the side of the Essex barracks building. Sergeant Wood was right. If the bomb had gone off during the night, when the building was full of sleeping soldiers, casualties would have been much greater.

He walked over to the two men he had seen earlier. They looked at him without much interest. He showed them his ID and asked them who they were.

'Weidemann. Inspector, Federal Prosecutor's Office,' the taller of the two said. He was rail thin, dressed in a windbreaker, turtleneck sweater, and slacks. 'My partner, Klaus Gottfried.'

'Any progress?'

Weidemann shrugged. 'We won't get far with this one. Hit and run. They stuck some Semtex against the wall of the building and set it off. No timer, as far as we can make out, so it was probably detonated by remote control.'

'This Red German Army that claimed responsibility. Ever heard of them before?'

'Never,' Weidemann said.

'How did they make contact?'

'The local paper got a call,' Gottfried said. All we know is that it was a man.'

'I'll check with BFV,' Garrett told him.

'Don't bother, we already did,' Gottfried replied. 'They ran it through the TREVI computer. Nobody ever heard of the Red German Army before.'

'Semtex, gunpowder, detonator, remote detonation,' Garrett mused. 'I'd have bet money that that was an IRA bomb.'

'The thought occurred to us, too.'

'One thing you might ask whoever took the call,' Garrett said. 'What kind of German the man spoke.'

Weidemann looked at him in surprise. 'I don't get it.'

'He might not have been German.'

'What makes you think so?'

'The pricking of my thumbs,' Garrett said. He saw Gottfried's scowl of incomprehension. Well, not everybody had read *Macbeth*. 'Intuition.'

'Lot of that about in this business,' the

German said. 'Okay, I'll check it out.'

'Thanks for your help.'

'No thanks necessary. You're not one of Colonel Shupe's people?'

Garrett shook his head.

'Thank Christ for that,' Weidmann said.

Garrett walked back to where Sergeant Wood was waiting. The man's face was impassive; Garrett wondered whether he had heard what the German investigators had said.

'They don't rate your boss too highly,' he remarked.

'I heard,' Wood said.

'What about you?'

'I just take orders, sir,' the sergeant said. 'I'm not required to think.'

Garrett grinned. 'Tell me, Sergeant, how would you feel if I requested that you be assigned to assist me on this case?'

'I wouldn't be overjoyed, sir. No disrespect.'

'You want to tell me why?'

'Well, sir, it's like this. When you've finished your investigation, you'll be going back to where you came from. I'll still be in the army. And so will Colonel Shupe.'

'Tends to hold a grudge, does he?'

'No longer than a century, sir,' Wood replied.

'I wish you'd reconsider, Sergeant,' Garrett said. 'I need all the help I can get.'

'Yes, sir,' Wood said. 'You certainly do.'

6

Twenty-four hours with BSSO computers got Garrett precisely nowhere. His interviews with personnel who had been involved in earlier investigations were equally inconclusive, perhaps because Shupe, apparently all at once freed from the enormous work load Cameron had suggested he was struggling with, insisted on sitting in on every one of them. It took Garrett no time at all to see that Shupe's presence clearly inhibited every one of the people he wanted to talk to.

'I can't see where you're trying to go, Garrett,' Shupe told him. 'You've checked all the investigation reports, read all the dossiers, talked to everyone. If there was a connection, you'd have found it by now. I told you, this is the work of some loony fringe group.'

'I wish I was as sure as you seem to be.'

'Cameron tells me you've been talking to Emil Fritz in Cologne.'

'That's right.'

'In the future, I'd like you to clear that with me beforehand,' Shupe said. 'Most of my people have a pretty solid work load, you know.'

Most of your people are under your thumb to such an extent they'd turn back somersaults before taking the chance of telling me anything I didn't already know, Garrett thought.

Maybe he was asking in the wrong places. He surrendered his computer security key to the orderly sergeant and headed purposefully back to his quarters, where he used the phone to request an interview with Brigadier General Leyland Irwin, commanding Rhine army, and chief executive officer of BSSO. To his surprise the general agreed to see him immediately. Sergeant Wood picked him up at his billet and drove him across to the NATO headquarters building.

'Nice day,' Garrett observed.

'Yes, sir,' Wood replied. 'Going to see the CO, I hear.'

'No secrets on an army post.'

'That's right, sir.' Wood left a little

silence there, enough for Garrett to appreciate the double meaning. 'I hear Colonel Shupe's given you the freedom of the base.'

'I asked him very nicely, Sergeant,' Garrett said.

Sergeant Wood continued to stare straight ahead through the windshield of the Jeep, but he was grinning. 'Yes, sir,' he said. 'You must have.'

'Sad, though,' Garrett continued. 'I got the distinct impression this morning that he still doesn't really like me.'

'Well, sir. Not making his day, really, are you?'

'How's that?'

'Well, he can control most things around here, sir. But General Irwin isn't one of them. So I don't imagine the colonel's exactly thrilled at the idea of you talking to him. Especially when he hasn't been invited to sit in on the conversation.'

'It was remiss of me, I know,' Garrett said. 'But I hate to tear him away from his filing.'

Garrett got out of the Jeep and watched

as Wood drove away. He went into the headquarters building and was taken by an orderly to General Irwin's office on the second floor.

Irwin looked about sixty, spare and handsome in his well-tailored uniform. His hair, his eyebrows, and his mustache were all iron gray; his eyes were kelly green. He had a warm smile and a strong handshake.

'Good to meet you, Garrett,' he said. 'Nicholas Bleke told me about you.'

Garrett raised his eyebrows. 'You know General Bleke, sir?'

'Quite well. I knew your father, too. Served with him in Aden. Out to pasture now, isn't he? Squire of Homefield Hall and all that?'

'Yes, sir.'

'Be my turn before long, I expect,' Irwin said. 'Be glad to be back in Blighty. See a few old chums. Well, hrrrmph, yes. What can I do for you?'

'I'm experiencing a little difficulty investigating these bombings, sir,' Garrett said. 'I need a little room to move around, and I'd like to enlist your assistance.'

'Shupe, eh?' Irwin said, worlds of meaning in the word. 'Tryin' to tie you up in red tape, is he?'

'He falls over himself to be helpful, sir,' Garrett said.

Irwin looked at him. A grin spread slowly over his face. 'You're like your father,' he said. 'Don't always mean what you say. You want Shupe out of the way, is that it?'

'That's right, General,' Garrett said. 'Is there any chance at all that you could get him off my back for a few days?'

Irwin swiveled around in his chair and looked out of the window. Then he swiveled back around to face Garrett. 'People around here might tell you I don't like Shupe,' he said. 'I want to disabuse you of that notion here and now. I hate the crawly bugger's guts. Trouble is, I can't break the man because he's unpleasant and inefficient. If someone offered me half an excuse for getting him transferred out of here, I'd trample twenty strong men to death to put my signature on the papers. But they're all afraid of the fellow.'

'That's why I'd like him out of the picture for a while,' Garrett said. 'It might loosen a few tongues.'

'Worth a try, I suppose,' Irwin said. 'How long do you need?'

'Three days ought to do it,' Garrett said.

'We'll make it five,' Irwin replied. 'Just to be on the safe side. What about Cameron?'

'Him too,' Garrett said.

'I'll arrange it at once. Time someone inspected the facility at Lüneburg, anyway. Keep the boys up there on their toes. Look here, young fellow, tell me straight, what's your assessment of those two?'

'I'll tell you the truth, General, I can't really put my finger on it. It's not just that they're an unpleasant pair, although that doesn't help. There's some kind of malaise there, and I'd like to know what it is.'

'Ha!' Irwin said. 'Knew you and I were going to hit it off, my boy. My feelings precisely. Know something's wrong, but I can't pin it down. Gut instinct, really. It's in the way they do things. The way they run the whole organization.'

'I'll see what I can find out,' Garrett said. 'I'm very grateful to you for your help, General.'

'I'd love to know exactly why Nicholas Bleke sent you over here, young fellow,' Irwin said reflectively. 'But I know you secret service johnnies don't give much away.'

'General Bleke wants these terrorists caught, sir. He thought I might be able to, ah, encourage BSSO to try harder.'

'Encourage, eh?' Irwin chuckled. 'I like that. You go ahead, Garrett. Encourage the hell out of them. Whole damned outfit needs a bloody good shakeup.'

'Then with your permission, General, I'll give it one.'

Irwin grinned like a mischievous schoolboy; it made him look ten years younger. 'Splendid,' he said. 'Splendid.'

★   ★   ★

The following morning, when Garrett appeared at the BSSO building, Shupe was busily slotting files into a leather briefcase lying open on his desk. He looked up as Garrett came in.

'Well,' he said. 'Nice work, Garrett.'

'What does that mean?'

'It means you've got the place to yourself. The old fart-arse is sending me on some stupid shakeout tour to Lüneburg.'

'Have a good trip,' Garrett said. He smiled at Shupe's poisonous glance and went out to the front of the building. Sergeant Wood was waiting outside in the Jeep. The sergeant gave him a sort of salute.

'Like to talk to you, sir. Private, like.'

'Changed your mind, Sergeant?'

'Off the record, right?' the soldier said. 'Nothing written down.'

'Okay,' Garrett said. 'What's Shupe up to?'

Wood's eyebrows went up. 'How d'you know?'

'Fish stinks from the head.'

'Never heard that one,' Wood said. 'But it's true. Shupe has got some sort of racket going with the Americans down at Wiesbaden. Him and Cameron.'

'Go on.'

'UKUSA liaison officer at Camp Pieri is an American named Paul Barton.' He held up two fingers, crossed one over the other. 'Barton and Shupe are like this.'

'Do you have any idea what they're up to?'

'Rather not go into details, sir,' Wood said nervously. 'Not here.'

'Where, then?'

Sergeant Wood's face suddenly became wooden. He ignored the question, staring straight ahead. Out of the corner of his eye Garrett saw Cameron on the steps of the BSSO building. How long had he been there? Had he heard what Wood was saying?

'There's a place on the river about two miles north of Wegberg called the Molzmühle,' Garrett said, keeping his back toward Cameron. 'I'll be there at eight o'clock tonight.'

Wood didn't reply; Garrett didn't expect him to. He was about to walk away when Cameron called his name.

'As you are no doubt well aware,' Cameron said coldly, 'Colonel Shupe and I will be in Lüneburg for a week. If for any reason you should need access to classified material, you'll need an authorization from either myself or the colonel.'

'When are you leaving?'

'In about ten minutes.' Cameron smirked. 'Is there anything I can do for you before I go?'

Garrett shook his head. 'I won't need access to the security area, Captain. I'll be elsewhere.'

'Oh,' Cameron said, with an alarmed look. 'In that case, perhaps you'd better give me a briefing before I leave. The colonel will want to know where this thing is going.'

'It would take longer than ten minutes, I'm afraid,' Garrett said regretfully. 'And I'd hate to keep you when I know how much you must be looking forward to the pleasures of Lüneburg.'

He clapped Cameron on the shoulder and walked away. Cameron glared at his back helplessly, twin red spots of anger coloring his cheeks. Sergeant Wood was staring fixedly at a Lufthansa jumbo passing overhead. Only the rapid movements of his Adam's apple revealed the struggle he was having not to laugh out loud.

The place Garrett had picked for his rendezvous with Wood was about a mile and a half outside of town, a converted watermill that stood on a quiet road on the bank of the river.

By the time he arrived, the place was already three quarters full, mostly with local people. There wasn't a uniform in sight, which was one of the reasons Garrett had chosen it.

'*Was darfen Sie?*' a pretty German girl in a dirndl asked him, her tray held at an angle against her hip. He asked her for the wine list, and when she brought it, he ordered a bottle of Kreuznacher and two glasses. She showed him her dimples and went away.

Garrett drank two glasses of the Kreuznacher — the bottle bore the colorful label of the Hungry Wolf Vineyard — and watched the people around him. No one evinced the slightest bit of interest in him; a big man sitting alone at a table in the corner. He waited an hour, then another ten minutes. No sign of Wood. He paid his bill and went out to the car park, faintly illuminated by the lights of the restaurant behind him.

A wind had sprung up and the trees were tossing their heads like wild horses. As he walked across the half-empty parking lot, he sensed, rather than saw, a movement and then they had him, three of them, dark shapes in the darker shadows. The first of them chopped him down hard and Garrett felt the hard bite of gravel against his cheekbone. Stunned and disoriented, he instinctively kicked out at the legs of his attackers. He heard one of them grunt in pain. As he tried to get to his feet, the one on his right kneed him in the face, hurling him back against a parked car. Blinded by pain, Garrett struggled to his knees, striking out hopelessly. He felt them grab his arms, two of them holding him while the third hit him again and again, smashing blows into his unprotected body. Garrett started to slip into deeper darkness, an echoing bottomless red pit full of pain, where a drum made a single awful sound, over and over and over. The deep red glare started to turn to black, and he no longer heard his pounding pulse. He wanted to let the blackness wash over him, but some instinct told him that if he did he would be dead.

'*Genug, genug!*' one of them shouted. 'Enough!' The man who had been hitting Garrett lurched back, panting, his eyes wild. The other two let go of Garrett's arms and he collapsed, facedown. The one who had done the beating kicked him in the kidneys for good measure and then they ran off. A car door slammed, an engine roared. Then there was silence.

★   ★   ★

He opened his eyes. It was pitch dark. His face was numb. Agony swept through his lower body. Memory flooded back: three men, dark clothes, ski masks. He tried to sit up and groaned with pain. They really worked me over, he thought. He started to shiver and could not stop; tremors shook his body like some terrible fever.

Got to move, he thought. He was lying on his back between two parked cars, his knees drawn up in a fetal curl. He straightened out, bracing the soles of his feet against the wheel of a car, then pushed himself until he felt his head touch the body work of another. Very slowly, he eased himself into a sitting position. Waves of pain ran through his chest, and he almost passed out. He pulled his knees back to his body and straightened them out again, fighting the nausea and pain that the movement produced. Again. Again. The nausea passed; the pain remained.

It took him nearly ten minutes to stand up. He had no feeling in his hands or his face or his feet. He lurched against the Mercedes, felt his way along it to the next car, and the next. Across the parking lot, only a million miles away, was the lighted doorway of the restaurant. He shambled toward it, reeling like a drunk. He got to the door of the restaurant, but he could not open it; his hand felt like a potato. He banged weakly on the door. Then again, harder.

The door opened and the pretty waitress with the dimples stood framed in the light. When she saw Garrett's face, she started screaming.

★   ★   ★

He opened his eyes. He was lying on a bed. He felt clean and warm. A white ceiling. The smell of antiseptics. Memory returned: blue flashing lights bouncing off concrete walls. A pudgy-faced man asking questions. Someone telling him to count backward from fifty.

'So, we are awake.'

The speaker was a man in a white coat, stethoscope looped around his neck, beaming at Garrett from behind horn-rim spectacles. To one side stood a nurse in a blue uniform, her face set in professional readiness.

'How are we feeling?' the doctor asked.

'Maybe we should get together and find out,' Garrett said. His mouth felt as if it were full of cotton wool. He lifted his hands and a dull ache started up in his belly. He touched his face. It was numb, as if he had been injected with novocaine.

'Where am I?'

'You are in Wegberg. The Bergspital. I am Dr.Sieben.'

'Am I badly hurt?'

'Some fractured ribs. Massive bruising. Fortunately, no internal injuries. You were very lucky.'

'It doesn't feel like it,' Garrett said. 'Where are my clothes? I have to get out of here.'

The nurse drew in her breath sharply, as if he had said something obscene. The doctor smiled forgivingly.

'You must remain,' he said. 'Then there is the matter of the police.'

'Just get me my clothes, nurse,' Garrett said. She looked at the doctor. He shrugged. *What can you do with such people?* his expression said. The nurse made an angry face and left the room, closing the door harder than was necessary but not quite slamming it.

Garrett pushed back the bedclothes and sat up. The dull ache in his midriff turned to an angry red pain. He tried to ignore it as he stood up, catching hold of the bedrail to steady himself. Dr. Sieben shook his head.

'Herr Garrett, for the last time, I request you to get back in the bed,' Dr. Sieben said. The nurse came in with Garrett's clothes and stood irresolutely by the door, waiting to see if he would do as the doctor asked. Garrett took the plastic garment bag from her and laid it on the bed. His clothes were mud-stained but otherwise in good shape. There was dried blood on the front of the shirt. It would do. He started to get dressed, nearly fell. The nurse made an impatient exclamation and came to help him. He was just putting on his jacket when the door opened and a man came in.

He was about thirty, slim, athletic looking, with a gunfighter mustache and swarthy skin. He showed Garrett an ID card that identified him as Alexander Ochs, detective grade three, Wegberg civil police. He took out a pack of Gauloises.

'It's okay?' he asked.

'Sure.' Garrett shrugged.

Ochs lit a cigarette, then took out a

notebook and opened it. 'You permit the taking of notes?'

Garrett smiled. 'What do you want to know?'

'Your name is Charles Frederick Garrett. You are a British citizen.'

'I'm sure you've checked all that, detective.'

Ochs looked up, his face expressionless.

'Do you have any idea who attacked you, Herr Garrett?'

'None at all,' Garrett said.

'Could you describe your assailants?'

'Other than that there were three big guys wearing dark clothes and ski masks, no.'

'Can you suggest a reason why you were attacked?'

'Robbery?'

Ochs shook his head. 'Your wallet was in your pocket. Nothing had been taken.'

Garrett shrugged. '*Rowdies*, then.' It was the word the Germans used for hooligans, juvenile delinquents.

'We do not have rowdies in Wegberg, Herr Garrett,' Ochs said stiffly, as if they were talking about leprosy.

'In that case,' Garrett said, 'you tell me.'

Ochs stood up and closed his notebook with a little snap. 'Do not make the mistake to treat me like a fool, Herr Garrett,' he said angrily. 'You were professionally beaten up by men who knew exactly what they were doing and exactly when to stop. It was not a robbery and it was not rowdies and both of us know it. However, if you will not help us, we cannot help you.'

'Help me do what?' Garrett asked innocently.

Ochs made an impatient sound. 'My department saw to it that your car was brought to the hospital,' he said, his tone of voice making it clear that he thought it was a great deal more than Garrett deserved. 'I may wish to speak with you again. Please do not leave Germany without reporting to my office.'

He marched out, his back stiff. Dr. Sieben's nurse looked as if she wanted to applaud.

'Thank you for all you did for me, doctor,' Garrett said. 'Is there anything you want me to sign before I leave?'

They gave him the usual waiver and he signed it; he would be in perfectly good hands at Rheindahlen, he told them. If that made the doctor and his nurse feel any better, their expressions didn't show it. Garrett limped out and followed the *Ausgang* signs. A clock on the wall in the tiled hallway told him it was two-fifteen A.M. He walked slowly, carefully down the stone steps to the parking lot. When he found the car, he got inside and just sat there, waiting until he felt strong enough to face the exhausting task of switching on the engine.

Detective Ochs had been right, of course; it was a professional beating, done by men who knew how to inflict exactly the right amount of punishment. That made it a warning: keep off. All right, *keep off what?* Whatever it was, his only lead was Sergeant George Wood. He started the car and headed back toward the base, driving like an old-age pensioner. The sentry at the gate eyed the dressings on his face curiously as he checked his ID, and was about to wave

110

him in when Garrett asked him a question.

'Sar'nt Wood? Yes, sir. He signed out about seven-forty-five last night. No, sir. Never said where he was going.'

'Do me a favor, will you? When he comes back, ask him to get in touch with me immediately.'

He drove over to the guest bungalow near the officers' enclave that had been put at his disposal. As he got inside and switched on the lights, he realized that he had not eaten since that morning. His whole body was throbbing with pain. He made some strong black instant coffee, took a couple of aspirin, and lay down on the bed, staring up into the darkness. After a while, he slept.

7

He no sooner seemed to have closed his eyes than he was awakened by the shrill, insistent sound of the telephone. He sat up, disoriented, and cursed as pain shot through his body. His fumbling hand found the telephone receiver. He put on the light. It was a little after five A.M.

'Lieutenant Pennyweather, sir. Duty officer. Could you come to the orderly room by the main gate immediately, please?'

'What is it?' Garrett asked, although something told him what was coming next.

'I've had a call from the police in Merbeck, sir,' the duty officer said. 'It's Sergeant Wood. Two hunters found his body in the forest. Dead.'

'I'll be right there.' Garrett got up painfully. His entire body felt as stiff as a board. He took two aspirin and then put on his clothes and went out to his car. He was at the gatehouse twelve minutes after putting the phone down.

'Mr. Garrett?' A young lieutenant snapped a salute. He was tall, thin, blond, and pleasantly good-looking, like one of those juveniles who used to come in through the French windows in 1930s' plays and say, 'Anyone for tennis?' 'Clive Pennyweather, 187th Infantry. Duty officer. I called you.' Garrett could see the curiosity on his face, but he made no attempt to explain the dressings on his face.

'What did the police tell you?'

'Pretty much what I told you on the phone. Two men out hunting stumbled across Wood's body. They found his ID in his pocket. And a luggage label around his neck that said: 'Compliments of the Red German Army.' I've got their names if you — '

'That can wait,' Garrett said. 'Get on the horn to the Nordrhein Criminal Investigation Division, Mönchengladbach. Wake up whoever you have to. Get them to send a meat wagon and scene-of-crime equipment to Merbeck.

Tell them to contact Inspector Weidemann or Sergeant Gottfried, Federal Prosecutor's Office. We'll meet them there.'

Pennyweather nodded and picked up the phone, talking rapidly. While he was talking, Garrett looked around until he found a powerful flashlight; as soon as Pennyweather got through, he led the way outside. They piled into the Mercedes and roared out of the base, heading west through the thin grayness of early morning. Pennyweather drove fast and well. There were only a few cars on the winding country road that led to the little hamlet of Merbeck. The town was just waking up; there were lights in the bakery and a postman was pushing his bicycle up the street. Pennyweather slid the car into a parking slot outside the police station and ran up the steps, followed more slowly by Garrett. A stolid-looking sergeant frowned at them across his counter.

'Military intelligence, Rhine army,' Garrett said, holding up his ID wallet. 'You've got two men here who — '

'Ja, ja, ja,' the sergeant said, holding up

a beefy hand. 'Not so fast, not so fast.'

He picked up the phone and talked to someone. A man wearing a raincoat over pajamas came out of the office at the rear. He was about forty, unshaven, tousle-haired.

'Losch,' he said, by way of self-introduction. 'Chief detective, state police. This is something, eh?'

'Where are they?'

'Our hunters?' Losch beckoned them to follow him. 'Inside, I'll show you.'

They went into a small back room that was obviously used as a canteen by the local police. It smelled of cigarettes and coffee.

'So,' Losch said in English with a thick German accent, 'here we are.'

On a bench near the potbellied stove, cradling tin mess mugs in their hands, sat two men. One was in his midfifties, the other was perhaps ten years younger. The older man wore a brown corduroy coat and brown trousers with high laced boots. The younger one had on a red blanket coat, with dark gray woolen trousers tucked into calf-high leather boots.

'Gentlemen,' Garrett said. 'I am Charles Garrett. This is Lieutenant Pennyweather.'

'Ernst Haldemann,' the older man said. 'This is my friend Jurg Klassner. What happened to you — an accident?'

'You found the body?' Garrett asked, ignoring the question. 'You're sure he was dead?'

'You don't believe?' the younger one said belligerently. It was clear he had been badly shaken by their discovery.

'Don't mind Jurg,' the older one said. 'First time he's seen a stiff.'

'Where did you find it?'

'I told them here already. We were out hunting. Dawn's the best time to catch deer, you know.'

'Where was this?'

'It's about a mile out of town, six or seven hundred meters off the road,' the older man said, nettled. 'We can take you there.'

'First, tell me exactly how you found the body,' Garrett said to Haldemann.

The German shrugged his heavy shoulders, rubbed his chin with a hamlike hand. His stubble rasped against his palm. 'It was as I said. Jurg and I went out, before dawn, after deer. We were walking through the forest when we saw the man lying there. I thought, damned drunks, they're everywhere. We went a bit closer and I could see he was dead.'

'What did you do then?'

'Checked for a pulse. He was as cold as ice cream. Stiffening up, too.'

'You didn't move him?'

'You think we're fools?' Haldemann growled. 'Of course not. I said to Jurg, feel in his pockets. See if there's a wallet or something.'

'He had army identification in his wallet,' Jurg said. 'I said to Ernst, he's a soldier. A sergeant.'

'Then we saw the label round his neck. The same people who did the bomb at Rheindahlen. We were going to telephone the base, report it,' Haldemann said. 'But then we thought it would be quicker to come here. That way we could take you right back to the place.'

'You were absolutely correct,' Garrett said. The older man looked at the younger one. *There, you see,* his expression said.

'Perhaps you could take us out there,' Pennyweather said. 'We don't want anyone else stumbling over the body before the coroner gets here, do we?'

'I'm not so sure — ' Losch began.

'I'll take full responsibility,' Garrett said, touching Losch reassuringly on the shoulder. It was a phrase that had always worked well in Germany, and it worked again now. They went out into the morning chill. Haldemann and Klassner got into a Peugeot 505 flatbed truck and swung right on the road toward Dalheim. Pennyweather followed close behind in the Mercedes until, about a kilometer farther on, he saw Haldemann's brake lights flash; he pulled to a stop behind the Peugeot, and they all got out.

'Through here,' the German said. He opened an iron gate and led the way down a stone path that turned into a track and then a woodland path. The trees were planted in neat, military rows. Moisture dripped noisily from the leaves.

Sergeant Wood was lying at the foot of

a big beech tree, wide-open eyes staring at nothing. The dead man's face shone eerily in the flashlight beam, his skin slick with moisture. Garrett noted that the forehead was strangely misshapen.

'Shot in the back of the head,' he said to Pennyweather. 'Close range, by the look of it.'

'Yes, sir,' the lieutenant said. He looked a little green around the gills. Well, there was a first time for everyone.

Kneeling down beside the body, Garrett lifted the luggage label with a twig. It was just as the two hunters had reported: 'Compliments of the Red German Army,' it read.

Somewhere off in the darkness, car doors slammed with a sound like silenced guns. Loud voices echoed flatly in the dank morning air. Garrett saw strong lights moving between the trees and then the dark bulk of an ambulance, bouncing over the uneven ground. Uniformed police seemed to materialize everywhere. In ten minutes the little glade was as brightly lit as Eintracht Stadium, fenced off with yellow plastic tape run through the loops of steel staves planted in a circle about forty yards from the corpse.

Ten minutes or so later, Garrett saw the slat-thin figure of Inspector Weidemann pushing through the mill of police personnel toward him. 'You again,' he said.

'In person.'

'What the hell happened to you?'

'It's a long story. I'll tell you later.'

'Why'd you ask for me? We don't have jurisdiction in local cases.'

'Look.' Garrett gestured toward the body.

Weidemann bent down and read the message on the luggage tag. 'So,' he said. 'This is linked to the bombing?'

'Or we're meant to think so,' Garrett said.

'Who's the dead man?'

'An army sergeant. Name of George Wood.'

'Let's talk to the medical examiner.'

The ME was a middle-aged man with a pudgy face and an unfortunate nose that gave him a piggy look. His badge proclaimed his name as Dieter Gunther, his rank as examiner, KuzK — *Krimina-linspektion und zentrale Kriminalin-spektionen, Nordrhein-Westfalen*.

'Dieter,' Weidemann said. 'What have we got?'

'One shot in the back of the head. Probably a nine-millimeter,' Gunther said, scratching his ear. 'Very close range. Not much blood. I'd say he was shot somewhere else and dumped here.'

'How long ago?'

'Rigor's just reaching the distal extremities now. At a guess, between eight and twelve hours.'

'That it?'

'Until the autopsy,' Gunther said. He fished in his pocket and brought out a pack of HB cigarettes, lighting one and inhaling smoke greedily. Weidemann turned away and took out a stick of spearmint gum, chewing on it morosely.

'Just given it up?' Garrett asked.

'Three weeks.' Weidemann nodded. 'It's always worst first thing in the morning. Have you got any ideas about this thing?'

'Only what I told you. The dead man is a sergeant on the staff of Rhine army intelligence at Rheindahlen. His name is — was — George Wood. He was supposed to meet me in Wegberg at eight o'clock last night,' Garrett said. 'He didn't turn up. Someone else did. Three of them. They did this.' He gestured at his bandages.

Weidemann raised his eyebrows and looked at him with fresh interest. 'Looks as if they did quite a job,' he observed. 'Did you report it to the police?'

'I talked to a detective named Ochs at Wegberg. Couldn't tell him much. There were no witnesses. I couldn't identify the men.'

'Are you all right? You look rocky.'

'That's one word for it.'

'Who do you think it was?'

'Good question. I wish I knew the answer.'

'What was the meeting with Wood about?'

'He told me there was some kind of racket going on between the Americans at Wiesbaden and the head of MI at Rheindahlen.'

'Colonel Shupe?'

'You know him, of course.'

'He's famous,' Weidmann said sourly. 'What kind of racket?'

'That was all he said. He was going to tell me about it when we met.'

'And instead he winds up with a bullet in the back of his head,' Weidemann mused. 'And you look as if you fell into a combine harvester. Are you telling me what I think you're telling me?'

'I'm telling you what I know,' Garrett said. 'I thought that way if you found out anything, you might return the compliment.'

'It's a thought,' Weidemann said.

Two ambulance men were putting Wood's body onto a stretcher. A policeman was switching off the lights. It was almost daylight now. Men stood around, smoking cigarettes, waiting to be told what to do next.

'I'll get a forensic team out here to check the place over,' Weidemann told Garrett. 'I don't expect we'll find anything, but it's worth a try.' He raised his voice. 'Has anybody sent for coffee?'

'On the way, Inspector,' one of the

uniforms called back.

'Thank God for that. All right, Garrett. Keep in touch, yes?'

Garrett found Lieutenant Pennyweather sitting in the Mercedes, his thin face pale and drawn.

'You all right, Lieutenant?'

Pennyweather tried for a smile. It didn't take. 'I'm all right. It . . . it just hit me, all at once.'

'It happens,' Garrett said. He got into the car and Pennyweather turned it around, heading back toward Merbeck. 'You want to stop, get some coffee?'

Pennyweather shook his head, his lips pressed close together.

'Who's going to tell Eileen?' the young officer said, almost as if to himself.

'Eileen?'

'Eileen Carson. The sergeant's sister.'

'I didn't know he had a sister.'

'She lives in the American sector. Wiesbaden.'

'Do you know her?'

Pennyweather nodded. 'I haven't seen her for a while.'

'You'd better give me her number,'

Garrett said. 'I'll catch her when we get back.'

'Yes, okay,' Pennyweather said, and Garrett wondered why there was so much relief in his voice.

★ ★ ★

Eileen Carson lived in an apartment house up in the hills north of Wiesbaden on a neat street near the Princess Elizabeth Park. She was a plump, prettyish blond woman of thirty-five, not at all what Garrett had expected from the dossier he had read on her. Eight years younger than her brother, she had stayed on in Germany after her husband, Keith, serving with Rhine army, was killed in a car accident in 1984. If Shupe's dossier on her was at all accurate, and Garrett had absolutely no reason for supposing otherwise, Eileen Carson had spent most of her time since the commencement of her widowhood pursuing American servicemen with a zeal — and a success rate — that many a younger woman might have envied.

'My name is Charles Garrett,' he said, showing her the Ministry of Defense ID card he carried for such occasions. 'I'm investigating the death of your brother.'

'Come in,' she said. He felt her eyes checking him over, like a housewife looking at pork chops in a butcher shop. They went into a sitting room with lots of plants along the sill of a big picture window that looked out over a communal garden at the rear of the block.

On the wall hung a reproduction of Van Gogh's painting of the bridge at Arles. Garrett remembered going there in the sixties. The bridge was out in the middle of a field, no road going to or coming from it, and the canal was dried up.

'I take it you've been informed about what happened,' he began.

'Poor George,' she said automatically. She didn't look particularly grieved.

'Have you been in an accident?'

'It wasn't an accident,' Garrett said. 'Did you see much of your brother?'

'Not a lot. Maybe once a month.'

'When was the last time?'

'About a month ago. He used to come

down to Wiesbaden a couple of times a week to see someone at Camp Patton.'

'You know why he went there?'

'Official business, I guess.' She shrugged. She had no trace of an English accent. If he had not known better, he would have said she was American.

'I had an appointment to meet him the night he was killed,' Garrett said. 'He said he was going to tell me about some racket he was mixed up in. Would you have any idea what he was talking about?'

She sat down in an armchair, then got up again and paced across the room and back.

'He didn't tell me anything, but that doesn't mean a lot. We weren't close, my brother and I. He didn't come here too often. He disapproved of me.'

'Oh,' Garrett said artlessly. 'Why was that?'

She gave him one of those 'are you kidding?' looks and let out a wry little laugh. 'Are you married, Mr . . . ?'

'Garrett,' he supplied again. 'I used to be.'

'Then you know the score.'

He shrugged. 'I'm new here.'

'You'll learn,' she said. 'S'all they do. Everybody's got a *schatzi*.'

'I understand that the man your brother dealt with at Camp Patton was a Major Paul Barton,' Garrett said. 'Do you know him?'

Her head came up, the little-girl eyes glittering with malice. 'I know him.'

'Popular guy?'

'Wiesbaden's answer to Al Pacino,' she said. 'Jus' ask him.'

'You don't like him.'

'I used to,' she said carelessly. 'Till the ointment wore off.'

'Was he one of the ones who came around after your husband died?'

She shook her head. 'He likes older women,' she said. 'He likes the kitty-kitty type.'

'What's that?'

Eileen Carson giggled. 'Kitty, kitty, who's got the kitty?' she said. 'You mean you really don't know?'

Garrett shook his head.

'You must be the only man in West Germany who doesn't,' she said. 'Barton is shacking up with Kitty Irwin. You know, Kitty *Irwin*!'

'General Irwin's wife?'

She nodded benevolently. 'There you are, see? Now you know, too.'

That nice old man, he thought. Well, maybe that was the problem. The world was full of nice old men whose wives were playing around, and there wasn't any point in adopting a high moral tone about it.

'Tell me about her,' he said.

'Kitty Irwin? What you want to know?'

He shrugged.

'Well. She's about forty-five. Full figure, bit blowsy if you ask me, but men seem to like her. Dresses like a million dollars: Karl Lagerfeld, Jasper Conran; you name the designer, she has the dresses.'

'How long has this ... affair been going on?'

'Year. Eighteen months. I don't know. You want a drink?'

'Wish I could,' he said. 'But I've got a long drive ahead of me. Is Barton married?'

'Sure. Lucy's her name.'

'She's here, in Germany?'

'Got a house up the valley,' Eileen Carson said 'Prolly got a *schatzi*, too.'

Love is sweeping the country, Garrett thought.

He stood up. 'I'll be in touch if there's anything else I need to know. Do you have any special wishes regarding the funeral?'

She frowned, as if she were trying to remember something. Then her brow cleared again. 'Oh, George,' she said. 'Nah.'

He got out of there and drove down into town, past pleasant villas and neat houses with shining BMWs parked outside of them. On the south side of town, he turned right onto the ring road, then left onto the pleasant tree-lined Schliersteiner-strasse. Just past the hospital was the imposing stone-pillared entrance of the old infantry barracks, christened Camp Patton after the war-time general. The usual striped pole barred the entrance; he stopped and showed his ID to the white-helmeted MP at the gate and waited while the soldier got clearance to admit him.

Garrett parked the Mercedes outside the administration building. It was a big old sandstone pile, three stories high, its yellow stucco façade mellow in the afternoon sunshine. Inside a lofty hall with stone staircases coming down in sweeping curves from above, he found a directory board that listed the offices. Major Paul Barton, Special Projects Unit and UKUSA liaison, was in 21, which meant second floor, first office.

He went up the stairs. A couple of young women with clipboards under their arms went by. Two GIs, tunics open, passed him on the landing, taking no notice of him whatsoever. So much for security, Garrett thought. Room 21 was on his right. The office doors were made of solid hand-carved oak. He knocked and waited. A man's voice called out for him to come in.

Paul Barton was a shopgirl's dream of an army officer. He was five foot six, with naturally wavy dark hair, liquid brown eyes, smooth tanned skin, and a mobile, good-humored mouth. Garrett recalled Eileen Carson's sardonic description: Wiesbaden's answer to Al Pacino. Come to think of it, he even looked a bit like the movie star.

Barton came around his desk to meet Garrett, hand extended. 'Mr. Garrett,' he said, 'I'm sorry we have to meet under such tragic circumstances.' He had a hand-shake like someone who once read a book about winning friends and influencing people. 'Sit down, please. Can I get you some coffee?'

'Coffee would be fine,' Garrett said. 'Black, please.'

'Excuse me,' Barton said. He picked up a phone and spoke to a secretary, then turned back to face Garrett, his face open and frank.

'Now, sir,' he said. 'How can I help you?'

'As I told you on the telephone,' Garrett said. 'I'm investigating the murder of Sergeant George Wood, 187th Infantry.'

'I read about it in the paper,' Barton said. 'Sounded like a nasty business. Terrorists, wasn't it?'

132

'So they say,' Garrett said. 'I gather you knew him quite well.'

Barton shrugged. 'Casually, not well. He was a courier. He brought classified stuff down here from NATO headquarters, took other material back.'

'I see,' Garrett said. 'You mind a few questions?'

'Fire away,' Barton said expansively. 'Ask me anything you like.' He settled in the leather armchair behind his desk, opened a silver cigarette case, and lit a cigarette, his expression open and friendly.

'I saw Wood just before he was killed,' Garrett said. 'He told me, and I quote, that you and Colonel Shupe of British military intelligence were tied up in some sort of racket and that he was acting as a courier between you. Would you care to comment?' He had tacked on his own deduction that Wood was acting as a courier to see what Barton's reaction would be. It didn't work.

Barton stared at him. 'What the hell is this, Garrett?'

Garrett shrugged. 'You told me to ask you anything I liked, Major. So I'm asking.'

Barton shook his head as if in admiration. 'You don't seriously think I plan to dignify such crap with the semblance of a reply, do you?' he said.

'You're telling me there's no truth in what Sergeant Wood told me?'

'That's exactly what I'm telling you!' Barton said. 'And if that's all you came here to say, consider it said and get your ass out of here before I have it kicked off the base!'

He stood up and heaved his chair back out of the way. 'Maybe I'll just kick you out of here myself.'

'Maybe,' Garrett said, smiling. He didn't move. Barton stared at him irresolutely. At that moment the door opened and a young woman came in. She wore a white blouse and a tan skirt, and her dark hair was tied back with a red ribbon. She looked about twenty.

'Your coffee, sir,' she said. She sensed the hostility in the air and looked uneasily from Barton to Garrett and back again.

'Put it on the desk, Hilde,' Barton said, thickly. '*Danke.*'

'*Bitte schön,*' the girl said, and went

out quickly, closing the door behind her. Barton still stood where he had stopped, halfway around the desk. Garrett could see the uncertainty in his eyes. He didn't want to back down and he didn't want to push this any further, either.

'Sit down, Major,' he said softly. 'Sit down.'

Barton went back to his chair and sat down in it. He frowned at Garrett, as if trying to identify something completely unfamiliar. Then he drew in a deep breath and sighed, shaking his head. 'I don't understand you, Garrett,' he said finally. 'You don't look dumb.'

'Now it's my turn not to understand,' Garrett said.

'Let me ask you a question. What happened to your face?'

'Ah,' Garrett said. 'Wegberg. That was you?'

'Did I say that? What I'm saying is, you don't seem to be getting the message. Let me spell it out for you: stay away from the George Wood case.'

'And if I don't?'

Barton stared at him disbelievingly.

'You cannot be serious,' he said harshly.

'That's what John McEnroe told the umpire, and he was wrong, too,' Garrett said. 'I'm serious. And I'll tell you why. When I walked into your office this afternoon, Major, I had nothing going for me but a hunch that you weren't kosher. Now I know it for a fact.'

'You don't know a thing, and you never will,' Barton said angrily.

Garrett smiled. He reached into his inside pocket and brought out the tiny Uher tape recorder. Its reels were still turning. Barton looked at it.

'Jesus Christ,' he said, his tone one of weary disgust.

'That's right, Major,' Garrett said. 'Every word. On tape.'

'A tape recorder?' Barton said scornfully. 'You think any court in the world would accept that as evidence?'

'You're not dealing with a court of law, Major,' Garrett reminded him. 'You're dealing with me.'

Barton stared at Garrett for a long moment. Then he nodded, as if coming to a decision. His whole demeanor had changed. Antipathy fired the dark eyes. He laid his hand flat on the desk in a gesture of finality.

'Okay,' he said. 'This interview is terminated.'

'God,' Garrett said, 'you're lovely when you're angry.'

To his surprise, Barton did not rise to the bait. Instead, he shrugged and spun his chair around so that he was staring out of the window. Somehow, his indifference was more impressive than anything he had said during the whole conversation. Garrett turned and left. As he closed the door, Barton spoke without turning around.

'Good-bye, Garrett,' he said.

8

It was about a hundred kilometers from Wiesbaden to Linz, slightly more via the scenic route. Garrett drove without haste, following minor roads to Niederbreitbach, above Linz, where the imposing sandstone gate pillars of the old estate of Schwarzenberg faced the country road like haughty sentinels from bygone days.

With its pillared façade draped with climbing vines of multicolored leaves, the old mansion looked like something out of a picture postcard. Its Baroque central dome reflected in a circular pool with a fountain facing the great porte cochere; the old house bravely faced its world as if the last hundred years had never happened.

Hans Kupfer was a short, ruddy-faced man in his early sixties, built like a beer barrel and nearly half again as wide across the shoulders as Garrett. His quizzical, washed-out blue eyes displayed wary interest as Garrett explained the reason for his visit.

'So old King Peter sent you, did he?' Kupfer said.

'Told me if anyone could help me, it was you,' Garrett said.

'And what's the name of this fellow you're looking for?'

'Jim Kitson. He's Irish. I heard he was working in this area as a *gastarbeiter*.'

'We don't employ many foreigners. What does he look like, this friend of yours?'

'He's about your height,' Garrett said. 'Not as big, though. Thirty-five or six. Stocky. Blue eyes, carrot red hair.'

Kupfer shook his head. 'We had a fellow here who looked like that. Early summer, as I recall. He had red hair and blue eyes, but his name wasn't Kitson. It was . . . wait a minute, I'll have to go and look in the ledger.'

He went into a stone outbuilding that leaned against the thick walls of the cobbled courtyard to one side of the big house. Garrett took a moment to look about him. Schwarzenberg was a handsome country residence of perhaps eighty rooms standing on the southern slope of the forested hills above Linz. He was surprised it had not been turned into a luxury hotel, with a sauna and a swimming pool and a helicopter pad. There were a lot of those in Germany these days, all of them as phony as a publisher's blurb.

He looked up as Kupfer hobbled out of his office, a heavy leatherbound book in his hand. He held it open so Garrett could see the entries, all written in a crabbed, old-fashioned hand.

'There he is, you see,' Kupfer said. 'From March until the end of July. I knew his name wasn't Kitson, though. It was Harwood. Robert Harwood.'

'And he fit the description I gave you?' Garrett said, concealing his reaction. Hennessy had used the alias of Robert Harwood before, in France. He kept his voice casual. 'I don't suppose you know where this Harwood went after he left here, do you?'

Hans Kupfer cocked shrewd eyes at him and shook his head. 'Look, young fellow, if there's something you want to know, come straight out with it. We've got nothing to hide here.'

'Sorry,' Garrett said. 'I should have told you the truth right at the start. I'm a sort of policeman.'

'Sort of?'

Garrett let that one go by him. 'This Harwood uses a lot of names. Kitson is one of them. Hennessy is another.'

'Ah, now I get it,' the older man said. 'Why are you looking for him?'

'He's lived too long,' Garrett said flatly. There was a little silence.

Hans Kupfer looked at Garrett reflectively, as though deciding what words to choose when he spoke. 'What is it, murder?'

'Among other things.'

'I had no trouble with him,' Kupfer said. 'He did his work, pulled his weight.'

'Where did he live while he worked here?'

'We've got a dormitory. Casuals sleep there.'

'He didn't leave anything?'

Kupfer shook his head. 'Nothing to leave. Casuals usually arrive in what they're wearing and leave the same way.'

'You say you've no idea where he might have gone?'

'I didn't ask. He didn't say.'

'That's what I thought,' Garrett said, with a wry grin. 'Well, thanks for your help, Herr Kupfer. Give my regards to the King when you see him.'

'Peter Heldorf,' Kupfer growled. 'That old bastard.'

'You know him well.'

'We served together. In the . . . army.'

'Intelligence?'

'Very good,' the old man said. 'How did you know?'

'The way you ask questions. The way King Peter asks questions.'

Kupfer grinned unrepentantly. 'Nobody likes to admit he was in the Dienst these days. The kids think we were the same as those Gestapo bastards.'

And a lot of you were, Garrett thought.

'I've got to be going,' he said. 'Thanks for all your help. I'll leave you a number. In case you remember anything.'

'Good luck,' Kupfer said, taking the card. 'I hope you find your man.'

He hobbled back toward his office, an embittered survivor of a war most of his countrymen had gladly forgotten.

It was about five-thirty when Garrett drove out of the imposing gateway of Schwarzenberg. The road curved in long hairpins down from the mountains to the valley. Late-afternoon sun gilded the tops of the trees.

It was only the fractional error in aim of the man in the white Audi that saved Garrett's life. He was coasting down a straight stretch of road, between high banks crowned with close-set conifers, when the big car surged alongside. Garrett glanced automatically at the passing vehicle and as he did the first bullet, fired from a distance of about ten feet and moving at about four hundred and fifty meters a second, smashed its hundred and fifty-eight grains of lead into the steel upright of the window a couple of centimeters from Garrett's head, tearing the metalwork out of its fitting in the same instant that Garrett saw the glint of light on the heavy barrel of the pistol inside the car.

Even as the window to his left starred and a sliver of metal flicked his cheek like a whispering finger that drew blood, Garrett was slamming on the hand brake. In the same moment he whipped the wheel hard down to the right. The Mercedes slewed almost completely around in a screaming hundred-and-forty-degree turn, coming to a stop facing back up the hill. Even before it had stopped moving, Garrett had rolled out onto the grassy bank alongside the road, the deadly Smith & Wesson ASP in his hand, snaked by reflex action from the shoulder holster, prone and ready to fire as the Audi, moving at about a hundred kph, whistled down the road ahead, already almost into the left-hand bend where the road crossed a small bridge that would hide it from his sight.

Garrett steadied the stubby little automatic, lining up the Guttersnipe sight without conscious thought, relaxing automatically as he fired two groups of three shots after the disappearing car. For a moment the shots seemed to have had no effect, and then the tail of the Audi moved violently to the right and back to the left as its driver fought to hold the car on the road. Garrett's face showed grim satisfaction. Using the partially hollow THV — it stood for *très haute vitesse,* very high speed — ammunition perfected by the Societé Française des Munitions, which delivered twice the stopping power and penetration of a .357 Magnum, he knew that a couple of millimeters of soft steel wouldn't stop his bullets. He had hit something, either the driver or one of the tires.

The car straightened and then swerved again. Steel screeched on concrete as a tire flayed from the front offside wheel. A violent report tore into the screeching as another tire burst under the tremendous stresses being exerted on the wheels, and in what seemed like slow motion, the Audi turned on its side, crashing into the iron guardrail of the bridge with a sound like a gigantic hammer hitting a huge steel plate. As it hit, the Audi flipped onto its nose, both front doors bursting open. One of the wheels leaped outward into the road and the lid of the trunk soared in a short arc ahead of the car as it cartwheeled forward and over into the ravine below. The tremendous crash of tortured metal ended in abrupt silence.

Garrett was already on his feet, running down the hill toward the bridge, when the silence was shattered yet again, this time by a sullen explosion from the ravine as the gas tank ignited. By the time he reached the bridge, fierce flames were already licking hungrily around the twisted chassis, lying in the dry ravine perhaps thirty feet below him. There was no sign of the driver. Garrett slid and skidded down, gun ready, getting as near to the blazing wreck as the intense heat allowed.

The car was scrap, a battered jumble of scorching metal. It was impossible to see inside it. Smoke that stank of burning leather and oil coiled upward like a funeral pyre. Garrett shook his head; the driver had never had a chance.

He climbed back up to the bridge, and retraced his steps up the hill to the Mercedes. On the way, a dull gleam of metal in the road caught his eye. It was the would-be killer's revolver, its deadly blue surface abraded from contact at high speed with the road. The phoenix trademark of Sturm Ruger glared balefully at him from its circle on the walnut butt of the gun. He got back into the Mercedes and flopped onto the seat, waiting until the other levels of his mind released the questions that had begun forming there almost from the moment the first shot was fired.

Who?

Only two people had known where he was going: Klaus Prachner at BFV, and Inspector Robert Weidemann at the Federal Prosecutor's Office, both of whom he had called before leaving Wiesbaden. It was outside the bounds of belief that either of them would have been party to an attempt on his life. Which left only one other possibility; that Colonel Paul Barton, the Al Pacino of Wiesbaden, had put a hit man on Garrett's tail, and that he had been followed all the way up to Schwarzenberg by someone waiting for the opportunity that had presented itself on the mountain road below Niederbreitbach.

He turned the car around and headed down toward the Rhine. When he got to the bridge that crossed the river to Weissenthurm, he pulled over to the side of the road and used the car phone to call Klaus Prachner again. It was something of a relief to hear the familiar dry voice; the reaction to the violent events of a half hour earlier was coming stronger now.

'You sound shaky, Charles,' Klaus said. 'Anything wrong?'

'Not anymore,' Garrett said. 'But I need an SS squad, Klaus.'

'Where?'

Silently blessing his friend for asking the right questions first, Garrett gave him the precise instructions for finding the wreck that the BFV cleanup team would need. Their name was a jargon joke: Once upon a time the SS had been the most feared organization in Hitler's Germany. Now the initials were used to designate the *Scheissestaffel*, the Shit Squad whose job it was to remove all trace of any mess the security services did not wish to advertise. They would locate the Audi, winch it out of its ravine, repair the damaged road, fix the bridge, and fill in the huge gouges on the sides of the gully so that no one would ever be able to guess what had happened there.

'I'll get them down there immediately,' Prachner said. 'Can you tell me what happened?'

'Somebody tried to blow me off the road,' Garrett replied. 'Took a shot at me from a car with a Ruger Speed Six.'

'A *what* Speed Six?'

'Ruger. An American gun manufacturer in Southport, Connecticut. It's a .357 Magnum revolver, double action, side-loading six-shot. Seventy-millimeter barrel, three-dot radioluminous sighting system.'

'Makes a change from shotguns,' Prachner said sourly. 'You've got the gun?'

'Right here.'

'Give me the serial number and I'll see if I can trace it.'

'Fat chance.' Sturm Ruger put serial numbers either on the frame or the bottom of the butt of their guns. There was no sign of one on the weapon Garrett had picked up.

'Had the acid-bath treatment, has it?

Okay, forget the gun. What about the driver?'

'He ran out of road,' Garrett said.

'You're a mine of information, aren't you?' Prachner observed. 'Can you give me a registration for the car?'

'F-49821-MK. White Audi A6 four-door sedan.'

'That should be easy. I'll call you back.'

Garrett drove across the graceful suspension bridge over the Rhine and turned north on the autobahn toward Mönchengladbach. The dull gray kilometers sped beneath his wheels. As he passed the Brohital service area, the car phone gave its urgent signal. It was Prachner.

'That Audi you asked about,' he said. 'It's an *Ausreisser*. A runaway.' In German police slang a 'runaway' was a stolen car.

'That figures,' Garrett said.

'Sorry, Charles. Maybe we can come up with something when they bring the body in. What about Hennessy, by the way? Did you have any luck?'

'Yes,' Garrett said. 'And it was all bad.'

'Where are you now?'

'On the way back to Rheindahlen. That would seem to be where the answers are.'

'Charles, listen, I found something out. Something you ought to know. BFV is working on something inside USFET.'

'Heidelberg?' The headquarters of United States Forces, European Theater (USFET), were in Heidelberg.

'Our man is using the cover of a translator at the consulate in Frankfurt.'

'Doing what?'

'There are a lot of drug barons in the American army. There's a big drug traffic between the south of France and Germany. It's mostly cannabis, but there's cocaine and heroin as well. The big wheels at USFET are worried about it, and I gather BFV was asked to assist.'

'Are Barton and Shupe involved?'

'I don't know.'

'But you think the BFV man might know something?'

'I don't know that, either. All I can tell you is that Section Two has a man checking it out undercover. His name is Manfred Roth. He had an apartment on the Riederbergstrasse in Wiesbaden.'

151

'Very interesting,' Garrett said.

'I thought you'd say that.'

'I'm just coming up to the Niederzissen exit. If I turn around, I can be back in Wiesbaden in a couple of hours.'

'I thought you'd say that, too,' Prachner said. 'Listen, Garrett. If anyone asks, you haven't heard from me.'

'No problem.' A thought occurred to Garrett. 'Just one thing: if we haven't talked, how did you find out about the Audi at Niederkirchstein?'

'I'll tell them I'm psychic,' Prachner said, and broke the connection.

* * *

When he got back to Wiesbaden, Garrett checked into the Oranien Hotel on Platterstrasse. The room he was given was as severe as a monk's cell, neat, clean, and utterly without personality. He picked up the phone and called Eileen Carson. She answered on the second ring.

'Eileen, this is Charles Garrett,' he said. 'I came to see you about your brother.'

'I remember.' Her voice was guarded,

as though she were afraid he was going to spring a surprise question.

'I know this is short notice,' he said, 'but I wondered if you'd have dinner with me.'

'You mean tonight?'

'Why not?'

'Where are you?'

'Downtown. We could meet somewhere if you like.'

'You know Westendstrasse? There's an Italian restaurant. Gino's.'

'Eight o'clock?'

'Fine,' she said, and he could hear the curiosity in her voice. *What does he want?*

He called the restaurant and made a reservation, then put on his Burberry trench coat and walked over to Riederbergstrasse, which rose steeply along the flank of a hill crowned by the city hospital. Roth lived in a four-story building at the corner of Knaurstrasse. Garrett checked the mailbox and discovered that the agent's apartment was on the second floor; no lights showed from the windows.

He walked down the hill to the

Sedanplatz and turned right. Half a block along Westendstrasse, he found the place he was looking for. It was one of those Italian restaurants that are more Italian than the ones in Italy. The tables were covered with red-and-white-checkered cloths, candles stuck in Chianti bottles, packets of *grissini* beside each plate. On the wall was a painting of the bay of Naples done with more enthusiasm than accuracy. The place was full, nearly every table occupied. It was very noisy.

A buxom, dark-haired girl of about twenty-two greeted Garrett and showed him to a table in the corner. He ordered a bottle of Frascati, poured himself a glass, and sat back to wait. After about ten minutes the door opened and Eileen Carson came in. She was wearing a fake fox coat, thigh-hugging slacks, and high-heel leather boots. The owner, a thickset, dark-haired man who doubled as a waiter, greeted her effusively. She saw Garrett and raised her hand, wiggling the fingers.

'Hello,' she said, in her breathy little-girl voice. 'This is a surprise.'

She had on enough perfume to stock a duty-free shop, but it didn't conceal the fact that she'd taken a couple of belts from the bourbon bottle before she arrived. She sat down and looked at him expectantly.

'Would you like some wine?'

She wrinkled her nose and made a moue of distaste. 'I'll have a real drink.' She raised her voice. 'Gino, *caro*, the usual, *per favore*.'

'*Subito, subito!*' Gino trilled as he waltzed between the tables with four plates of food, one in each hand, the others balanced on his forearms. A few minutes later he brought over a large bourbon on the rocks and put it in front of Eileen Carson.

'*Grazie*, Gino,' she said.

'*Prego, prego!*' he said, and hurried away.

As she sipped her drink, Eileen Carson felt Garrett's eyes on her and she self-consciously fluffed her frizzy blond hair. She was wearing a sleeveless black blouse with a scalloped neckline that showed plenty of cleavage.

'Well,' she said, leaning forward so he could see more of it. 'And what brings you back to Wiesbaden, Mr. Garrett?'

'Unfinished business,' he said. Her eyes widened.

'That's right,' he said. 'You're the unfinished business, Eileen. I thought, that day at your apartment, what a shame we should pass like ships in the night. So I came back. And here I am.'

'Oh, how sweet,' she said.

'You want to know something? I sat by the telephone for an hour, trying to get up the nerve to phone.'

'You should have called earlier,' she said. 'I'd have dressed up. We could have gone somewhere nice.'

'There'll be plenty of time for that,' he said, reaching across the table and touching her hand.

The buxom girl brought them menus. Her name was Carla. It was clear from the way that Eileen talked to her that the two women knew each other well. To Garrett's surprise, the menu was interesting and inventive, something no Italian restaurant had to be in Germany, where people were generally much more interested in how much was on their plate than whether it was good.

'What do you feel like eating?' he said.

Eileen Carson looked at him boldly and smiled. 'Whatever you think I'd like,' she said, rolling her eyes to emphasize the innuendo.

He drank some more of the Frascati and ordered another Jack Daniel's for Eileen. She lit a cigarette with her slim gold lighter.

'So tell me about you,' she said. This time she reached across to touch his hand. Her eyes were slightly glazed.

'No, no,' he said, taking her pudgy fingers in his hand. 'You're much more interesting. You're a mystery woman.'

'Think so?' she said, preening. The idea obviously appealed to her. She was about as mysterious as a Big Mac. 'Well, don't you go gettin' any ideas, big feller.'

'Can't go to jail for what you're thinking,' he said. Maybe I should pant and let my tongue hang out, he thought. Carla brought them their first course and Garrett ordered another drink for Eileen.

Any other time he would have felt pretty lousy about what he was doing, but he told himself that it was worthwhile if it led him to whoever had killed George Wood.

'I met your friend Paul Barton the other day,' he told her as they ate the antipasto. The bread was fresh and good.

'I told you already, he's no friend of mine,' she said tartly.

'What's his wife like?'

'Lucy? She's okay.'

'You said Barton was two-timing her.'

'That bastard. He two-times everyone.'

'Has she got a boyfriend, too?'

She grinned blearily. 'Everybody's got a schatzi. Nothin' else to do in this borin' fuckin' hole, excuse my French.'

Carla took the dishes away and came back with their main course.

'This boyfriend of Lucy Barton's. Is he a serviceman?'

'You kiddin'?' she said. 'Even if Lucy were dumb enough to fool around with a serviceman, nobody would take the chance.'

'What's his name?'

'Rauth, Roth, something like that.

Dunno what she sees in him. He's a little shrimp of a guy, with a doll face and a wispy mustache.'

'Does Barton know about him?'

Eileen raised her eyebrows at him. 'You crazy?'

'Barton's a tough cookie, huh?'

'Not just him,' she said. 'All of them. The Four Horsemen.'

'Who?'

' 'S what they call them. Four Horsemen of the Apol — Acolo — '

'Apocalypse?'

'You bet ya bippy,' she said, poking the food on her plate around with her fork. 'Bet ya bippy.'

There were four of them, she said. Besides Paul Barton, there was a great lumbering bear of a man from Arizona called Walt Gilchriese; Donald Rogers, who was senior executive officer, CIC; and last, but by no means least, Colonel Max Northrup, commanding. Someone had dubbed them the Four Horsemen of the Apocalypse and it had stuck.

'All b'long to the same unit,' she said. 'Some hush-hush operation nobody's

159

allowed to talk about.'

'Something to do with CIC, I suppose,' he said artlessly.

'Na,' she said, shaking her head. 'Special Operations Unit. Nobody knows what it does, but that's what they call it. Headquartered at Jefferson barracks.'

'In Bad Kreuznach?'

'Right. Northrup runs things in Kreuznach. That fat pig Gilchriese in Darmstadt. Rogers in Heidelberg. And little old Al Pacino right here in Wiesbaden. Why d'you want to know all this stuff, anyway?'

'No special reason.' Garrett shrugged. 'Let's talk about something else. You, for instance.'

She giggled, and reached across the table to take his hand. 'You're sweet. You ask a lot of questions, but you're sweet.'

'You forget, I'm a stranger. I don't know all these people the way you do.'

Eileen Carson snorted. 'You don't want to know them,' she said vehemently. 'None of them.'

He had the feeling that she wanted to say more, but the moment passed. She ran the tip of her tongue over her lips and leaned forward so that he could see the swell of her breasts.

'Get the check, darling,' she said conspiratorially. 'Then we'll go back to my place for a nightcap, yes?' She put her hand on his thigh beneath the table.

'Sounds great,' he said. He signaled Carla, who brought the check and promised to call for a cab right away. It arrived soon after they finished their coffee, and they went out onto the street pursued by a burst of *arriverdercis* from Gino. In the taxi, Eileen's lips were hot and feverish.

They went up the stairs to her apartment and she unlocked the door. She threw her fake fur coat at the sofa and wobbled toward the bedroom, stopping in the doorway to look back at him with her chin on her shoulder, her eyelids slumbrous.

'I'll jus get inna somethin' comf'ble,' she said. 'Pour us a drink.'

He took two glasses from the liquor cabinet and measured out a stiff bourbon. Into his own glass he poured some mineral water and a dash of liquor. Well, I'm driving, he thought with a wry grin. Eileen appeared in the doorway, striking a pose. Her body beneath the filmy nightgown was silhouetted against the light. There was plenty of her.

'See anythin' you like?' she said, coming across to the sofa. She put both her arms around his neck and fastened her mouth on his, molding her body against him. He disentangled himself from her arms, stood up, and took off his jacket, unfastening his shirt purposefully. She looked up at him, her mouth slack.

'Finish your drink,' he said. 'I'm taking you to bed.'

She downed her whiskey and stood up. 'Take me,' she said woozily. Garrett swept her off her feet into his arms and whirled her around. Her head lolled, and he saw the whites of her eyes; her head was probably spinning like a gyroscope. He took her into the bedroom and laid her on the bed. She managed a weak smile. Her eyes were as blank as water.

'Be gentle, lover,' she said, and passed out.

9

As soon as he was certain that Eileen was asleep, Garrett systematically searched her apartment. He lucked out almost immediately; she kept a diary. Correction: diaries. When he noticed a locked drawer under the desk in the wall unit in the sitting room, a picklock from the slim wallet of them that he always carried opened it in seconds. It contained four leatherette-covered books, each page filled with her sloping script.

Garrett took them across to the sofa and started reading.

Each of the many names that appeared in Eileen Carson's jottings was marked with coded signals. Some of these clearly indicated sexual prowess: one-, two-, three-, four-, or five-star performance, by the look of it. Others were less obvious. What, for instance did the symbols '<->' or '½' or '///' mean? He grinned. None of your damned business, Garrett, he told himself.

There were a lot of names he didn't know, and a lot of initials that didn't mean anything to him at all. He found what he was looking for in the third book. The diaries indicated that as long ago as May 14, a year ago, she had noted a visit from her brother.

Geo. here today. He wants to get out of Rhine army, but says if he tries, they'll fix it so he gets dishonorable discharge, and no pension. I told him to go to his CO but he says they've got him tied up as well.

The next entry mentioning George Wood was in July.

Geo. here again. He was in some sort of trouble. He wouldn't tell me what it is. Says if anyone knew I knew, I would be in danger, too.

Garrett turned the pages rapidly. After three volumes, it was no hardship to skip through Eileen Carson's bodice-ripper accounts of her life on the mattress. He reached October of the preceding year when a name caught his eye.

October 12
Wine festival dance at Rudesheim. Shupe and that wimp Cameron there. S. sucking around. Bastard. Does he think I'll ever forget? Clive Pennyweather. Only 31.**
Very British: just thank you, ma'am, no wham bam.

So Pennyweather had been another of Eileen Carson's many conquests. He turned the pages rapidly, scanning the entries with one part of his mind while another asked questions he couldn't answer. What sort of trouble was Wood in? What had Shupe done that Eileen Carson would never forget?

Pennyweather's initials — either as 'C.P.' or later, as the affair ran down, just 'P.' — appeared frequently until the following April. The last entry read:

165

April 12

P. v. tiresome. He has got into some kind of trouble with S. I told him not to come around anymore. G. here again. Says he is in over his head, but he won't tell me any more. I don't know what he expects me to do about it.

Kurt S. **** He is fabulous ////. C. joined us as arranged. ½. K. fucks like a steam engine. I thought it was going to come out of my ears.

Obviously Pennyweather had been given the gate, and his place had been taken by Kurt S., whoever he was. Eileen Carson clearly didn't waste any of her time crying over spilled milk. Could the 'C' stand for Carla? Did the notation '½' mean three in a bed? Keep your mind on the job, Garrett, he thought. The next mention of Sergeant Wood was dated October 3, the day before his murder.

G. called. Someone arrived at Rh.dahlen from UK he thinks he can trust. He is going to tell him everything. Says dangerous to talk but must do something. His exact words: 'What I'm mixed up in is bad enough but Project 23 is beyond criminal.'

'Project 23,' Garrett muttered. 'What the hell is that?'

He kept on reading until the first faint gray light of dawn filtered into the apartment. Eileen Carson was still snoring gently in her king-size bed. He put on his jacket and made some instant coffee in the kitchen. Before he left, he gently mussed up the bedclothes on what had been intended to be his side, taking care not to waken her. He found a lipstick and used it to write a message on her dressing-table mirror.

'You were wonderful,' he printed. After all, he thought, she had her pride, too. He wondered how many stars she would award him in her diary.

By seven-thirty he was parked outside Manfred Roth's apartment on the Riederbergstrasse. He recognized the German from Eileen Carson's description. Roth was wearing a loden coat and a narrow-brimmed black leather hat. He reversed his Volkswagen Passat out of the garage below the apartment and set off down the hill.

Garrett stayed behind the black VW all the way down the autobahn to Frankfurt. Roth turned uphill past the Senckenberg Natural History Museum and the university and cut through to the tree-lined Siesmayerstrasse. A few hundred meters up on the left, he swung into the parking area beside the modern building that housed the American consulate.

Garrett watched Roth show his ID to the marine at the barrier, park the VW, and go into the consulate. He looked at his watch: eight-thirty. Assuming an eight-hour day, Roth would be in there until four-thirty. He drove over to the parking lot in front of the old opera house, parked the car, and found a telephone booth. Emil Fritz came on the line almost at once. He sounded surprised to hear Garrett's voice.

'We heard you got beaten up, Charles,' he said. 'I thought they had you in the hospital.'

'I was and they did,' Garrett replied. 'Who told you about it?'

'Three guesses,' Emil said dryly. 'He wasn't prostrate with grief, either.'

'So that's why I didn't get any flowers. Listen, Emil, I need a favor.'

'Name it.'

'I'm in Frankfurt. I want to see the dossier of a BFV operative named Roth, Manfred Roth.'

'Does Shupe know you're back in the field?'

'Why?'

'He told us all requests for assistance from you were to be cleared with him before activation.'

'Let's not tell him, then.'

'He'll find out soon enough,' Emil said. 'He's got informers everywhere.'

'Is Ralph Summers still running the outstation in Frankfurt?'

'You've got a good memory.'

'Call him. Tell him I'm coming in to use the facilities. How long will it take you to get the dossier?'

'A couple of hours.'

'Fax it to me there. And thanks, Emil.'

'*Nichts zu danken*. Are you all right, Charles?'

'So far, so good,' Garrett said. '*Schuss*.'

The BSSO outstation was a scruffy-looking office building in Krögerstrasse, near the Eschersheimer Tower, one of the city's old medieval gateways.

Ralph Summers came bustling out of his office, a tall, slim, dark-haired man in shirtsleeves, with horn-rim spectacles on the end of his nose. He gave Garrett a bear hug and then held him at arm's length to look at him.

'Good God, Charles,' he said. 'What happened to you?'

'It's a long story,' Garrett said. 'How are you, Ralph?'

Summers shrugged. 'You know how it is in a place like this. Nothing but excitement.'

As they went through to Summers's office, Garrett cast a glance over the personnel working industriously at their desks, computer screens flickering. Most of them were leggy, long-haired young women in their middle twenties, 'good-lookin' gels' who had gotten their jobs in

BSSO because their parents knew someone who knew someone in Foreign and
Commonwealth, someone able to get
these Fionas and Annabels the 'glamor-
ous' overseas job they all seemed to covet.
Of course, the pay was lousy, but they
didn't need the money; Daddy took care
of all that.

'Come into my office,' Summers said.
'Tell me how we can help.'

They went into the glass-walled office;
Summers shut the door behind him. The
plastic chatter of the computer keyboards
was blotted out. Apart from the faint
sounds of traffic on the street below, the
room was silent.

'I want some checks run on American
military personnel serving here in Germany,' Garrett said. 'Is there any way we
can get sight of their service jackets?'

'I take it you don't want them to know
you're checking up on them?' When
Garrett didn't reply, Ralph Summers
nodded as if he had. 'In that case, we have
to go around the houses. What are these
men — army, air force, marines?'

'Army,' Garrett said. 'Current service.'

The records of all serving American personnel, Summers told him, were held at the Military Personnel Records Center in St. Louis, Missouri. Access was, of course, restricted.

'What we have to do is play a game we call leapfrog,' Summers said. 'For a start, we plug ourselves in to the R2 computer in London.'

'Neal McCaskill and his happy band,' Garrett observed.

'Mac' McCaskill, as he was known, was the dour Scot who ran the security service computer complex in the DI5 Operations Division, which was sandwiched conveniently — but by no means accidentally — between the computer banks of British Telecom and the Department of Health and Social Security, on the twenty-fifth floor of Euston Tower on London's Marylebone Road.

'That's right. They've got a thousand times the computer power we've got here. What might take us all week will take them only a few minutes. We'll ask them to scan their networks to find us a computer we can talk to, which talks to the computer we want to talk to.'

'Run that by me again,' Garrett said.

'Leapfrog,' Summers said again. 'Let's say you wanted to get inside our computer. This one here. First you'd have to get your computer to communicate with one that we're already talking to. Then you would have to break into its codes, which might take the average hacker a couple of weeks, or a couple of months, or forever. But let's say you get lucky and hit the right numbers. You can then use that computer to get into ours. That's why it's called leapfrog.'

'Sounds too good to be true,' Garrett said. 'Is it really that easy?'

'I didn't say it was easy,' Summers replied testily. 'I said it can be done.'

Garrett gave him the names. Summers wrote them down and went outside to talk to leggy brunette with long hair tied into a loose ponytail. She looked over her shoulder at Garrett and smiled. Summers came back into the office.

'Okay, Vanessa is through to London now. They'll ask who this is for. I told her to use your name. Is that okay?'

'Fine,' Garrett said. 'I'm expecting some stuff from Cologne. Emil Fritz said he'd Fax it to me here.'

Summers picked up an intercom, pushed a button.

'Daphne, has anything come through from Cologne? Nothing yet? Okay, listen. Something will be coming through for a Mr. Garrett. Bring it in here as soon as it arrives. Good girl.'

He reached over to a side table and unscrewed the top off a thermos bottle, filling a thick mug with coffee. He lifted the thermos and raised his eyebrows at Garrett.

'Thanks,' Garrett said. 'Black, one sugar.'

Garrett looked at the clock on the wall of the office outside. It was close to midday.

He turned as a young woman knocked on the glass door of Summers's office. She was carrying a folder that contained a sheaf of papers.

'Daphne, this is Mr. Garrett,' Summers said.

'These are for you, sir,' she said,

174

handing him the folder. Garrett thanked her and she went out, closing the door gently.

'Whose are those?' Summer asked as Garrett riffled through the papers.

'Manfred Roth, the BFV agent I mentioned to you,' Garrett said. 'He looks clean.'

'Did you have any reason to think otherwise?'

Garrett shrugged. 'Can I use your phone?'

'Go ahead.' Summers got up and went out of the office without being asked. A pro, Garrett thought. You had to tell the amateurs. He dialed the London number and waited. It rang four times and then the familiar voice of Derek Warren came on the line.

'On scrambler, please sir,' Garrett said. Brigadier General Warren was a senior liaison officer to the joint intelligence chiefs at the Ministry of Defense in Whitehall. Garrett pushed down the scarlet control button on his own phone and waited until Warren did likewise in London.

'All clear,' he heard him say. 'What is it?'

'I've run across an American project here that nobody seems to be able to tell me anything about, General,' Garrett said. 'All I know about it is that it's called Project 23.'

'That all you can give me?'

'USFET has a Special Operations Unit based at Bad Kreuznach, commanded by a Colonel Max Northrup. There appear to be outreaches in Heidelberg, Darmstadt, and Wiesbaden. It's possible Project 23 has something to do with them. I wondered if you could do a little poking around. See if anyone at JIC knows anything about it. It would seem to have a pretty high security rating.'

'I'll do what I can,' Warren said dubiously. 'Can't promise anything, of course.'

'Thank you, sir. I'm grateful,' Garrett said. He hung up and redialed, this time using the number that would put him straight through to Nicholas Bleke.

'Bleke.'

'Garrett, sir. Have you got time for a

176

situation report?'

'Fire away, Charles,' Bleke said, his voice noticeably friendlier. Garrett depressed the scrambler button again and made his report, omitting nothing. Once or twice Bleke interrupted the flow of words with a request for clarification of this point or that, but in main he listened without comment until Garrett was finished.

'Do you want me to talk to Dick Snyder?' Bleke asked. 'Maybe he could cut a few corners for you.' Snyder was head of the CIA's London station, based at the Grosvenor Square embassy.

'I think I'd prefer to keep the Company out of things at this stage, sir,' Garrett hedged. 'If I need to involve them, I'll let you know.'

'Good,' Bleke said. 'Keep in touch.'

Garrett hung up, a faint smile on his face. It was one of the things he liked about the Old Man; he was all business and no bullshit.

Ralph Summers took him to lunch in a restaurant called Alt Nürnberg where they ate spicy, strong-tasting Nuremberg sausages on pewter plates and drank

Henniger *dunkelbier* from stoneware tankards served by buxom girls in national dress.

When they got back to the office, there was another dossier waiting. Garrett went through it quickly. Clive Pennyweather was a career soldier: Wellington school, Sandhurst, a good regiment. He lived in bachelor officers' quarters, but was engaged to a nice girl back home. The dossier gave no indication of what, if any, trouble Pennyweather might be in with Colonel Paul Shupe, nor why, with a pretty fiancée waiting for him in Beaconsfield, he had gotten himself involved with someone like Eileen Carson. Garrett laid down the dossier with an impatient sound. Ralph Summers looked at it over his shoulder.

'No good?' he asked.

'That's the trouble with dossiers,' Garrett said. 'You can't ask them questions.'

Summers left him to his own thoughts.

The afternoon wore on; at about four o'clock, Summers came back in to report that the girl doing the 'leapfrogging'

— her name was Fiona; Garrett smiled at the predictability of it — had not yet been successful in connecting with St. Louis.

'I've taken a room at the Oranien in Wiesbaden,' Garrett said. 'Courier whatever you get up there as soon as they come through.'

He walked back to the opera house, got into his car, paid the ransom to the attendant at the parking lot, and drove across to the American consulate. At four-forty, Manfred Roth came out of the building and got into the black Volkswagen. Garrett tailed it back along the autobahn to Wiesbaden, evincing no surprise when instead of going back to his apartment, the German headed up the valley through the spa quarter and made a left into a tree-lined cul-de-sac, where he parked the car. He went into a large two-story house with a well-kept front garden.

Garrett drove on down the wide, tree-lined avenue until he saw a restaurant on his right-hand side. He pulled into the parking lot and went in. The telephone cabin was just inside the door, a phone book on the shelf below it. It was the work of only a few moments to confirm that the house Roth had just gone into belonged to Major Paul Barton.

He got back into his car and drove back up the hill, turning around so that he was parked on the right facing the way he had just come. After about an hour and a quarter, Roth came out of the Barton house, got into his car, and drove down the hill. Garrett followed at a respectable distance, confident Roth was headed back to his apartment. Garrett drove on down to the Sedanplatz, found a telephone, and dialed Roth's number.

'My name is Charles Garrett,' he told the German. 'I'm a friend of Klaus Prachner. He suggested I call you.'

'What can I do for you, Herr Garrett?'

'I'd like to talk. Have you any free time this evening?'

'I can make some.'

'How about the Kurhaus Restaurant? Say seven o'clock?'

'How shall I recognize you?'

'Trench coat, Donegal tweed hat. *Frankfurter Allgemeine* under my arm.'

'*Stimmt,*' Roth said. 'See you later.'

At about six-thirty, Garrett walked downtown through the crowded pedestrian precinct that opened out by the town hall into what had once been the old marketplace, bought a copy of the Frankfurt newspaper from a newsstand and walked around the Kursaal to the restaurant.

'Herr Garrett?'

Close up, Manfred Roth was even smaller than Garrett had thought, with a face so smooth-skinned that he looked like a doll. Shrewd gray eyes shone behind rimless spectacles. He looked like the senior clerk in an insurance company. A waitress showed them to a table in a corner at the rear and looked at them expectantly as they sat down. Garrett ordered black coffee.

'*Kaffeinfrei,*' Roth told the waitress primly. He tapped his stomach by way of explanation to Garrett. 'Can't drink it unless it's decaf,' he said. 'Damned stuff keeps me awake all night.'

'Thanks for coming,' Garrett said.

Roth shrugged. 'Any friend of Klaus's,' he said.

181

'How long have you known him?' Garrett asked casually.

Roth grinned. It made him look ten years younger. 'Longer than you, Mr. Garrett,' he said. 'Don't look surprised. You knew damned well I'd call him.'

'What did he tell you?'

'He gave me a message for you. He said the man in the Audi was . . . wait, I wrote it down.' He took out a small notebook, leafed through it. 'Age between thirty and forty, white, male, Caucasian. It hasn't been possible to identify him yet, because everything burned. Okay?'

His eyes betrayed his curiosity. Garrett made no attempt to satisfy it. 'Okay,' he said. Everything burned, he thought dispiritedly; another dead end. 'Did Klaus tell you why I'm here in Germany?'

'Something to do with the bombings at the British bases up north, isn't it?'

'That's what brought me here. Since then a sergeant in the army has been found murdered. You read about that?'

'Wasn't it the same group that did the bombing at Rheindahlen?'

'That's what it said in the papers.'

'But you don't think so.'

'The MO of the bombers at Rheindahlen was copybook IRA. There was an IRA hit team operating somewhere between Antwerp and Düsseldorf. They killed some soldiers in Holland, then disappeared. Our people felt pretty sure this was them.'

'But instead you got the Red German Army.'

'I don't think there's any such organization as the Red German Army,' Garrett said flatly. 'I think what happened is that the IRA did the bombing, but someone else, someone calling themselves the Red German Army, claimed they did it to give credibility to the name. Then, when they killed George Wood, they were already, as it were, a fully-fledged terrorist group.'

'It's an interesting theory,' Roth said. 'Have you got anything to back it up?'

'Nothing you could call proof,' Garrett said. 'Wood was frightened. He told his sister he was involved in something dangerous that he couldn't get out of. He told me it concerned an officer in Rheindahlen called Shupe and another

183

here in Wiesbaden called Barton. We had arranged to meet so he could tell me the rest of it. That was when he got killed.'

'Shupe and Barton.' Roth grimaced.

'You know them?'

'I work as a translator for the military attaché of the United States consulate in Frankfurt,' Roth said. 'Sooner or later you meet everyone.'

For military attaché, read CIA, Garrett thought; interesting. 'Have you ever heard of something called Project 23?'

Roth frowned. 'Never,' he replied. 'What is it?'

'I don't know. It might have something to do with a unit at Bad Kreuznach called the Special Projects Team, commanded by a colonel named Max Northrup.'

'This is all news to me,' Roth said. 'Of course, the Americans don't feel the need to tell us everything.'

'Can you tell me anything about what you're doing down here?'

'What do you want to know?'

'General parameters would do.'

'Okay, general parameters. Last spring,

USFET became concerned about drug abuse after a missile launch control team was discovered smoking dope on duty. The more they dug, the worse it got; it was an epidemic. They figured it had to be organized, and if it was organized, it had to be international. If that was the case, it was more than Army Criminal Intelligence Corps could handle alone. So, on a strictly unofficial basis, they asked BFV for help. USFET made some positions available to our people in appropriate places: Frankfurt, Heidelberg, Munich, and so on.'

'Big traffic?'

'Big enough. The market in the States is about at saturation, so the Colombians have switched their attention to Europe. Army personnel are an obvious target. We think that about ten million dollars' worth a year, street value, is coming into Germany alone.'

'That's a lot of snow.'

'It doesn't all go to the military. There are plenty of civilians ready to buy as well. We're trying to establish exactly where it's coming in, and whether it's the military that's running the stuff.'

'Are the drugs reaching British troops as well as Americans?'

Roth shrugged. 'Probably.'

'Are any of the officers I named part of your investigation?'

Roth shrugged. 'Until we nail whoever is running the narcotics, everyone is suspect.'

It wasn't so much an answer as an evasion. Garrett didn't push it. 'Do you know a lady named Eileen Carson?' he asked.

Roth grinned. 'Everybody knows Eileen,' he said. 'Although not all of them call her a lady.'

'What about Lucy Barton?'

Roth's face stiffened.

'You're making a mistake, Garrett,' he said. 'It's not the way it looks.'

'If you say so,' Garrett said. 'Tell me how it really is.'

Roth shook his head.

'Let's just say it's outside the parameters I agreed upon.'

'Is that what they're calling it now?' Garrett said. 'Parameters?'

Roth flushed, and Garrett saw anger kindle in his eyes.

'I told you the matter is not open for discussion, Garrett,' Roth said, putting his hands on the arms of his chair and making as if to stand up. 'Drop the subject, or I'm leaving.'

'All right, all right, I'm sorry,' Garrett apologized. 'Please, sit down. Let me ask you something else.'

Manfred Roth hesitated for a long moment, then sat down again. 'You can ask,' he said warily. 'I don't promise to answer.'

'I've been told Paul Barton is having an affair with Kitty Irwin, the wife of General Leyland Irwin, commanding Rhine army. Is that true?'

'There's more to it than that.'

'Such as?'

Roth shook his head. 'No comment.'

'Of course,' Garrett said. 'You're using Lucy Barton as a source, aren't you?'

'No comment,' Roth said again.

'A source for what?' Garrett wanted to know.

Roth just looked at him and made no reply.

'We're supposed to be on the same side, you know.'

'You're investigating some bombings in Rheindahlen and the shooting of a British soldier. Lucy Barton could not possibly have any connection with either event.'

'What would you say if I told you that I suspect Paul Barton tried to have me killed?'

'Why would he do that?'

'You're not that näive,' Garrett said. 'But I'll spell it out anyway. Barton is involved in the drug racket. Wood was a courier. He looked as if he were going to spill the beans, so they killed him. I went to see Barton, told him what I just told you. Within twenty-four hours, someone tried to kill me.'

'Even if it's true, that's not the reason for my interest in Lucy Barton.'

'What is?'

Roth shrugged. 'I can't tell you that,' he said, getting up and putting on his coat and hat. 'And listen, Garrett. I've got enough problems without you getting under my feet. Don't call me again, and more importantly, don't follow me. Understood?'

'I don't know what you do to the enemy, Manfred,' Garrett said, 'but, by God, you frighten me.'

'Think positively,' Roth said unsympathetically. 'You've got more now than you had when you came in here.'

'Thanks,' Garrett said. 'Thanks a lot.'

'My pleasure,' Roth said. Garrett watched him go without anger or surprise. There were a lot of people like Roth in intelligence work, people with tunnel vision and compartmentalized minds. Whatever Roth knew, he wasn't sharing. Garrett looked at his watch. It was nearly eight-thirty. He went to a telephone and called Jessica.

'Where are you?' she said.

'Wiesbaden,' he said. 'That toddling town.'

'You sound miserable.'

'I wish you were here,' he said. 'I need your expertise.'

'I wish I were there, too,' she replied, and he could almost see that devil dancing in her eyes. 'You could have it.'

'I've met a woman here,' he told her. 'I'm trying to figure out what makes her tick.'

'You're asking my professional advice, I take it?'

'Be serious, Jess,' he said. 'Her name is Eileen Carson. Thirty-five. Her husband was killed in a road accident in 1984. On the face of it, she is making a determined effort to get into the *Guinness Book of Sexual Records*.'

'How do you know all this?'

'I read her diaries.'

'You read her *diaries*?'

'It's a dirty job,' he said. 'But someone has to do it. Any thoughts?'

'It's hard to say without knowing the woman, Charles,' Jessica said. 'Maybe she had a frigid husband and she's making up for lost time.'

'I'm disinclined to think so. She told me he hadn't been buried two days before every soldier in West Germany was trying to get into her pants.'

'You do have a way with the ladies, Charles.'

'She was drunk,' Garrett said.

'Did she proposition you?'

'Sort of. It was more like she let me know that if I made a pass at her, she wouldn't fight me off.'

'And what did you do then, my dear?'

'I got the hell out of there.'

'I'm relieved to hear it.'

'So, what do you think?'

'As I said, I can only make a guess. What you or I might shrug off as a slight might humiliate someone else utterly. What we might consider merely humiliating could drive another person to the edge of suicide.'

'But you think the basic problem might be a lack of self-regard.'

'The important word to remember is 'might',' Jessica emphasized. 'It might be that if she has no belief in her own worth, she sleeps around to make herself feel desired, loved even. The drinking would be so she doesn't have to think about what she's doing. Is all this any help?'

'Yes,' he said. 'I think it is. Look, I'll send over a dossier. Do a psychological profile on her for me. Get Pat Miller to give you a hand if you need help.'

'You think I can't manage it on my own?'

'No offense, kiddo,' he said. 'I need it fast, and two heads are better than one.'

'Not just two heads,' she said. 'Talking about which, when will you be back?'

'Hard to tell. Not soon.'

'Oh.' She was silent for a moment. 'Well, let's not ask for the moon. We have the stars.'

He walked slowly back through the brightly-lit streets, playing back in his mind the tape of his conversation with Manfred Roth. *You've got more now than you had when you came in here.* He went through it all again step by step. What had he got? Assume Roth was using Lucy Barton as a source. If she were giving Roth information it could only be on one subject: Paul Barton and/or Kitty Irwin. Roth had said there was more to Barton's affair with Kitty Irwin than just romance. That was information he could only have gotten from Lucy. Now for the big question: was Lucy Barton supplying Roth with information voluntarily or involuntarily?

There was an important distinction between the two. If she was actively spying on Barton and Kitty Irwin, that meant she either knew or believed both of them were involved in the narcotics racket. But if Roth was exploiting a relationship with Lucy Barton to find out what he wanted to know, she was just another innocent bystander being used by a manipulative agent. Priority number one, therefore, was to establish just how well Manfred Roth knew Lucy Barton.

He looked at his watch and shrugged. *If God had wanted everything done today, He wouldn't have invented tomorrow.* He stopped at a liquor store and looked along the shelves for a bottle of wine. At a delicatessen a little farther up the street he picked up some bread, some rough country pâté, some of the thin slices of meat known as *aufschnitt*, and mustard. He took the food up to his room and spread it out on the small table beside the window. It wasn't Le Manoir Aux Quat' Saisons, but it was good; he was wiping his fingers on a paper napkin when the phone rang and the desk clerk told him a courier had delivered a package. He went down to the foyer and signed for the bulky parcel. The black leather-clad dispatch rider was a good-looking youngster of about twenty-two, with tousled blond hair and a cocky smile.

'Any message?' he asked.

'Say hello to Fiona,' Garrett said.

The cocky grin got even wider. 'It's Daphne, actually,' the courier said. Garrett took the package up to his room, locking the door behind him. He poured some more wine into the glass he had brought in from the bathroom and sat cross-legged on the bed, reading the U.S. Army service dossiers on Paul Barton, Donald Rogers, Walter Gilchriese, and Max Northrup with scrupulous care. It was well after ten o'clock when he finished. He laid the papers aside and poured himself one more glass of the Rhône wine. He caught sight of himself in the mirror and raised the glass in a mock toast.

'Here's looking at you, kid,' he said, and thought of Jessica.

* ★ ★

He was running across a field toward a copse of conifers and beech. The ground was rough and heavy, newly plowed.

He reached the shelter of the trees and turned around. The field he had just run across mocked him with its emptiness. Rooks cawed overhead somewhere. Off to the left the ground sloped sharply downhill to a road.

He eased back into the deeper shadow of the close-planted trees, placing his feet carefully. The butt of the Smith & Wesson AP felt greasy in his hand. He was moving forward when he heard the heart-stopping crack of a dry branch snapping and whirled around to see Sean Hennessy crouched behind him, an AK47 cradled in his hands, his face alight with hatred.

'I told you we'd settle this one day, Garrett!' he shouted. 'I told you I'd find you!'

Garrett started to bring his gun up, but he knew he was always going to be too late and he watched Hennessy's finger tighten on the trigger of the Kalashnikov. As flame blossomed in the muzzle of the gun, a telephone began ringing. Garrett opened his eyes. The phone beside the bed shrilled again, loud and persistent, banishing his nightmare.

'Garrett.'

'Klaus Prachner, Charles. It's Manfred Roth.'

'What about him?'

'He's dead,' Prachner said flatly. 'Dead as a mackerel.'

10

The usual crowd of people was moving purposefully through Manfred Roth's apartment in Riederbergstrasse: fingerprint and forensic specialists, some uniformed police, photographers. It was not a very big place, just two rooms, bathroom, and kitchen; there was hardly any room to move. The body was lying in the center of the room. It looked like dead bodies always look: not quite real, something humanoid with nothing living in it. The off-white carpeting beneath the body was dark with blood. The sharp technical tang of chemicals mingled with the odor of tobacco. You should have told me what you knew, Manfred, Garrett thought.

Inspector Robert Weidemann came out of the bedroom, the sturdily built Gottfried behind him. Weidemann looked peevish and out of sorts, like a man awakened from a sound sleep and forced to go out on a cold night. He looked at

Garrett expressionlessly, and then waved a hand, come over.

'Well, Garrett,' he said. 'You're turning into a regular Typhoid Mary. Everywhere you go, corpses. Who told you about this?'

'BFV called me,' Garrett said, without being specific.

'Why you?'

'I talked to Roth last night. About eight o'clock.'

'What about?'

'Our mutual interest,' Garrett replied. 'What exactly happened here?'

'Someone broke in and shot him. Simple as that. It wouldn't have been difficult; these places have locks a kid could spring. Roth never even knew what hit him.'

'Nobody in this building saw or heard anything?'

'Nobody ever does anymore. They're all asleep in front of the TV.'

'Our Red German Army again, I take it?'

'Ah-uh,' Weidemann said, gloomily. 'Same caliber weapon, same luggage tag.'

'Who called you in?'

'We're the agents of choice,' Gottfried said. 'The Red German Army is our case. We get all the good ones.'

'Have you come up with anything on these people yet, Garrett?' Weidemann asked.

'I'm beginning to think they don't exist,' Garrett said.

Weidemann looked at him sharply. 'Your thumbs pricking again?'

'Exactly,' Garrett said.

Weidemann looked up. A detective was gesturing from the bedroom doorway. 'Don't go away,' he said. 'I want to hear the rest of this.'

Weidemann and Gottfried went into the bedroom. Inside, detectives were carefully going through Roth's clothes and possessions, unfolding the neatly folded sweaters and shirts, checking each jacket and pair of pants. You lost any right to privacy by getting murdered. Klaus Prachner came in from the bedroom. He had on the same tan leather jacket that he had been wearing the last time Garrett saw him. Garrett started to say something, but Klaus held up a hand. As he did, a large fat man came through the doorway behind him. He wore a tan gaberdine suit, a pale blue cotton shirt with French cuffs linked by chunky gold cuff links, a yellow silk tie, and alligator loafers with gold chains. He looked at Garrett with flat, incurious gray eyes.

'Who are you?' he said, his voice hostile. Prachner stepped forward.

'Garrett, this is Gerhard Leiche. Head of Amt Two, BFV. Gerhard, this is Charles Garrett, attached to British Security Services Overseas.'

'*Freut mich*,' Leiche said, although if he were pleased to meet Garrett it didn't show on his lardy face. 'What brings you here, Herr Garrett?'

'I asked him to come over,' Prachner said. 'He was probably the last person to see Roth alive.' His eyes caught Garrett's. *Nothing I can do about this*, they said.

'So?' Leiche said, drawing the word out like someone doing an bad imitation of a German. 'Where was this meeting, Herr Garrett? And at what time?'

'In the Kurhaus. Seven o'clock last night.'

'You knew Roth well?'

'I'd never met him before.'

'Who put you in contact with him?'

'It looked as if there might be a connection between some inquiries I was making and the matter Roth was investigating,' Garrett said. 'Klaus suggested I get in touch with him.'

'How very helpful,' Leiche said, with a thin smile at Prachner. 'And what inquiries exactly are those?'

'I'm investigating the bombing of the British army base at Rheindahlen,' Garrett replied. 'And the murder of a British soldier. The Red German Army claimed credit for both.'

'Yes, yes,' Leiche said testily. 'But what had Roth to do with that, Herr Garrett?'

'Until now, nothing,' Garrett said. 'But if the Red German Army killed him, there must be a connection.'

'*If?*'

'You must know that we have not been able to establish the existence of any such terrorist cell.'

'Tcha, there's a new one every ten minutes,' Leiche said. 'Disaffected kids, radicals, hippies. They get hold of a copy of *The Anarchist's Cookbook* and start blowing things up just for the hell of it.'

'They don't usually do serial murders,' Garrett pointed out.

'Let's explore the connection,' Leiche said. 'What have you got?'

'Not a hell of a lot,' Garrett admitted. 'The dead soldier was a courier. Just before he was killed, he told me he was mixed up in a racket that concerned Colonel Shupe of BSSO, Rheindahlen, and a Major Paul Barton at Camp Patton here in Wiesbaden. I established that Wood — the dead soldier — made frequent courier runs between Shupe and Barton.'

'You mean deliveries? Of what?'

'I don't know. The sergeant was killed before he could tell me. I was hoping Roth might have some clues.'

'Ah,' Leiche said. 'But he was unable to help you, you say?'

'Or unwilling.'

Leiche smiled. 'Always a possibility,' he purred. 'But surely, these courier runs could have been made to deliver intelligence material, of interest only to the military?'

'Maybe,' Garrett said. 'Maybe not.'

'Tell me, Herr Garrett, why didn't you ask Colonel Shupe or this Major Barton what they were?'

'The sergeant who was killed said it was some sort of racket and that it was dangerous. I didn't want to endanger his life.'

'Very commendable,' Leiche said. 'You mentioned it to no one?'

'No one.'

'Yet he got killed anyway. Curious, wouldn't you say?'

'Someone might have overheard us talking.'

'Of course,' Leiche said smoothly. 'And Roth? Did anyone know you'd had a meeting?'

'No.'

'Yet here he is with a bullet in his brain. It might lead one to wonder whether there is more here than coincidence, Herr Garrett.'

'Gerhard, you're not suggesting Garrett . . . ?' Prachner interrupted.

Leiche swung around on him, eyes glittering with malice. 'I'm examining possibilities,' he hissed. 'And I'd like to do so without interruptions, if you please!'

Prachner shrugged. *Nothing I can do about this, either,* his eyes told Garrett.

'Let's get on,' Leiche said impatiently. 'Did Roth provide you with any link between his investigation and yours?'

'No,' Garrett said. 'He said BFV was investigating a drug-smuggling syndicate, but that there were no common denominators between his investigation and mine. When I asked him for more details, he refused to discuss it further.'

'I'm relieved to hear it,' Leiche said heavily. 'What time did you leave the Kurhaus?'

'A little before eight.'

'Just for the record, where were you at two A.M.?' Leiche's smile continued to lack either warmth or sincerity.

'You don't mind if I ask?'

'I don't mind. I was in bed. The Oranien Hotel. You can check.'

Leiche made a note in a small notebook; he would do it, too, Garrett thought. Never underestimate the methodicality of a German policeman.

204

'Two o'clock,' he said. 'Is that when Roth was killed?'

'Close enough. The medical examiner will give us an accurate fix after he does an autopsy.'

A stretcher team was putting Roth's body into a tubular plastic container, which they then lifted onto a trolley, clipping the whole contraption together with metal snaps that made sharp, spiteful, final sounds. They looked across at Weidemann, who lifted his hand, okay. It looked like some sort of rocket launcher being rolled out through the door.

Gerhard Leiche watched it go, then turned back to Garrett. 'Is there anything else you wish to tell me, Garrett?' he asked.

'I don't imagine you'd want to hear my theories,' Garrett said.

'I don't think so,' Leiche said, with elephantine politeness. 'We seem to have rather a lot of those.'

Garrett was about to make a sharp reply when hc caught Klaus Prachner's infinitesimal shake of the head. He shrugged his shoulders and turned to go.

Leiche caught him by the arm. 'One more thing, *Herr* Garrett,' he said coldly. 'I suggest you leave this business to us from now on and confine yourself to matters that concern you directly.'

'How could I refuse,' Garrett said, disengaging his arm, 'when you ask so nicely?'

'You know the way out,' Leiche said, ignoring the gibe. Garrett went out of the apartment and down the stairs to the street. He waited on the sidewalk until Prachner appeared.

'Mr. Charm,' Prachner said bitterly. 'Sorry, Charles. I didn't even know the bastard was around until he turned up and took over.'

'What brings the heavy guns down here?' Garrett asked.

Prachner grinned at the small play on words; in German, they could also mean 'fat big shots.' 'Leiche's ambitious. He sees this USFET investigation as his passport to the big time,' Prachner explained. 'He's bucking for promotion to the *Bundesnachrichtendienst*, the foreign service. If he cracks this, he might get it, so he's not going to let some *auslander* steal any of his thunder. Watch out for him, Charles. He's a treacherous son of a bitch.'

'And pretty, too,' Garrett observed. 'Can't you make him see he's barking up the wrong tree with this Red German Army thing?'

'He doesn't ask my opinion.'

I may have my faults, but being wrong isn't one of them.

It was on a poster of a charging rhinoceros that Diana bought and thumbtacked to the larder door. It was the first time he realized that something was very wrong.

'Why didn't you tell me?' he asked her.

'What difference would it have made if I had?' she retorted, bitterly.

'All you care about is terrorists and killing and death. It's all you ever think about.'

'Why are you unhappy, Diana?'

'What do you care?' she screeched. 'What do you care?'

'Can you keep Leiche off my back for a

little while longer?'

'I can try. Why?'

'Roth told me he was using Lucy Barton as a source. I want to find out who she was spying on.'

'Didn't Roth tell you?'

'I tried to get him to. He wasn't having any.'

'He was a feisty little bastard,' Prachner said. 'Liked to play his cards close to his chest.'

'That's what got him killed,' Garrett said. 'If he'd told me what he knew . . . well, no use crying over that. He did say one thing. When I told him I thought maybe Barton was behind the attempt to kill me, he said even if it were true, that wasn't the reason for his interest in Lucy Barton.'

'What the hell does that mean?'

'He wouldn't tell me that, either. But ask yourself this: who could Lucy Barton have been giving Roth information about?'

'I give up.'

'The sergeant who was killed, George Wood, has a sister. Her name is Eileen

Carson. She told me Barton was having an affair with General Irwin's wife.'

'Kitty Irwin?'

'That's what she said. I asked Roth. He said there was more to it than that.'

Prachner shook his head. 'Let me get this straight, Charles. You're suggesting Kitty Irwin, the wife of the general commanding Rhine army, was one of Roth's suspects?'

'You have access to his reports. You tell me.'

Prachner sighed. 'If Leiche even knew I was talking to you, let alone that I sent out an SS squad to clean up after you, he'd cut my balls off, Charles.'

'Then you've got nothing else to lose.' Garrett grinned.

Prachner sighed. 'Roth was pretty sure the drug-running cartcl inside USFET was headquartered in the Rhine Valley. He suspected the facilities of the Special Operations Unit might be being used to move the stuff around.'

'What about surveillance?'

'We were just about to set it up when Roth was killed.'

'Did he name any names?'

'Walter Gilchriese in Darmstadt and Donald Rogers in Heidelberg.'

'What about Northrup?'

'So far, he looks clean. It's the others who have the profile. Think about it. They can fly anywhere, cross any border, and come back into Germany as often as they please with complete immunity against search. Roth figured they could be using that immunity to bring in the drugs.'

'And Shupe?'

'He could be their conduit to the British market,' Prachner said. 'As head of BSSO he'd be able to come and go as he pleased, too, wouldn't he?'

'Okay, I'll buy all that. But what about Kitty Irwin? How is she mixed up in it?'

'As far as I know, her name never came up.'

'There's something missing, Klaus. Something we haven't got a handle on.'

'I'll keep you posted,' Prachner promised. 'You do the same, okay?'

'Okay.'

'I've got to get back. Mustn't keep the corpse waiting.' It was another small joke.

Leiche's name translated into English as corpse. He hurried back up the stairs, passing Inspector Weidemann and his assistant Gottfried, who were just coming down. They sauntered across to where Garrett was standing.

'You said something interesting up there,' Weidemann said. 'You want to tell us the rest of it?'

'What would you say if I told you I thought this whole Red German Army thing is a cover?'

'I'd say, tell me more.'

'You know BFV is investigating a drug-trafficking operation inside USFET.'

'You think they tell us stuff like that?' Gottfried said harshly. 'We're just flatfeet.'

'Let me try something on you. Among others, Roth was watching Major Paul Barton, who is stationed here in Wiesbaden. Suppose Barton is a member of a syndicate trafficking in narcotics. Sergeant Wood is a courier running drugs from Wiesbaden into the British sector, where the distributor is Shupe. Barton finds out that Wood is going to talk to me and so they kill him.'

'Having first blown up an army barracks so as to throw us off the track,' Gottfried said ponderously. 'Very convincing.'

'I think the bombing may have been done by real terrorists, probably the IRA. Whoever killed Wood dreamed up a phony terrorist group and claimed they did it, to lend credibility to the killing.'

'Quite an hypothesis,' Weidemann said. 'I suppose it would be too much to hope you have some evidence to support it?'

'I interviewed Colonel Barton shortly after the death of Sergeant Wood and suggested he might have been involved.'

'You interrogated an American officer?' Weidemann said disbelievingly. 'On whose authority?'

'My own,' Garrett said impatiently. 'What's important is that within thirty-six hours of that interview someone tried to kill me.'

'Really?' Weidemann said smoothly. 'I don't recall seeing any report of an attempt on your life, Garrett. Where did all this happen?'

'Near Linz. I didn't report it. Nothing

to report, really,' he lied. 'A car went past me like a bat out of hell and someone in it took a shot at me.'

'What were you doing in Linz?'

Garrett told him about his conversation with old Kupfer at Schloss Schwarzenberg and the probability that the man who had worked there was Sean Hennessy.

'I think he or some of his unit were responsible for the bomb at Rheindahlen, but someone else killed George Wood. I've got no proof, but I believe there is a link between Shupe, Barton, the drug smuggling, and this Red German Army gang.'

'And what about Roth? Why did they kill him?'

'I don't know,' Garrett said. 'Not yet.'

'You're lucky, Garrett,' Weidemann said, his voice tired. 'You can fly all these kites as much as you like. We, unfortunately, have to deal in facts.'

'Inspector, Roth had a label round his neck that said the Red German Army killed him, right?'

'Right.'

'But Roth wasn't investigating the Red German Army,' Garrett said. 'He didn't even know it existed. He was investigating drug smuggling in USFET.'

'Go on.'

'Prachner just told me that Roth suspected a group of officers, all members of the Special Operations Unit based at Bad Kreuznach. He was particularly interested in Major Paul Barton.'

'And?'

'I think Barton and his partners are the Red German Army.'

'Good, good,' Weidemann said. 'I like it. Give us some proof and maybe we can do something.'

'What, for instance?'

'We can take it to General Harknett at Heidelberg and close this thing down.'

Oh, sure, Garrett thought. He could see the United States Army standing idly by while banner headlines all over the world proclaimed that a group of senior officers were drug traffickers. Let Heidelberg get one breath of what Garrett suspected, and the Pentagon would ship in so much whitewash the Rhine Valley would look like the white cliffs of Dover.

'I'll see what I can come up with,' he told Weidemann. 'If you'll do something for me.'

'What's that?' Weidemann said.

'Find those goddamned Irishmen,' Garrett told him.

11

German trains were clean, comfortable, and punctual. Traveling in them was a pleasure, as was leaving the grim gray valley of the Ruhr, so Davy McGinnis and Pat Mullan sat back and enjoyed the three-hour excursion.

When they got to Hannover, Davy walked out of the back of the station and under a tunnel that led to a car park alongside the old Palace of Justice, and half-inched a nice clean dark blue Mercedes CLK. It was so easy it almost made him laugh. He was back in front of the Hauptbahnhof within fifteen minutes.

'Nice motor,' Pat Mullan said as he got in.

'Nothing but the best.' Davy grinned. He followed the yellow signposts that pointed him first to Isernhagen and then onto the autobahn north. They drove north through featureless countryside, stands of pine and fir lying like buffalo pelts between long expanses of water-logged moorland. Army signposts all along the right-hand side of the road warned that the land beyond the fences was a *sperrgebiet*, a closed-off portion of the dreary, torn reaches of Lüneburg Heath.

'This is where the Jerries surrendered in 1945, you know,' Davy told Mullan. 'Somewhere around here. About fifteen miles over there is Belsen, where the concentration camp was.'

'Bastards,' Mullan said, and spat out of the window.

Skirting Lüneburg, McGinnis headed north through pretty countryside to Lauenburg, a small town of about eleven thousand inhabitants, which stood on the River Elbe. A few kilometers farther on, he eased off the accelerator as they approached the neat, whitewashed curb-stones flanking the entrance to a large army establishment. Beyond the fenced perimeter, the standard red-brick build-ings of the post stood in orderly rows. The gatehouse was manned by armed sentries. Davy coasted slowly past the entrance and came to a stop about fifty yards farther on.

'This is the place,' Mullan said, squinting back at the sign facing the road. 'Buckinghamshire barracks, headquarters of the 1185th Infantry Regiment.'

'Lots of trucks,' Davy observed, pointing with his chin to an apron in front of a large, hangarlike building off to one side.

'There's eighteen hundred men stationed at this camp,' Mullan told him.

'Our brave lads,' Davy said sourly. 'Keeping the world safe for democracy.'

'Most of them are bored out of their fuckin' skulls,' Pat told him. 'Sitting in a half track, day in, day out, staring at nothing.'

'You know what they say: if you can't take a joke . . .'

'You shouldn't have joined. Poor bastards. They do two weeks in the field, then they get a week off. They're trucked up here via Lüneburg from the Langenhagen barracks outside Hannover. Off-duty personnel are taken back in the same trucks.'

'Aha,' Davy said. 'I see your drift.'

'Good,' Mullan said. 'Then drift us out of here before that sergeant in the gatehouse whistles up someone to come and ask us what we're doing sitting here.'

Davy turned the car around and headed back into Lauenburg. It was a pretty town with streets full of old-fashioned, red-roofed houses sloping steeply down to the river from the *Schloss* that crowned the hill. They drove slowly around to get the feel of the place, noting the locations of the smaller hotels: one called Möller on Elbestrasse, in the lower town, and the Bellevue, up on the hill looking out over the river. What decided them was seeing soldiers sitting at tables outside an old inn near the canal called *Weisser Schwan*, the White Swan.

'Looks good,' Mullan commented as they drove past. McGinnis slid the car into a parking slot and they went inside. It was one of those places with oak beams and dark corners, like an English country pub. Dinner was served in the dining room from seven until nine-thirty.

By the time they had eaten, the bar was filling up with young soldiers from the nearby camp, and the two men wandered out to mix with them. The plan was bonehead simple, but it always worked. Set yourself up as an open-handed tourist passing a few pleasant days in northern Germany. Get to know some of the lads, see to it that their beer steins were never empty. And every once in a while, over a period of a few evenings or even a week, ask your questions.

It was always a slow process. One question too many, or too soon, or too direct, and you were blown. So it had to be done carefully, in among the badinage and the dirty jokes. Softly, softly. Did the convoys leave for Lüneburg at the same time every Sunday? How many men, how many trucks? Did they always take the same route? Did they make any stops on the way? Was the convoy escorted? Where were the trucks kept between their arrival and departure? What was security like? Were the fences electrified? What were the times of the guard watches at the barracks? How many men? Was the perimeter patrolled? How often?

The information would be recorded in

minuscule lettering on Rizla cigarette papers; in any emergency they could be eaten in a trice. They would purchase 1cm=1km scale Landesverwaltungsamt-Landesvermessung topographical maps of the area around the barracks, and reconnoiter it on foot. At one shop here and another there, they would buy the other things they would need: stone chisels, a steel mallet, waders, yellow fluorescent jackets like the ones used by autobahn engineers. The important thing was to take no chances, to avoid drawing attention to themselves or what they were really doing in Lauenburg. Ask. Learn. Watch. And wait until the target Sunday in November.

Remembrance Day, they called it.

They'd give the bastards something to remember.

★   ★   ★

Garrett drove back north in a thoughtful mood.

By the time he reached Cologne, a plan was already beginning to form in his mind. He drove into town and parked in the same lot he had used a few days earlier. Before going up to the BSSO building, he went into a computer supply shop and purchased a couple of floppy disks. Ten minutes later he was in Emil Fritz's office, smiling as Emil shook his finger at him as if he were an errant schoolboy.

'For God's sake, Charles, where have you been?' Emil said testily. 'Shupe has been phoning me twice a day from Lüneburg trying to find out what you were up to.'

'And what did you tell him?'

'The truth: that I had no idea.'

'I bet that wasn't what he wanted to hear.'

'It was strange. He sounded . . . odd. I expected him to rage like a bull. If I didn't know it was impossible, I'd have said he sounded apprehensive.'

'Maybe he is,' Garrett said. 'I'm willing to bet our Colonel Shupe is a bad apple, Emil. I'm just not quite sure yet how bad.'

'I wish I could say I'm sorry,' Emil said. 'I wish I could even say I'm surprised. I always thought the bastard was a bastard. What have you found out?'

'Nothing concrete, yet. That was what I was doing in Frankfurt.'

'I heard you'd been there. Shupe nearly blew a gasket when he found out.'

Garrett frowned. 'Summers told him?'

'I don't know if Ralph told him or someone else did. The end result was the same; Ralph was suspended. Shupe also sent each head of outstation a memo saying you were not authorized to operate independently and that you weren't to be afforded any assistance without his personal authority.'

Garrett shook his head. 'He doesn't really think he can make that stick, does he?'

'You know Shupe. He's a throwback to the time when a man's tongue weighed more than his brain.'

'Emil,' Garrett said, 'you're going to be a busy man.'

'It sounds as if maybe the ordure is going to hit the air conditioner.'

'No maybe about it,' Garrett said grimly. 'Pick up the phone, Emil. Call this number.'

'London?' Fritz said, frowning at the slip of paper. 'Who is it?'

'Sir Richard Brook,' Garrett said. 'Coordinator of intelligence and security, joint intelligence chiefs.'

'What do I say?'

'Tell him that I have asked you to put the complete resources of BSSO at my disposal, effective immediately. Tell him I understand that you cannot do so without authorization. He will ask you why you cannot obtain that authorization from the officer commanding BSSO. Tell him that I believe Colonel Shupe is seriously compromised, that I wish to place him on suspension, and that I will assume command until his status has been clarified.'

Emil stared at him wide-eyed. 'Are you serious?' he asked softly.

'Make the call,' Garrett said.

Emil made the call, asked the questions, said 'Yes, sir,' a couple of times, and then put the receiver down. He stared at Garrett for a long moment, then shook his head. 'It's yours,' he said. 'Effective immediately, he said.'

'I thought he would. When is Shupe

due back at Rheindahlen?'

'Tomorrow. He'll probably come here first. Are you going to tell him . . . ?'

Garrett shook his head, no. 'As of this moment, only you and I know that Shupe is suspended. Let's keep it that way. I don't want to scare Shupe off.'

'What has he done, Charles?'

'Like I told you, I'm not completely sure,' Garrett said. 'But Shupe is on the spike. Probably his friend Carbolic Cameron, too.'

'All this time,' Emil said softly. 'All this time we've been jumping through his hoops . . . I can't believe it, Charles.'

'Believe it,' Garrett told him.

'You're really going after the bastard?'

'I'm really going after the bastard,' Garrett confirmed.

'All this time,' Emil said again, shaking his head as if he still couldn't believe what he had heard. 'What do you want me to do?'

'Did you get a package for me in the diplomatic pouch?'

'VIPAR status, Your Eyes Only. It's in the safe.'

'I'll need to use the mainframe. Who's in charge down there?'

'Her name is Ursula Bender.' Emil allowed himself a small smile. 'You'll find working with her . . . interesting.'

'Tell her to clear a machine for me,' Garrett said. 'While we're waiting, tell me what you know about Kitty Irwin.'

'Kitty Irwin?' Emil looked puzzled. 'You mean General Irwin's wife? What do you want to know?'

'The works.'

'Her private life is a mess,' Emil said. 'Has been for years. There seems to have been a boyfriend at every post: Singapore, Auckland, Hong Kong.'

'Is she having an affair now?'

'The scuttlebutt is that she's shacking up with an American officer who's based down at Wiesbaden. It's been going on for about eighteen months or so. It's all very discreet, but it's an open secret at Rheindahlen.'

'You think the general knows?'

'If he doesn't, he's the only one.'

'What's the boyfriend's name?'

'Paul Barton. He's UKUSA liaison officer.'

'It couldn't be something else? Mutual interests?'

Emil shook his head. 'Paul Barton is a prick, but he's not a stupid prick. If he's shacking up with Kitty Irwin, he's not just doing it for intellectual reasons.'

'She's a good-looking lady?'

'Everybody's ideal mature woman. Intelligent, good-looking. Not beautiful in the conventional sense. But . . . there's a German word, *saftig*. You know what I mean?'

'Stop drooling. Where would I find her if I wanted to talk to her?'

'The general bought a villa in the Schwalmtal, about three miles from Wegberg. When she's not traveling, that's where she spends most of her time.'

'Traveling?'

'She takes excursions like other women take vitamins. Bus trips, train trips, airline packages. This week Amsterdam, next week Munich, she never seems to touch the ground.'

'Okay,' Garrett said. 'Let's change the subject. What do you know about the U.S. Army Special Operations Unit at

Bad Kreuznach?'

Emil shrugged. 'Not in our brief,' he said. 'UKUSA rules.'

He was referring to the protocol drawn up by the security services of the United Kingdom and the United States in 1947, under the terms of which all espionage was coordinated and it was mutually agreed that neither country would spy upon the other.

'Has Shupe ever spent time down there?'

'Not to my knowledge,' Emil said. 'But he doesn't check his social calendar with me. Who's in command? Maybe I've heard the name.'

'The commanding officer is a Colonel Max Northrup,' Garrett said. 'I pulled his dossier while I was in Frankfurt. He's like one of those old feudal princes up there in his *Schloss*. The Special Operations Unit functions outside the parameters of day-to-day USFET operations. Northrup reports directly to the Pentagon.'

'That's unusual, isn't it?'

'The whole damned setup is unusual. They've got a top security enclave, their own private *Sperrgebiet* about twenty or thirty kilometers west of Kreuznach. Nobody knows what they do there.'

'But there are plenty of rumors,' Emil said.

'Rumors?'

'You know how we Germans are about the ecology. They had a couple of scares down there, dead fish in the river, stuff like that. It made headlines for a few days, then the water authority or the army or somebody made some kind of statement and the papers lost interest.'

'Have there been any cases like that in this area?'

'Not to my knowledge. If there have, it'll be in the file along with the stuff about Kreuznach.'

'While I'm using the computer, I want you to pull those files for me,' Garrett said. 'I'll need that package from London, too.'

'Go on down,' Emil said. 'As soon as we've got everything together I'll bring it to you.'

Garrett took the elevator to the basement. The computer complex was a large, square, open area, brightly lit by banks of fluorescent lamps, its austere matt white walls and featureless carpeting as cool as the constant breath of the air conditioning. Aisles flanked on both sides by sophisticated analysis and information-retrieval machinery radiated outward like gray-carpeted spokes, which joined at a hub formed by a central island of offices.

A cardboard nameplate in the slot outside the frosted glass door of the central office announced that the head of the computer and analysis facility was Ursula Bender. The owner of the name turned out to be a strikingly attractive woman in her early thirties, with long streaky blond hair, cornflower blue eyes, and the kind of figure that would make a monk reconsider his vows of celibacy.

'Mr. Garrett?' Her voice was husky, as if she smoked too much. 'I've cleared a PC for you. You'll need this security key, of course. Oh, and here is your package from London. Is there anything else you need?'

'Just point me at the machine. I know how it works.'

She led the way to a small office — they were known as 'safe rooms' in the service — simply furnished with a teak desk, a swivel chair, an adjustable high-intensity lamp, and the computer: an IBM PC with a Canon laser printer. Venetian blinds covered the glass windows and door. The way she walked made it impossible not to notice her tight, high backside. Garrett wondered whether she knew.

'Being head of C&A is a big responsibility,' Garrett observed. 'I expected someone older.'

'I started when I was twenty,' she said. 'I've got a lot of experience.'

There was more in the words than the mere words themselves. She smiled and ran her hand through her long blond hair. Her lissome body moved beneath the crisp white semitransparent blouse. She saw his eyes following the movement and smiled as she went out the door, leaving behind the faint trace of Nina Ricci perfume. She knew, all right, Garrett decided. He turned the key in the lock before opening the secret package sent to him by Brigadier Derek Warren in London.

There was no note, just two disks with their security rating and content codings printed on the labels with black felt-tip pens. Garrett slid in the first disk and waited as the machine went through its litany of hums and buzzes. The screen cleared, and the cursor blinked steadily at the end of a sentence: *Awaiting Access Code.*

All secret information on disks was scrambled. This meant that it would appear on screen as meaningless gibberish unless paralleled with a security key such as the one that Ursula Bender had given to Garrett. This was a resin block, about six millimeters thick, containing a radio receiver, transmitter, and microprocessor. Garrett inserted this into the interrogator and keyed in the current VIPAR code clearance. Because the security key was interactive, it would retain a record not only of who had used the computer but what information the user had requested.

Clearance sanctioned; key personal

password, the cursor demanded. Garrett keyed in his secret personal code and the machine blinked once, twice, and then filled the screen with lines of information. Garrett scanned it avidly.

MINISTRY OF DEFENSE
Old War Office Building, Whitehall,
SW1A 2EU.

Origination: BG/14GG8875/SM Warren.
Army Adviser, Special Matters.
Destination: Garrett,
PACT via BSSO Cologne.

CLASSIFICATION: VIPAR BLACK
ULTRA.
NO COPIES NO CIRCULATION NO
OTHER EYES.
CORRUPT AFTER READING.

PROJECT 23

Project 23 was inaugurated early in 1950. It was a joint Anglo-U.S. -Canadian operation, initiated by General Kenneth MacIntyre, head of munitions supply at the ministry, and chairman of the chiefs-of-staff committee on biological warfare, and organized by Dr. Henry Davidson, head of establishment, and a staff of fifty specially selected scientists based at Porton Down Research Establishment, Porton, Wiltshire. The aim of this project was to construct, if feasible, a biological bomb capable of aerial delivery, and was itself an outgrowth of Dr. Davidson's wartime experiments with anthrax on the island of Gruinard.

In June 1952, a four-thousand-ton tank landing ship, the *Ben Machree*, was converted into a floating laboratory and anchored near Cellar Head on the island of Lewis in the Hebrides. Over a four-month period, experiments involving pneumonic plague bacilli were conducted by the team. Acting as observers for their respective countries were Lieutenant Commander Michael Rafferty, RCN, and Major Theodore Hertz, U.S. Army.

In brief, the experiments involved

the use of aerosol sprays distributing pneumonic plague bacilli over a large area, in the center of which were dispersed a number of cages of monkeys, each floating on a large pontoon. As these experiments were in progress, it was discovered that *Suzy Hawkes*, a fishing trawler bound for Iceland, had steamed into the exclusion area, ignoring the notified safety zone, and passed directly through the target area in which the plague bacilli had been distributed.

The destroyer *HMS Indomitable* was dispatched immediately from Royal Naval Dockyard, Glasgow, carrying sufficient vaccine to inoculate all members of the crew of the trawler should the necessity arise. *Indomitable* was ordered to stay out of sight, but to remain tuned to the trawler's frequency. In the event of distress signals, the trawler would be boarded, the ship's doctor given the serum and told the reason for its use. A Department of Health emergency officer was also sent to the trawler's home port, Fleetwood, Lancs.

Indomitable remained on station twelve days, during which time the incubation period (six days) and the ensuing life-interruption period (three-four days) passed without incident. No adverse effects were then or subsequently experienced by the crew of the trawler, which indicated in turn that the aerosol droplets dispersed over very short distances, a fact confirmed by the survival of the monkeys. It was concluded that the system was therefore ineffective as a weapon, and the project was abandoned. It was, however, agreed that studies should be continued on aerosols and that all three countries would concentrate on the search for new types of incapacitating and lethal agents of this nature.

At the UKUSCAN conference held in Victoria, B.C., in 1958, it was decided that Britain would continue to carry out pure research at Porton

Down, passing its discoveries to Canada and, more especially, to the United States, which alone could afford to manufacture weapons. Field testing, insofar as it was necessary, would henceforward be effected by the U.S. Army.

Since the last UKUSCAN conference, held in Lake Placid in 1984, military interest has focused upon genetic engineering. This was in main the result of signal failures in other experimental areas, notably the use of strontium 90 to poison food, the use of LSD as a drug, and the release of bacteria in the New York subway to test their dispersal. After the DNA breakthrough in 1974, when the first animal genes were cloned with viruses and multiplied for study, research has been concentrated in this area.

In 1988, a major program of genetic experimentation and biochemistry, with particular emphasis upon the insect transmission of viruses and the factors effecting virulence, with a budget in excess of one hundred and fifty million dollars a year was undertaken at the Pentagon, Washington, under the umbrella classification of Environmental Research Project. Its aim is to produce a debilitating but not fatal virus capable of incapacitating a potential enemy for a period of up to four days. Field trials have been carried out clandestinely in top-secret underground test sites in White Sands, New Mexico, in West Africa, and in Europe. As has been remarked earlier, Project 23 was abandoned in 1953. It would seem probable that the appellation Project 23, if still in use, would designate some program of a similar nature, but if it does, its present status is classified at the highest level.

After he had read the transcript for the fourth time, Garrett leaned back in the chair, rubbing his eyes. He picked up the intercom and dialed Emil Fritz's number.

'Did you get those newspaper cuttings I asked you about?' he said.

'Just coming in with them,' Emil said. 'Do you want some coffee?'

'Black,' Garrett said automatically. 'One sugar.'

He read the transcript one more time, then typed the word 'corrupt' into the computer. The machine was still buzzing and humming when Ursula Bender opened the door and came across to the desk with a neat tray on which were a cup and saucer, sugar bowl containing cube sugar and silver tongs, a plate with a fan of Kambly Butterfly cookies, a small white porcelain pot of coffee, and a slender glass vase containing one deep red carnation.

'Pretty,' Garrett said.

'Call me Ursel,' she said. 'You looked pleased.'

'I am.'

'What time will you be through?'

'Another hour, maybe two. Why?'

'I thought you might like to buy me a drink. Celebrate.'

Garrett just looked at her.

'Think about it,' she said, turning toward the door. 'We could have a nice time. Dinner, wine. After that . . . ' She raised her eyebrows and shrugged.

'Wouldn't you say I was a bit too old for you?'

'I prefer older men.' She smiled, showing perfect teeth. 'They take you to the right places.'

'I can't, Ursel,' Garrett said.

'Think about it,' she said, and went out as Emil Fritz bustled in, a ring binder under his arm. He looked at Garrett and then back at the door through which Ursula Bender had just exited.

'Yes, she did, and no, I didn't,' Garrett said.

'Where's your sense of adventure, man?'

'In my day, the girls used to wait until you asked them.'

'Ah, the *Fräuleinwunderschaft* isn't what it was,' Emil said. 'Nowadays, the girls have to compete with the sex-grannies. Germany is full of rich widows prowling the streets looking for young flesh to take into their beds.'

'Makes the blood run cold,' Garrett said. 'Is that the newspaper file?'

'It's mostly rubbish,' Emil said, laying the file on the table in front of Garrett. 'Why are you interested in this stuff?'

Garrett made no reply. Emil shook his head. 'Don't even trust me, do you, Charles?'

'The classification is ULTRA VIPAR BLACK, Emil.'

Fritz whistled. 'It must be dynamite.'

'It might well be,' Garrett said. 'Now get out of here, Emil, I've got a lot more work to do.'

Garrett took the corrupted disk out of the machine and slid in the second one. He went through the same clearance procedure to access the information, then waited while the machine purred and hummed and the lines zipped across the screen. What he had in front of him now were computerized personal dossiers on the four men he was interested in: Paul Barton, Walter Gilchriese, Donald Rogers, and Max Northrup. He knew their service dossiers inside out. He hadn't expected to find what he was looking for in them, and he hadn't been disappointed when he didn't. This material was different; it covered their private lives, their movements, their extracurricular activities, friends, associates, finances, and business arrangements. Garrett was not interested in their individual lives, the details of where they were born or had gone to school, their family background, and the rest of it. He was looking for common denominators, and using a computer was the way to find them. First things first.

#Search all dossiers for any occurrence of the name SHUPE.
Nothing found.
#Search all dossiers for dates any visit NATO HQ Rheindahlen.
Ready.
List.

A long column of dates striped down the screen beneath the name of BARTON, Paul Francis, two more beneath the names GILCHRIESE, Walter John, and ROGERS, Donald Michael.

#Nothing found for NORTHRUP, Max?
Nothing found.

Well, even nothing was something. Garrett was beginning to get a glimmering of what he had stumbled into. Something had been nagging away at the back of his brain ever since the clumsy attempt to kill him on the road below Schwarzenberg; even such bizarre details as the use of the Ruger pistol were beginning to make a certain warped kind of sense.

He returned to his research.

All four men had at different times received special training at the White Sands Missile Range Testing Facility near Tularosa, New Mexico, the computer reported.

List.
Negative. All information on this training is classified and USFET clearance is required before access can be permitted.
Q: List procedure for authorized

access.

Initial clearance General T. Harknett, USFETCOM, Heidelberg, Germany. Second clearance General P. P. Haining, USA-INTELCOM, Fort Meade, MD.

Third clearance General A. Wells, Pentagon, Washington, DC.

Fourth clearance General L. S. James, CIA, Langley, VA.

Garrett whistled softly. Whatever Northrup and his officers had been trained for, they had top-level security protecting their secret: the Army Intelligence and Security Command, the Pentagon, and most interesting of all, the spooks at Langley.

He cleared the screen and typed in another query.

Q: Had any two or more of the subject officers at any time had related military interests of any kind? Nothing found.

Q: Had any two or more of them at any time had related business or financial interests of any kind?

Nothing found.

Q: Had any two or more of them at any time had related personal interests of any kind?

Nothing found.

Q: Had any two or more of them any special qualifications in common?

Yes.

List.

This information is classified and USFET clearance is required before access can be permitted.

Q: List procedure for authorized access.

Initial clearance General T. Harknett, USFETCOM, Heidelberg, Germany.

Second clearance General P. P. Haining, USA-INTELCOM, Fort Meade, MD.

Third clearance General A. Wells, Pentagon, Washington, DC.

Fourth clearance General L. S. James, CIA, Langley, VA.

'Surprise, surprise,' Garrett muttered.

Q: Was any place prior to their

military service common to any two of them?

Nothing found.

Q: Had any of them had any financial difficulties?

Nothing found.

Q: Was any event common to two or more of them?

Yes.

List.

The machine whirred and ticked. Northrup and Barton had appeared as witnesses at a 1986 court-martial in Heidelberg. The cursor blinked on an invitation:

For résumé of transcript and other records key 2:HDLBG JACKSON — SHIPSTONE.

Garrett typed in the code. An index scrolled down the screen, listing the records of a court-martial hearing before a military tribunal in Heidelberg in April 1986. By reading the salient documents, Garrett discovered that a Sergeant Leroy

Jackson, Special Operations Unit, had been accused of murdering PFC Lester Shipstone, 115th Ordnance Corps. Evidence was presented by the Judge Advocate General's Office that Shipstone had called Jackson 'a boneheaded nigger' at a Frankfurt disco named Lucky Luke's and they had a fight. Witnesses said Shipstone was getting the worst of it when his friends ganged up on Jackson and he took a bad beating.

Three days later, at about nine P.M., Shipstone was shot to death in an alley off Moselstrasse in Frankfurt's red-light district. Witnesses claimed to have seen Jackson in the area that night. Appearing for the defense, Major Max Northrup and Captain Walter Gilchriese swore Jackson had been with them at SOU headquarters in Bad Kreuznach on the night of the killing. In the face of this airtight alibi, all charges against Jackson were dismissed and he was returned to duty. A verdict of murder by a person or persons unknown was rendered in the case of Lester Shipstone.

Garrett made a note on the ruled pad

beside the computer: 'Determine exact cause of death of Lester Shipstone.' He was almost willing to bet he already knew the answer. He added another note: 'Determine whereabouts of Leroy Jackson.'

More? the computer blinked.

More, indeed, Garrett thought. Once again he typed the word 'list' and once again the computer hummed and hawed as it disgorged the information.

In May 1987, Colonel Max Northrup, together with Captains Gilchriese and Rogers, had participated in an inquiry, conducted by the Oberstein Water Control and Purification Board and the council of the district of Reichenheim, into the suspected contamination of a mountain stream called the Glessbach that ran through the village. Depositions from officials of the OWCPB established that the contamination could not have emanated from its systems. Speaking for the Special Operations Unit, U.S. Army, Northrup had testified that its activities in the closed exercise area above the town were of a purely military nature and could in no way have brought about the contamination of which the townspeople complained.

Garrett turned to the thick binder Emil Fritz had brought in and leafed through the cuttings, neatly pasted to blank sheets of foolscap paper and filed in date order. They ranged from the sober to the sensational.

Garrett turned the pages until he came to the slip Fritz had inserted to mark the places for him. The first was dated May 1987. Cuttings from the *Obersteiner Tagesblatt* and the *Kreuznacher Zeitung* had the story he was looking for. Forty-two-point headlines and graphic photographs accompanied the text. The details were simple: Over a two-day period hundreds of dead fish were found in the swift-flowing Glessbach, a stream coming down out of the mountains above Reichenheim, a town of about four and a half thousand people standing where the mountain stream joined the River Nahe. The Oberstein water authorities conducted tests and concluded that 'a toxic element' might have been responsible, but that in spite of 'extensive tests' no trace of any such element could be found in the water.

The computer cursor was still blinking on the word '*more?*'

List, Garrett typed.

A new dossier of information flowed across the screen. In July 1988, Northrup had again appeared before a public meeting, this time in Eschenau, just a dozen kilometers south of Reichenheim. Several hundred townspeople had been affected by a mysterious 'bug' that caused diarrhea, stomach pains, sickness, and skin irritation. The local water supply was tested and no trace of contamination was found, and once again, all eyes turned to the mysterious *Sperrgebiet* in the mountains. Colonel Max Northrup, accompanied again by Gilchriese and Barton, stood up and told the good burghers of Eschenau that although he was not permitted to disclose what the secret activities being conducted in the closed area were, he would assure them that the U.S. Army was in no way to blame.

A cross check with the newspaper file filled out the story. MYSTERY ILLNESS LAYS LOW THREE HUNDRED AND SEVENTY, the headlines shouted. Doctors were baffled; the virus, whatever it was, could not be isolated or identified and therefore, of course, could not be treated. Such infections were particularly dangerous to the elderly and the sick. Not unnaturally, the newspapers linked this occurrence with the earlier one at Reichenheim, but once again the Oberstein Water Control and Purification Board stated categorically that no trace of any 'foreign substances' had been found and that the water supply was safe to use and to drink. What else could it be, then? the newspapers wanted to know. There was only one explanation. What were the Americans up to in the mountains? It was a scandal that no inspection of the American *Sperrgebiet* was permitted. The local councils should insist that the base be opened to the public at the earliest opportunity.

More?

List.

October 1988. General Terence Harknett, commanding USFET, and members of his staff, assisted by Colonel Max Northrup, Captain Donald Rogers, and Captain Paul Barton were hosts at a USFET/SOU open day. The festivities took place in a marquee erected on the onetime village green of what had been the little village of Wieselbach, in the center of the Special Operations Unit's *Sperrgebiet*.

The newspaper file filled out the details. Professor Dr. August Kautz, burgermeister of Idar-Oberstein, honored guests, and dignitaries from all the nearby towns and hamlets, were taken on a tour of the facilities. This was followed by a buffet luncheon prepared by master chefs of the U.S. Army driven up specially from Heidelberg for the occasion. A great deal of wine and schnapps were drunk, a great many toasts given and received, a large number of long-winded and flowery speeches made.

The cursor blinked emptily on the screen, awaiting instructions. So there were no more common denominators.

Well, perhaps what he had was more than enough to be going on with, Garrett thought. The next item on the menu was Colonel Paul Graham Shupe. Garrett set to work, oblivious of place and time, keying in question after question, making occasional notes in his neat, well-formed script. He worked nonstop for perhaps two hours before closing the dossier. What he had, although far from conclusive, supported his theory, but that was still all it was, a theory. Time to toss a dead cat into the doghouse, he thought. But first, find your dead cat.

The 'corrupt' warning appeared when he typed in his code, and the screen blanked out as the computer carried out his instructions. While he was waiting, Garrett took the two disks he had bought at the shop in the Heumarkt out of his coat pocket. Using felt-tipped pens he found in the drawer, he made a reasonable facsimile of the special codings that had been written on the now-corrupted disks that had come from London. He put both the original disks into his raincoat pocket, then spent perhaps another twenty minutes programming the two dummy disks, which now looked like originals, before putting them into the padded security envelope that they had arrived in from London. Then he went back to Emil Fritz's office.

'All finished?' Emil asked.

'Nearly,' Garrett said. 'Your turn now.'

'What do you want me to do?'

'Listen,' Garrett said. 'While I was in Wiesbaden, I found out that BFV is investigating the possibility that some USFET officers are involved in trafficking drugs. One of those officers is your friend the chocolate soldier.'

'Barton?' Fritz frowned.

'My theory, for what it's worth, is that Shupe is tied up in it as well. George Wood was coerced into running the stuff between Wiesbaden and Rheindahlen. When he looked as if he might spill the beans, they killed him. At the same time, they worked me over, with a view to discouraging me from digging any deeper.'

'But — '

'The Red German Army, I know. It

doesn't exist, Emil. They dreamed it up as a cover. The IRA planted the bomb at Rheindahlen, and it gave them a way to get rid of Wood without implicating themselves. At the same — '

'Charles, you're saying that Shupe . . . ?'

'One of them did it,' Garrett said grimly. 'Whether it was Shupe or the Americans remains to be seen. My money is on Barton. When I made it clear I wasn't going to be frightened off, he tried to have me killed.'

'I didn't know any of this.'

'There wasn't any way to tell you without it getting to Shupe,' Garrett said. 'I haven't been able to make a move he didn't know about.'

'I told you he had informers everywhere in the organization.'

'Wait, there's more,' Garrett told him. 'Yesterday, a BFV operative named Manfred Roth, the one who was investigating the drug smuggling, was killed in the same way as George Wood; a bullet in the back of the head, a label around his neck saying the killing was done by the Red German Army.'

'There was nothing in the papers.'

'I know,' Garrett said. 'That's what bothers me.'

'It must have been the Americans,' Emil said. 'We know for a fact that Shupe is still in Siberia.'

'I'm returning an open verdict on Roth,' Garrett said. 'We'll find out soon enough who killed him. In the meantime, I want you to give Shupe and Cameron the works. Hit them with everything. Comprehensive surveillance. Sound and vision. Fiber optics, phone bugs, RDFs on cars, footmen all around him. I don't want either of them taking a leak without someone telling us the exact amount in fluid ounces.'

'That's going to tie up a lot of people.'

'It won't be for long,' Garrett promised. 'As soon as I leave, I want you to call Shupe. Fall over yourself to tell him I was here, what I said, everything I did.'

'All right,' Emil said. 'But why?'

'I need a dead cat,' Garrett said. He ignored Emil's blank look and laid the package containing the two blank disks on Fritz's desk. 'Put this somewhere safe.'

'What's in it?'

'Two floppies from R2 in London. One is a dossier on Northrup's Special Operations Unit. What it is, what it does. The other is a TREVI assessment of the narcotics-trafficking ring operating inside USFET: names, dates, the business.'

'TREVI? The Europolice network?'

'That's right.'

'I don't get it,' Emil said. 'If I tell Shupe what you did while you were here, the first thing he'll try to do is see what's on these disks.'

'I know,' Garrett said.

'Is that all you can say, I know? For God's sake, Charles, if Shupe gets these disks to the Americans, they'll mount a brute force attack on them. Intense validation, they call it. Breaking your access codes wouldn't even make them sweat.'

'I know,' Garrett said again. He looked at Emil and Emil looked at him. Then the German shook his head.

'I should have guessed.' He sighed. 'You're up to something, aren't you?'

'I told you I needed a dead cat,' Garrett

257

said. He tapped the envelope containing the disks. 'This is it.'

'My God, Charles,' Emil Fritz said. 'You're a devious bastard.'

'I know,' Garrett said.

12

Colonel Paul Shupe was in a foul temper.

With Cameron strutting behind him, he marched straight through to Emil Fritz's office and unceremoniously thrust open the door. He took off his overcoat and threw it on the couch. Fritz rose to greet him, hand outstretched.

'Colonel,' he said. 'Good to see you back.'

'I can do without the grease job, Fritz,' Shupe growled.

'Did you think because we were stuck up in Lüneburg we didn't know what you were doing?'

'I don't understand, sir.'

'I don't understand, sir,' Shupe mimicked to Cameron. 'Tell him, George.'

'Were you or were you not given specific orders not to extend assistance to Charles Garrett without the colonel's written authority?' Cameron snapped.

'Yes, sir, but — '

'No buts, Fritz! Are you going to deny that you deliberately disobeyed that direct order, and permitted Garrett to use the facilities of this office?'

'No, sir, I'm not,' Emil said. 'I had no choice in the matter.'

'No choice?'

'I'm afraid I have bad news for you, sir,' Fritz said. 'I am required to inform you that orders countermanding yours arrived direct from London. We were instructed to render unrestricted support to Mr. Garrett. And that you and Major Cameron were to consider yourselves under indefinite suspension.'

Shupe's jaw fell open.

'Who issued these orders?'

'Sir Richard Brook, sir. Coordinator of intelligence of the joint chiefs.'

Shupe and Cameron exchanged a glance that Emil Fritz affected not to see. The name of Sir Richard Brook had given them a clearer idea of just what caliber gun was pointed at them.

'Why weren't we informed of what had happened?' Shupe asked.

'Sir, Mr. Garrett gave me strict

instructions not to discuss the matter with you or — '

'Garrett, Garrett, Garrett!' Shupe exploded. 'You listen to me, Fritz. If you don't want to be walking the streets looking for a job as a shoe clerk, you'd better tell me exactly what the hell Garrett has been doing here the last few days!'

'Sir,' Fritz said, getting up from behind his desk and going across to close the door. 'I repeat, I am instructed not to discuss the matter with you. You and Major Cameron are ordered to return to Rheindahlen and hold yourself in readiness for a court of inquiry into your conduct.'

As he closed the door, Emil touched first his eyelid and then his ear, and then looked up at the ceiling. Shupe's eyes widened as he got the message. He looked at Cameron, who inclined his head to one side, let's get out of here.

'I see,' Shupe said, hamming up a thoughtful tone of voice. 'If those are our orders, we have no choice but to obey them. We'll leave at once. Look, Major Cameron and I haven't eaten since six

A.M. I think we'll go across the street to that little restaurant, what's it called, George?'

'The Tessiner Stubchen,' Cameron said.

'That's it,' Shupe said. His forehead was glistening with sweat. 'Why don't you join us?'

'It would be my pleasure, Colonel,' Fritz said. 'I'll just get my coat.'

The staff of BSSO kept their heads down as the three men went out of the office; sighs of relief were heard as the doors closed behind them. Emil Fritz led the way across the Heumarkt to the restaurant on the corner of the Salzgasse. The three men took a table in the corner far enough away from the other patrons not to be overheard. Shupe leaned across the table, his heavy face dark with unease.

'What the hell is going on upstairs, Emil?' he asked urgently.

'Garrett,' Emil said. 'While he was in Frankfurt he learned BFV is investigating a major narcotics-smuggling ring based inside USFET. They told him someone at BSSO may be involved. Garrett is making it his number-one priority to find out whether there is anything in it.'

Once again he affected not to notice the covert glances exchanged by the two officers. Garrett was right, then; Shupe and Cameron certainly knew something.

'I thought his job was to find this Red German Army gang,' Shupe said.

'Garrett seems to think that the whole thing is a hoax, and that the murder of Sergeant Wood may be connected to the narcotics smuggling.'

'Has he got any evidence?'

'He must have. You remember I told you he had a package from London. Highest security classification, ULTRA VIPAR BLACK, no other eyes. Two disks. He spent about five hours in the safe room working on them.'

'Did he give you any idea what was on the disks?'

'I gather one of them concerns some secret project he was investigating. The other is a TREVI assessment report on the USFET drug traffic. Names, places, dates, everything.'

'TREVI?' Shupe said hoarsely. 'I

thought they were only concerned with terrorism. How did they get involved?'

'Garrett,' Emil told him. 'Apparently he's cleared to access their computers. As you know, the Europolice network has direct access to the data banks of all the European security agencies: DGSE and DST in France, DI5 and 6 in Britain, SIS in Sweden, BFV and BND here in Germany, and so on.'

'Did he give you any idea of what TREVI have?'

'No, sir.'

'We could get Emil here to hack into his Cryptags,' Cameron said thoughtfully. 'They'd tell us what he accessed.'

'Problem there, sir,' Emil pointed out helpfully. 'The entire computer complex is wired. Sound and video. If I accessed his Cryptag, it wouldn't take Garrett two seconds to figure out why.'

Shupe made an angry noise and looked at Cameron as much as to say, *Come on, think of something.*

'Where are these disks he got from London?' Cameron asked.

'In the security safe,' Emil said.

'Maybe we ought to have a look at them.'

'That's impossible, I'm afraid, sir,' Emil said, working hard to make sure that none of his enjoyment was showing. 'They're access-protected by Garrett's secret personal codes, sir.'

'That's no prob — ' Whatever Shupe had been about to say, he stopped in midsentence as Cameron again touched his arm warningly. Shupe heaved in a deep breath, mopping the perspiration out of his eyes. He put persuasion into his voice the way another man might have put grease on a wheel.

'All right, let's forget the disks for a moment. What I'd like you to do is give us a complete rundown of everything Garrett did while he was here. What exactly was he looking for?'

'He asked a lot of questions that didn't make much sense to me,' Emil replied. 'About Mrs. Irwin, for instance.'

'Kitty?' Shupe said, unable to conceal his surprise. 'What did he want to know?'

'Everything. He'd accessed her dossier, of course. But he wanted to know about her trips abroad. Who she goes with, who her friends are, things like that. He also asked a lot of questions about her . . . friendship with Colonel Barton at Wiesbaden.'

'Did he say why he was interested?' Cameron asked.

'I gathered the colonel is a named suspect in the drug-trafficking investigation.'

Shupe could not conceal his reaction. Cameron covered it with a small laugh that sounded like a heron dying. 'Did Garrett mention anyone else?'

'No, sir,' Emil said.

'I think we'd better get on to Rheindahlen,' Shupe replied. 'One more thing before we leave.'

'What's that, sir?'

'You said the disks Garrett was using are in the safe?'

'Yes, sir.'

'Did he make backups?'

'I don't think so.'

'All right,' Shupe said. 'I want you to sign those disks out to General Irwin on my authority.'

'Sir, that would be highly unorthodox. Under the circumstances, you have no authority — '

'Trust me, Emil,' Shupe said, putting his hand on Fritz's shoulder again. 'This isn't a matter of who has authority. As commanding officer, General Irwin has a right to know what is in those disks. I'm sure you agree.'

'I suppose so, sir,' Emil said dubiously.

'You know so,' Cameron said smoothly. 'You go up there and get those disks. Make out a confiscatory release docket and bring it down here. We'll sign the docket, you hand over the disks.'

Shupe nodded confirmation. 'Emil, it's very important you get the disks out of the office without anybody seeing you do it. Do you think you can manage that?'

Fritz got up from the table and put on his raincoat. 'I'll be back as soon as I can,' he said. He paused for a moment in the doorway of the restaurant then hurried across the square and around the corner. When he was out of sight of Shupe and Cameron, he let out a whoop. Then he ran up the stairs into his office and grabbed a telephone, a wide smile on his face as he dialed.

'Mission control,' he said breathlessly. 'We have lift-off.'

★ ★ ★

Although it was over an hour since he had left Heidelberg, Paul Barton was still seething with anger. He forced himself to think clearly, replaying the events of the preceding twenty-four hours over in his mind, as if by doing so he could somehow reverse them: Shupe's urgent phone call, the clandestine meeting in the motorway restaurant at Lorsch, the story of Garrett's investigation and the disks containing the information off the TREVI computers, his meeting with Don Rogers, all of it.

'We're in bad trouble, Paul,' Shupe had said, mopping the sweat off his forehead. 'I'm telling you, Garrett knows about us. About the syndicate. He's probably even guessed who killed Wood.'

'Shut up, you goddamned idiot!' Barton snapped, glancing hastily around

268

to see if anyone had noticed Shupe's outburst. 'You want the whole fucking world to hear you?'

'I've brought the disks,' Shupe told him. 'If you can access them, we'll at least know how much he's found out. But, listen, you've got to get them back to me within twelve hours.'

'Twelve hours!' Barton said angrily. 'Are you crazy? Do you know what's involved here?'

'They've got to be back in the safe before Garrett gets there,' Shupe insisted. 'If he finds out they're gone, he'll know I took them.'

'If he doesn't know already,' Barton said contemptuously.

'No, it's all right. Apart from George Cameron, only one other person knows I've got them. He's one of my best people. He won't talk.'

'You'd better be right,' Barton had said. 'Or we'll all be up shit creek without a paddle.'

And now that was exactly where they were, he thought. Anger at having allowed himself to be stampeded by Shupe's panic surged through him again. Garrett had put the bait under the Englishman's nose, and the stupid fat bastard had gone for it like a pike after a tiddler.

Well, I fell for it, too; the thought made him angrier still. After leaving Shupe at Lorsch, Barton had taken the disks directly to the USFET computer facility at Heidelberg and laid them on the desk of his friend Captain Mort Shapiro, head of the research and analysis facility. The lanky, balding Californian had a typically laid-back style, but he sat up straight when he saw the codings.

'Where the hell did you get these, Paul?' he asked, looking around as if he were afraid someone might be watching them. 'Do you know how high an ULTRA VIPAR BLACK security rating is?'

'Ask me no questions, I'll tell you no lies,' Barton said. 'I want to access them, Mort.'

Shapiro whistled.

'I'll need special authorization, Paul. I don't suppose there are more than ten people in USFET cleared to read at this level. Who's going to sign the docket?'

'Log it as a Special Ops priority-access requirement.'

Shapiro shrugged. 'It'll be your balls in the wringer if anyone checks the Cryptags, babe. I can't cover you on something like this.'

'Just do it,' Barton said.

'Okay,' Shapiro said, and ambled off with the disks. By virtue of the nature of its secret work, Special Operations Unit had on-demand any-hour access to the computer facility. Barton was confident he could lose the details of this transaction in the records of the hundreds of others that came down from Bad Kreuznach each year. He paced up and down impatiently in Shapiro's office, chain-smoking until his mouth felt like a felt tea cosy, watching the white-coated technicians go unhurriedly about their work. After perhaps half an hour Shapiro called him on the intercom.

'We ran into something damned peculiar, Paul,' Shapiro said. 'Is this some kind of a joke, or what?'

'Uh, I . . . no. No, no joke. What's wrong?'

'We subjected the disks to intense validation,' Shapiro said. 'They bounced it off. We couldn't believe it. Then one of the technicians asked a dumb question: are there actually any codes on these disks? We checked. He was right. The disks aren't coded, Paul. There's nothing on them at all except a simple listing program that wouldn't stretch the mind of a ten-year-old. Take a look.'

He gestured to a young technical specialist who slid one of the disks into his computer and tapped a few keys. Barton stared in total disbelief at the message that blinked at him from the screen.

HELLO, SUCKER!

'The other one is just the same,' Shapiro said, his voice aggrieved. 'What the hell is all this about?'

'A mistake,' Barton mumbled. 'Must have picked up the wrong validation. I'm sorry, Mort. Just forget the whole thing, will you?'

Shapiro shrugged. 'All right, boys,' he said to his technicians. 'Fun's over. Back to work.'

Barton snatched the disks out of the computer technician's hands and hurried out of the facility. Shupe had been well and truly had. Garrett had programmed him beautifully, leaking the information that BFV was investigating narcotics trafficking within USFET, pretending to whistle up a dossier on this investigation from the Europolice network, which was known as TREVI because of its James Bond-ish French title, *Terrorisme, Radicalisme, et Violence Internationale*, and then letting it be known that the dossier named him, Paul Barton. The moment Shupe took the disks and brought them to Lorsch, he confirmed the suspicions that Garrett had voiced that day at Camp Patton. *When I walked into your office this afternoon, Major, I had nothing going for me but a hunch that you weren't kosher. Now I know it for a fact.* The jeering message programmed into the disks had been put there to let Barton know that Garrett knew.

He got into his Opel and drove across to the headquarters building and ran up the stairs to Dan Rogers's office.

Sleek, well built, clean shaven, with wavy dark hair and alert green eyes, Rogers was a shrewd, careful, and well-organized man. He listened without interrupting as Barton poured out his story, his expression imperturbable.

'So Garrett set the whole thing up,' he said when Barton finished. 'You know what this means, Paul. You're out of it.'

'What am I supposed to do now?'

'Get out,' Rogers said coldly. 'Go to Switzerland, collect your pension, disappear. How much have you got?'

'About half a million.'

'Then you won't starve,' Rogers said, with the ghost of a smile.

'What about . . . my house. My wife?'

'What do you think this is, for Christ sake?' Rogers snarled. 'Do what I tell you. Get the fuck out while the going is good. The syndicate will do what it can to cover for you.'

His tone was dismissive, almost as if he had lost interest the moment he stopped

274

talking. A feeling of betrayal, that he was being abandoned, welled up inside Barton like water.

'You better make fucking sure they don't take me, Don,' Barton said. 'I go, we all go.'

Rogers gazed at him levelly for a few moments before speaking.

'Don't even think it,' he said coldly. 'Open your mouth about the syndicate and there is no place on this earth where you'll be safe.'

Barton stared at him, mouth slightly open.

'I thought we were friends, Don,' he said, hurt in his tone.

'Did you really?' Roger's voice was bored. 'Whatever gave you that idea?'

Barton stamped down to the parking lot, got back into his car, and drove out of the base and up on to the autobahn heading north, his mind seething. Behind the feeling of betrayal was another sensation, a larger version of the premonition he had felt in the computer facility, a sense of things coming apart.

'I knew that bastard Garrett was

dangerous,' Barton muttered to himself. It had been a major error of judgment to delegate the job of getting rid of Garrett to Paul Shupe. Shupe was a windbag who made extravagant claims and then, when he couldn't deliver, instead of admitting the inability and letting someone else take the strain, compensated by doing a sloppy, messy, undisciplined job. It was like everything else in life; if you wanted a job done properly, the only way to do it was to take care of it yourself.

The big car ate up the miles in the gray drizzle. Weinheim. Bensheim. Pfungstadt. Darmstadt. Well, maybe Rogers was right. Maybe the smart thing to do was get out. It wasn't all downside. He had a few thousand tucked away in a shoebox in back of a wardrobe at home, and there was more than half a million in the Schweizer Kreditbank on the Paradeplatz in Zurich. After all, what was he leaving behind?

At the Frankfurter-kreuz he swung west, leaving the crowded highway at the Niedernhausern exit and taking the steep, winding Sonnenbergstrasse down through

Rambach, where the ruined castle on its hill stood stark against the heavy gray clouds. He turned left past the Catholic church and left again onto Liebenburgstrasse, driving to the far end where the stony road petered out at a farm gate leading into a field. His house stood on the right-hand side, a handsome two-story villa with a big fieldstone patio that commanded a fine view of Wiesbaden. He got out of the car and stood for a moment, looking at it. He wasn't even angry anymore. It was all down to survival now. Look after number one, and fuck everybody else.

If anyone was coming out of this with a whole skin, it was going to be Paul Barton.

'I'm in a hurry,' he said to Lucy when she opened the door. Her face was flushed from the heat of the oven and she had a streak of flour on her cheek.'

'I have to go away for a few days,' he said. 'I'll throw some things in a bag and grab a shower.' He went into the sitting room and she heard him mixing himself a drink. Whiskey and Canadian Dry, she thought; it always was.

When Barton came back downstairs, he was wearing civilian clothes: a Harris tweed jacket, a pale blue dress shirt with a narrow silk tie, tan slacks, and the black Bruno Magli loafers he had bought on a trip to Rome two years earlier. He put the suitcase he had packed in the hall and came into the kitchen.

He looked at her, as if seeing her for the first time. I wonder what you'd say if I told you, he thought.

'What's wrong?'

'Why should anything be wrong?'

'Just . . . you look so tense. So angry.'

'You want me to stop looking tense and angry, stop asking dumb questions.'

'I only . . . ' Lucy Barton didn't bother to complete the sentence. 'When will you be back?'

'Don't hang upside down waiting,' he said savagely, and went out of the house, slamming the door behind him. He stood outside in the drizzle for a moment, breathing heavily. Then he smiled. It's all over, he thought. Easy. It was like a weight being lifted off his back. He patted his inside pocket, feeling the bulk of the envelope containing the cash and the passport he had taken out of the wall safe upstairs. All he had to do now was get his passbook off Kitty and head for the tall timber.

He got into his car and turned it around. He took one last look at the house, shrugged, and headed down to the main road and on into town. On the radio, Simon and Garfunkel were offering to be a bridge over troubled water; he sang tunelessly along with them. Twenty minutes later he pulled up outside the familiar apartment house on Adlerstrasse. He ran up the steps, pushed the bell beneath the card for number three. The intercom made its tinny little sound.

'It's me,' he said. The door lock clicked and he pushed it open, bounding two at a time up the stairs to the first floor. Kitty Irwin was waiting at the top. She was wearing a silk nightdress the color of skimmed milk and he could see every line of her body silhouetted against the lights in the apartment behind her.

'Darling!' she said.

13

Garrett watched impassively as Paul
Barton's car barreled down the road,
whirling a spiral of dried leaves in its
wake. It was a pretty safe bet that the
American was going to see Kitty Irwin.
She would pay him off or give him an
account number in Switzerland that he
could use, and Barton would make his
run for it. It didn't matter. There was no
place he could go that the boys at Fort
Meade couldn't find him. What was it
that Joe Louis once said? 'He can run, but
he can't hide.'

He got out of the car, walked up the
path to the front door, rang the bell, and
waited. The woman who opened it was
perhaps five two or three, with a good
figure, dark brown hair framing a
heart-shaped face, wide-spaced brown
eyes, an expressive mouth. She was not a
raving beauty by any means, but if she
took the trouble to take care of her hair

and put on some makeup, men would find her attractive.

'Mrs. Barton? Mrs. Lucy Barton?'

'Yes. What is it?'

'My name is Charles Garrett, Mrs. Barton,' he said, holding up his MOD identification. 'I'm an officer of the British Ministry of Defense. May I come in?'

'Is it something to do with my husband?' Lucy Barton asked, frowning. Her voice still held the faint trace of a German accent that eight years of marriage to Barton had never completely ironed out.

'No,' Garrett said. 'It's something to do with Manfred Roth.'

The big brown eyes widened momentarily, then he saw caution hood them. 'What about Manfred Roth?' she said warily.

'He's dead, Mrs. Barton,' Garrett said softly. 'Someone murdered him.'

Shock stiffened her entire body. She closed her eyes and leaned against the doorjamb, and he thought for a moment she might faint. She put her face into her hands and took a deep breath, held it for a moment, then let it out. He reached out to steady her.

'I'm sorry,' he said. 'I should have broken it to you more gently.'

'It's all right,' she said, pulling back. 'I'm all right.'

'Perhaps we ought to go inside,' Garrett suggested.

'Yes,' she replied absently. 'Of course. Come in, come in.' She led the way into the living room. It was comfortably furnished, modern without being stark.

'Just give me a moment,' she said, brushing her hair away from her forehead with the back of her hand in an appealingly feminine gesture. 'I think I need a cup of coffee. What about you?'

'Coffee would be good.'

She went into the kitchen. He watched her through the pass-through window in the wall of the adjoining dining room as she filled the coffee machine. He could see a D-ended oak dining table and chairs, an étagère with plants on it, a wall cluttered with amateur-looking oil paintings, and a glass-fronted china cabinet with some nice pieces on it.

Taking up one whole wall behind him was a floor-to-ceiling bookcase crammed with art books, dictionaries, antique price guides, and an idiosyncratic selection of paperbacks. In front of the bookcase was a high-backed antique leather chair and a Pembroke table that looked eighteenth century. On it lay a cased 1847 Dragoon Colt .44 revolver, with bullet mold and powder flask, all in perfect condition. Serious money, Garrett thought.

Lucy Barton came in with a tray holding cups, sugar and milk, and a red thermos. She put it on the table, unscrewed the top, and poured the coffee, handing a cup to Garrett. He sat down in one of the armchairs facing the fireplace. She sat in the one opposite. She lifted her chin, as if in defiance, and looked him straight in the eyes, as much as to say, *I'm ready now.*

'All right,' she said. 'Tell me what happened.'

'Nothing much to tell,' Garrett said. 'A cleaning woman found him dead in his apartment. Someone had shot him in the back of the head with a nine-millimeter automatic pistol.' He watched her reactions carefully.

Lucy Barton shuddered. 'How awful,' she said. 'When did it happen?'

'Two nights ago.'

'There was nothing in the papers.'

'I believe not,' Garrett said, avoiding that. 'What exactly was your relationship with Roth?'

'I don't know that it's any of your business.'

'You're absolutely right,' Garrett said. 'And you don't have to talk to me if you don't want to. Of course, if you don't, I'll have to pass you on to the Federal Prosecutor's Office, and they're much less polite than I am.'

Lucy Barton stared at him for a moment, as if making up her mind about something. 'I've got nothing to hide,' she said. 'Manfred and I were . . . friends. Nothing more.'

Cynics said there was no such thing as a platonic friendship between a man and a woman. In Garrett's trade you learned to be a cynic early on. *Everybody's got a schatzi*, Eileen Carson had said when they talked about Barton's wife. She didn't look the type, but then, what did the type look like?

'How did you meet him?' he asked.

'At painting classes. We got talking. He wasn't much of a painter. Neither was I. After school we would have a coffee in the canteen. It was nice to have someone to talk to. I was alone a lot of the time. Paul was away on army business.'

'What did you talk about?'

'You know, the usual things. Books, TV. We went to a couple of exhibitions together. I know what you're thinking, but it wasn't like that. There was no romance. In fact it was nice to be with someone who didn't want to make a pass at you.' She grimaced. 'There are more than enough of that kind in the army.'

'Did you meet any of his friends?'

'He didn't seem to have any. He was from Munich, you know. He didn't know many people in Wiesbaden. I introduced him around, got him invited to some of the parties on the base.'

'Did he ever ask you about your

husband's work?'

She frowned. 'Once in a while. Never anything specific.'

'And Kitty Irwin?'

'He . . . he liked to gossip. I used to say to him, Fredi, you're an awful gossip. He wanted to know all the scandal.'

'And you told him.'

She bit her lip and stared at the floor, keeping her eyes averted as if by doing so she would never have to answer the question.

'He's dead, Lucy,' Garrett said. 'You can tell me now.'

'You make it sound as if I were spying on her. It wasn't like that. He used to ask me about her trips, where she'd gone, with who.'

He didn't doubt it was the truth. Roth had used the standard, classic ploy. The neglected wife going to evening classes, the friendly fellow student who just happens to have enrolled in the same class and is fun to talk to, who likes to gossip about people you know. Later, if necessary, Roth would have become her lover; that was how the game was played.

An undercover man used whatever weapon fate handed to him. Unhappiness was a handle, grief a key. Loyalty was something on a belt buckle; love was what women read about in magazines.

'Roth was an intelligence agent, Lucy,' Garrett told her. 'He worked for BFV, the German secret service.'

'An intelligence agent? I don't understand.' She was watching him the way a child will watch an adult when the scary part of the bedtime story is coming next.

'I'll try to explain it to you,' Garrett told her. 'The USFET high command believed there was a syndicate of American officers selling narcotics to servicemen in Germany. Army intelligence wasn't able to pin down who the kingpins were. So they asked BFV for help. Roth was sent down here to work undercover. The Americans gave him a job as a translator.'

'He told me he'd done some work for the army,' she said softly. 'That was how he knew Paul.'

'Your husband is a member of the drug syndicate,' Garrett said, hitting her with it. Unless she was a consummate actress, the shock on her face could not be anything but genuine.

'I used to ask him,' she whispered. 'Where did all that money come from? He said he won it at the casino.'

'He had to say something, Lucy. There can't be many officers of his rank who can afford to buy fifty-thousand-dollar Colt revolvers and leave them lying around as if they were paperweights. Can I ask you something very personal?'

She lifted her head to look him squarely in the eyes. 'Go ahead.'

'What exactly is Paul's relationship with Kitty Irwin?' She flinched slightly, as if he had moved to strike her. 'You don't have to answer.'

'It's all right. I'm not a child. Besides, you already know the answer, don't you?'

'How did it start?'

'She came down here with her husband, General Irwin. There was a lot of gossip about her. They said she liked men.'

'And Paul made a pass at her?'

'Or she made a pass at him,' Lucy said bitterly. 'It doesn't make much difference, does it? She likes men, Paul likes the ladies. Kismet.'

'When did you find out they were lovers?'

'He didn't make much of an effort to conceal it. It was quite a coup, you know. A general's wife.'

'I see,' Garrett said quietly. 'And you?'

'I did what I always do. I stayed home and waited for him to get tired of her.'

'This sort of thing has happened before, then?'

'Yes,' she said wearily. 'Yes, yes, yes.'

Why do they do it? he wondered. Why do some women hang on, hoping against any reasonable hope that the hurting will end? He remembered Jessica talking about a case she was handling. Although she never used names, he sometimes thought she told him about them to clarify them in her own mind.

'It's all there in Aesop's fable,' Jessica said. 'The frog and the scorpion. That's the way some people are.'

'How?' he asked her.

'The frog was at the riverside, preparing to swim across. The scorpion asked for a ride. The frog refused. 'You'll sting me to death,' he said. 'No, no,' the scorpion told him. 'That would be insanity. I sting you, we both drown.' That allayed the frog's fears, and he set off across the river. Halfway, the scorpion stung him. The dying frog turned despairingly to the drowning scorpion and said, 'Why did you do that? Now both of us will die.' 'I know,' the scorpion told him, 'but I can't help it. It's my nature.''

People who could not break the destructive patterns of their own life were like the frog and the scorpion, Jessica had said, each a necessary part of the other's inevitable destiny. I destroy you, even though I know that in doing so I destroy myself. You know I will destroy us both if you let me, and still you let me.

'You're not American, are you?' he asked Lucy Barton.

'I'm a GI bride,' she said, with a wan smile. 'Isn't that what they used to call them?'

'A long time ago.' He smiled. 'Where are you from?'

'Stuttgart. Ludwigsburg, actually. I met

Paul soon after he came over to Germany, in 1980.'

'That was when the Special Operations Unit was established?'

'Yes. It was at Stuttgart first. Patch barracks. We moved up here in '84.'

'Was that when he started playing around?'

'You men!' she said bitterly. 'You use such phrases. He was betraying his marriage vows and he was betraying me! He wasn't playing around, as you so nicely put it!'

'I'm sorry,' Garrett said.

She shook her head angrily. 'You'd think I'd learn, wouldn't you?' she said. 'But the funny thing is, I still get angry about it.'

'Is he still seeing Kitty Irwin?'

'Not the way he used to. At first it was — well, we all know what it's like at first. He was with her all the time, night after night after night. I couldn't . . . There had been others, I told you that. But it was never for long. A few weeks, two months, and then he got tired of them. This was different. It went on and on. I began to

291

think maybe he was going to leave me. I didn't know what to do. Then it stopped. I thought, Thank God, it's over, he'll come back. But it wasn't over. She rented an apartment downtown. She thinks nobody knows about it, but of course, it's common knowledge.'

'Frau Liebling, Adlerstrasse twenty-two,' he murmured.

'That's right,' Lucy said. 'She even called herself Mrs. Darling, the bitch. Paul was seeing her there, twice, sometimes three times a week.'

'They were still sleeping together?'

'You have to understand about Kitty,' Lucy Barton said. 'She's very casual about sex. It's something nice you can do to pass a little time if there's nothing much on TV.'

She said it with a certain bitterness that made him wonder if it was not tinged with a little jealousy. Some women could never quite cast off the straitjackets their upbringing had placed upon them.

'And then Manfred appeared on the scene.'

'He was so nice, so kind. I think if it

hadn't been for him, I'd have gone crazy. And all the time . . . ' Her shoulders slumped and she sighed; his heart went out to her. Roth had used her loneliness as a weapon, and now, from the grave, he was twisting it in her heart.

'He never told you anything about his investigation?'

'Not a word. It was as I told you earlier. Gossip. Where Kitty went, who she went with, how long she stayed. Of course, I see now why he wanted to know.'

'I think she's part of the syndicate, too,' Garrett told her. 'I suspect that's really the reason your husband visited her so often.'

'I wish I'd known,' Lucy said sadly. 'It would have made my life a lot easier.'

'How well do you know her?'

'Quite well. Not intimately, but better than casually.'

'Then tell me something. Why do you think someone like Kitty Irwin — someone with so much to lose — would get mixed up in a thing like this?'

Lucy shrugged. 'It could have been anything. Money, perhaps. She loves expensive clothes, champagne, the best restaurants, travel. I don't know, Mr. Garrett. Does anybody ever know why another person goes down a certain road?'

'Perhaps not,' Garrett said. She wasn't talking about Kitty Irwin; she was talking about her husband. 'I'm grateful to you for being so frank.'

She gave him a wan smile. 'If you were a shrink, I'd have to pay you a lot of money. Can you tell me something now?'

'I'll try.'

'What's going to happen to Paul?'

'The very best he can hope for is that he'll go to prison,' Garrett said. It was an evasion, but it was a kind one.

'You're honest,' she said, and he smiled at the irony of her words.

'It's not always a virtue.'

She had answered not only his overt but his unasked questions. It was quite clear she was not and never had been Roth's spy, merely a source. In some obscure way, he found he was glad about that. He wished that there was some way he could ease the pain, but he knew there wasn't. She was a nice, decent, warm, friendly human being who had found herself married to a heartless, conniving, self-centered shit who had performed entirely according to expectations. Frog and the scorpion. Happened all the time.

'Lucy, I want you to leave this house. I'll take you to a hotel in town, and I want you to stay there until I come back to get you.'

'Why?' she frowned. 'What's this all about?'

'Listen to me carefully,' he said, taking both her hands in his. 'There's a lot more to this thing than just the drugs. Your husband is also implicated in the murder of a British army sergeant, and it's even possible he had something to do with the death of Manfred Roth.'

She stared at him, shaking her head slightly from side to side as if what he was saying was beyond the bounds of anything she was prepared to believe.

'It . . . this is like some nightmare,' she whispered. 'I keep thinking, there can't be any more, but it goes on getting worse and worse and worse.'

'Lucy, trust me, please. Do what I ask.'

She nodded numbly. Who else was she going to trust? he thought. In short order he had destroyed what little faith she still had left in her husband, any remnant of affection she might have felt for Manfred Roth, and most of what little regard she had for herself. You do a great job, Garrett, he thought.

'Can I use your telephone?'

'Of course,' she said, waving a hand. 'It's in the hall.'

He went out, closing the door of the sitting room behind him. The phone was one of those replicas of the kind they had in fin-de-siècle Paris. More flash trash. He picked up the receiver and dialed.

'Inspector Weidemann, please,' he said when the call was answered. He tapped his fingers impatiently on the table until the detective came to the phone.

'This is Charles Garrett, Inspector.'

'Not another corpse, I hope.'

'Not this time. I've got some news for you.'

'And I for you,' Weidemann said. 'We

checked up on the phone calls made by the Red German Army. You were right. In both cases, the caller spoke German with an accent.'

'That fits,' Garrett said. 'How are you doing with the Roth case?'

'Lousy,' Weidemann told him sourly. 'Apart from the fact that somebody shot him, we haven't come up with a thing.'

'I imagine Gerhard Leiche told you that Roth was conducting an investigation inside USFET?'

'Leiche was not what you might call generous with his information,' Weidemann replied dryly. 'Refresh my memory.'

'The story I was told was that USFET had a drug problem, but army CIC was getting nowhere finding the traffickers, so they asked BFV to help them. BFV got Roth cover as a translator at the American consulate, and he began poking around.'

'I remember all that. He suspected the officers of the Special Operations Group. Your theory was that the Red German Army was a cover.'

'It looks like my theory was right,' Garrett said. 'Barton is one of the ringleaders of the drug gang. Shupe is in it, too. Barton's mistress, Kitty Irwin, the wife of the British general commanding, Rhine army, is also involved.'

'Christ on the cross, Garrett, you don't waste any words, do you?' Weidemann said. 'How do you know all this?'

Garrett told him about his ploy with the disks, and how Shupe had brought them to the American. 'The only reason they can have wanted those disks was to find out how much I knew about them. The fact that Shupe took them ties him to the syndicate, and probably gives us the murderer of George Wood.'

'You're telling me Shupe murdered Wood?'

'Or had him killed,' Garrett said.

'What for?'

'Because Wood had figured out what they were up to. He was going to tell me. They couldn't permit that, so they removed him.'

'How much of this can you prove, Garrett?'

'Meet me at Rheindahlen at noon tomorrow and I'll have it all on paper for you.'

'You sound very confident.'

'Oh, I am,' Garrett said. 'I am.'

He looked at the telephone and took a deep breath. There was one more call to make, and he wasn't looking forward to it. Your day to brighten people's lives, Garrett, he thought. First Lucy Barton. Now Leyland Irwin. The switchboard at Rheindahlen put him through. He told the old man what he had to tell him, and then told him what he wanted him to do.

★　★　★

The detention cells at Rheindahlen were solidly built, rather like the jails one sometimes sees in western movies, with iron bars from floor to ceiling, huge flat locks on the doors, stone floors, and slat beds that were little more than perfunctory. When Garrett presented himself at the security door, he was surprised to find that Lieutenant Clive Pennyweather was the officer in charge.

'General Irwin's orders, sir,' he told Garrett. 'He said he wanted someone over here he trusted. Since he knew

Shupe and I loathed each other, he selected me.'

'Which cell is Shupe in?'

'The first one on the left. Cameron's two doors down.'

'When did the disks arrive?'

'About an hour after you telephoned. They came by courier from Heidelberg, max-sec package addressed to Shupe. General Irwin had the pair of them arrested while they were opening the container.'

'Anybody talked to them?'

'Not yet. Shupe keeps demanding an attorney.'

'That'll be the day,' Garrett said. 'Give me the keys to his cell.'

'I'll come with you,' Pennyweather offered.

Garrett put a hand on his shoulder and pushed him back down into his chair. 'Call me Garbo. I want to be alone.'

'Sir, that's technically — '

'Shut up, Pennyweather,' Garret said tiredly. He took the keys and went down the corridor jangling them. When he got to Shupe's cell, he made a lot of noise opening the lock. Shupe was sitting on the slat bed, hands between his knees, shoulders slumped. He looked up as Garrett opened the door, his face tight with unease that he attempted to mask with anger.

'Come for a gloat, Garrett?' he hissed. 'Come to tell me how fucking clever you are, have you?'

His voice was defiant, but his piggy eyes glistened with apprehension. He was scared. Garrett remembered the advice of the psychologist who had taught him interrogation techniques at the DI6 training school in Borough High Street. *Play dirty. If they're scared, scare them some more. If they're afraid of being hurt, hurt them. Find out what they fear the most, then do it to them. Like the man said, once you've got them by the balls, their hearts and minds will surely follow.*

'No,' Garrett said. 'Only how stupid you are.'

Shupe turned his head away angrily. 'Get the hell out of here,' he said. 'I don't have to talk to you.'

'Wrong,' Garret said, and slapped

Shupe off the bed into the corner of the cell, where he sprawled in an ungainly heap, shocked and stunned. Garrett saw fear flood the close-set eyes; He bent down and bunched Shupe's shirt in his fist, dragged him to a sitting position, then rocked his head left and right with a series of flat slaps.

'Now,' he gritted. 'Have I got your complete attention?'

'Don't ... don't hit me,' Shupe croaked, lifting his hands in front of his face and cowering behind them. 'I'll tell you anything, anything you like, only don't hit me.'

'You know what I want, you despicable tub of lard,' Garrett grated contemptuously. 'Who killed George Wood?'

'It wasn't me, it was Cameron, he said he'd take care of it, I didn't know he was going to kill him!' Shupe blurted. 'I didn't know and then it was too late.'

'What about the man you sent to kill me?'

'Barton telephoned, told us you were dangerous.' Shupe was practically groveling, so anxious was he to please.

'Cameron knew someone. In Cologne. He arranged it all.'

'And you had nothing to do with it.'

'What will happen to me, Garrett?' Shupe quavered. 'What will they do to me?'

'They don't put your sort in ordinary prisons, Shupe,' Garrett said. 'You've been a keeper of secrets. They'll send you to what they call Far Isolation, an island without a name in a place that isn't on the map, and for the rest of what passes for your life you'll be a number in a book nobody reads.'

'Oh, God,' Shupe whined. 'I thought . . . if I cooperate. If I tell you everything, you'd . . . help me.'

'You miserable bastard,' Garrett snapped. 'I wouldn't piss on you if you were on fire. Get over there to that table. Pick up the pen and start writing. The whole story, right from the beginning. Everything you know.'

'Oh, God,' Shupe said again. Without warning he started sobbing, great, dry, gulping noises that brought no tears. 'Oh, Jesus Christ.'

'Do it!' Garrett said relentlessly. 'Unless you want me to kick your ass over there!'

Shupe stared up at him, his chest heaving. Very slowly, he got up off the floor and sat on the bentwood chair by his little table, his head in his hands, still racked by great dry heaving gulps.

'Write!'

Shupe nodded numbly and hunched over the pad that Garrett had brought in and started writing. Garrett left him to it; the smell of defeat and despair in the tiny cubicle was more than he could bear.

14

'I'm filing a recommendation that Lieutenant Pennyweather be given temporary command of MI until London confirms his appointment, General,' Garrett told Irwin. 'I imagine they'll send a team of dredgers out to debrief Cameron and Shupe.'

'I expect they'll want to talk to me, too,' Irwin said.

'Yes, sir,' Garrett said. 'They will.'

He had made Irwin's office his first call on returning to Rheindahlen, hoping somehow to find a way of humanizing the bare and brutal facts he had given him on the telephone, and maybe make it halfway possible for the old man to live with himself. Irwin rejected all thought of sympathy.

'My fault, the whole damned mess,' he said, standing by the window and staring out across the deserted parade ground. 'Could have stopped it before it got started, I suppose. But . . . she's a lively gel, my Kitty. I just couldn't . . . ' His voice trailed away. He looked older, frailer than the last time Garrett had seen him. Self-delusion was an astonishing thing; it was impossible to believe that the old man had not known about his wife's infidelities — she had done precious little to conceal them from him — but somehow or other, he had managed until now to persuade himself that what was happening in front of his eyes was not really happening at all.

'It's pretty clear to me she was in it for the money, sir,' Garrett said. 'I think the . . . other part of it was incidental.'

Irwin shook his head. He wasn't having any of Garrett's attempts at damage limitation. 'No, no, my boy. She liked the men. Loved the men, Kitty. Always has.'

'They used her, sir,' Garrett told him. 'She gave them perfect cover, you see. She wasn't even American.'

'I know you've explained it, but I still don't quite understand how it all worked,' Irwin said querulously. 'What was it you said she was, a bag lady?'

'It's a term the old gangsters used to use to describe a woman who moved money around for them,' Garrett replied. 'A lot of people were being greased — bribed — and the syndicate needed someone who could travel to Zurich or London whenever necessary and pick up funds from special accounts they kept there.'

'I still don't understand the connection between the drugs and this . . . this other thing.'

'I'll explain that later, sir,' Garrett said. 'As soon as Inspector Weidemann gets here. His office has an interest in what has been going on.'

'What will happen to Shupe and Cameron . . . afterward?'

'I think we can leave that to London, General,' Garrett said. He didn't get into the question of what would happen to General Irwin. All he could hope was that with the old man so near to retirement anyway, the powers-that-be at the ministry would simply pension him off without further ado and that would be the end of it.

After his confrontation in the cell with Paul Shupe, Garrett waited in the headquarters building until Weidemann and Gottfried arrived. He felt like an island surrounded by a sea of silence. Word had long since spread throughout the camp that Shupe and Cameron had been placed under close arrest and confined in the guardhouse. The base was abuzz with rumors, and Garrett was conscious of the wary, curious looks headquarters personnel directed at him as they went by his chair.

'I brought you some coffee.'

'He looked up to see Lieutenant Pennyweather standing beside his chair, a tray with a coffeepot and cups on it in his hands, a hesitant smile on his face.

'I appreciate it,' Garrett said. 'Sit down and join me.'

'Yes, sir,' Pennyweather said uncertainly. 'Can you tell me exactly what's going on, Mr. Garrett?'

'Not yet,' Garret said. 'You'll hear it all soon enough. Can you get the conference room set up for a meeting?'

'How many people?'

'You, me, General Irwin. Inspector Weidemann and Klauss Gottfried,' Garrett said.

'You said a meeting. Not a hearing.'

'There won't be any hearing, Lieutenant,' Garrett told him. 'Neither Shupe nor Cameron will ever come to formal trial.'

'What will happen to them?'

'Nothing good,' Garrett said, and left it at that.

Pennyweather sipped his coffee, then asked what time the meeting would start.

'As soon as possible after Inspector Weidemann gets here. He's due at noon,' Garrett told him. 'Do you want to tell me about Eileen Carson before he arrives?'

'Sir.' Pennyweather's face was almost scarlet with embarrassment. 'Is this relevant to — '

'Don't worry, I don't want the gory details. I just couldn't figure out why you were so relieved that night when I said I'd tell her about her brother being killed.'

'I didn't want to see her if I didn't have to. You see, I blamed her for something that happened to me, and it turned out it wasn't her fault.'

'Explain.'

'I had a few run-ins with Shupe and Cameron about the way they were running things. I was prepared to go over their heads if they didn't make some changes. I told Eileen about it. Next thing I knew, Shupe called me in. He knew all about Eileen and me. He threatened to make it public if I made any waves. I jumped to the conclusion it must have been Eileen who told him.'

'Why?'

'The story is that Shupe, uh, forced himself on her, sir. Right after her husband died. I can't vouch for it, of course. But there have always been stories. They certainly had some kind of love-hate relationship. I know Shupe found her that apartment in Wiesbaden. And I'm pretty sure he was using her as an informant.'

There's been some sort of trauma. What sort of trauma we don't know. Maybe you can find out. Even though it was only scuttlebutt, Pennyweather's story fulfilled the criteria raised in the psychological profile on Eileen Carson that Jessica had compiled. If she was his informant, it also meant that in all her loveless love affairs, she was effectively whoring for Shupe. That would account for the diary entries, it would explain the drinking, the lack of self-esteem. It would also explain why Eileen had lied to him about her brother's relationship with Shupe and Barton.

'I have to say, Lieutenant, Eileen Carson doesn't strike me as being your type at all. How did you get involved with her?'

'I was a damned fool,' Pennyweather said stoutly. 'I never should have gone near the woman. I kept trying to break it off, but she told me I was being tiresome. In the end, she found a new boyfriend, fellow by the name of Kurt Schneider, and that let me off the hook.'

'With Eileen. But not with Shupe.'

'Not Shupe. As I told you, he called me into his office. He and Cameron. They had it all, chapter and verse, photographs, a complete surveillance dossier. They gave me an ultimatum. Toe the line, or else. I had no choice, of course. If they . . . it

311

would have seriously embarrassed me. Uh, back home.'

Of course, Garrett thought. The family, the military tradition, the fiancée in Beaconsfield; Pennyweather would have been easy meat.

'Blackmail,' he said. 'Did Shupe gag General Irwin the same way?'

'She was up here one weekend. There was a party at the officers' mess. She got tight. Eileen always got tight. Well, to cut a long story short, General Irwin took her home.'

'He did what?'

'It's not the way it sounds,' Pennyweather said. 'There was Eileen bombed out of her skull, talking about driving back to Wiesbaden, and there was Shupe telling her he couldn't take the responsibility. The general stepped in and told Eileen he couldn't allow her to drive. Kitty was away on a trip, she could sleep in her bedroom. He took her back to his bungalow and she stayed the night.'

It had probably never even occurred to him that he was compromising himself, Pennyweather went on. The man was too much of a gentleman. Of course, the situation was tailor-made for Shupe. He told the general he had photographs and tapes of him and Eileen together; whether it was true or not was irrelevant. It was more than enough to keep the old man in line.

'Funny, really, isn't it?'

'Sad,' Garrett said. While Kitty Irwin was gratifying herself any way she wished, her doting husband put himself into the sleazy hands of Paul Shupe rather than have her think he might have been unfaithful to her. If he had confessed, she would probably have laughed out loud, but of course, Leyland Irwin couldn't bring himself to believe that. Whatever shape or size somebody else's love came in, it never failed to surprise the onlooker.

'I'm going to give you a clean bill of health in my report, Clive,' Garrett told the young officer. 'I'm also going to recommend that you be appointed acting commanding officer of military intelligence here until a permanent appointment can be made. You'll probably get your captaincy at the same time.'

'Yes, sir,' Pennyweather said, glowing with pleasure and pride. 'Thank you, sir.'

One for the angels, Garrett thought. At least he wasn't ruining every life he touched today. He looked at the clock: 11:45. Weidemann would be arriving anytime. He got up and walked through to the conference room, which was situated directly opposite General Irwin's office. Weidemann arrived as punctually as a train, the thickset Gottfried one step behind. They assembled for the meeting, the big maps on the wall with their pins and flags and little wooden tanks and guns giving it a curiously military air; it was as if they were preparing a battle plan. Well, in a way they were.

General Irwin sat at the head of the table, with Weidemann and Gottfried on his right and Garrett and Pennyweather on his left. Garrett gave each of them copies of Shupe's written confession and stood looking out of the window while they read them. It didn't take long. Weidemann was first to finish; he laid the papers down on the table and shook his head in sad disbelief.

'What a *stumperei*,' he said disgustedly. 'Did they really think they were going to get away with it?'

'They were getting away with it,' Garrett reminded him.

'Mostly because I was too damned spineless to stop them,' Irwin said. Whatever dark thoughts had assailed him earlier seemed to have been dispelled. The old air of command was back; it showed in the challenging assurance of the old man's posture. Well done, General, Garrett thought; it could not have been easy.

'Very well, Charles,' Irwin went on. 'Let's begin.'

'Shupe's confession says nearly all that needs saying,' Garrett told them. 'We really don't need to go into chapter and verse, but some background information will put it all into context for you. The story begins about 1980, when someone at the Pentagon initiated new research into something the scientific whiz kids call 'genes wars' — genetic engineering applied to viral infections, microorganisms, bacilli, and so forth. They needed a name for it so they used one that had been discarded sometime previously, Project 23.'

'Wait a minute,' Gottfried said. 'What has all this got to do with drug trafficking?'

'I'm coming to that,' Garrett said. 'The Pentagon trained the personnel for Project 23 at the White Sands base in New Mexico. They were then formed into a Special Operations Unit and posted to Germany, first at Patch barracks in Stuttgart, and then, when the project moved into its operational stage, to the *Sperrgebiet* near Bad Kreuznach.'

'Operational stage?' Weidemann said. 'You mean they were experimenting with genetically engineered viruses up there? I thought all that nerve-gas stuff was banned.'

'That's just it, Inspector,' Garrett said. 'It isn't nerve gas, or even a form of chemical weapon. This is something new. You don't kill the enemy with it, you just make him so damned sick he can't fight you.'

'And Shupe and Irwin were part of it,'

General Irwin said, with a contemptuous gesture. 'In it up to their necks.'

'The research and development was carried on at Porton Down in England. What better way of getting the material directly to the end users than through British security channels? The stuff came from Porton to Cameron here in Rheindahlen, then it went from Rheindahlen by courier to Major Barton in Wiesbaden, and from there up to the experimental area. Absolutely foolproof, and if it hadn't been for the fact that they all got greedy, none of us would ever have been any the wiser. But one day one of them — Shupe says it was Barton — had a brain wave. What if they used the same channels to bring in drugs?'

'Of course,' Pennyweather said softly. 'The Porton consignments would always be covered by an absolutely maximum security blanket, so they could ship in anything they wanted under the same protection.'

'That's how it started.' Garrett nodded. 'The problem was that the drug market grew bigger than any of them had expected.

The kind of spending they could do without drawing attention to themselves wasn't even making a dent in their takings. So they set up a laundering operation.'

'My wife,' General Irwin said, his voice toneless. Weidemann flashed a surprised look at him and then frowned a question at Garrett. Garrett shrugged. He was going to have to lay it on the line, whether it twisted the knife in the general's wounds or not.

'Kitty Irwin wanted a good time, plenty of money, clothes, travel,' he explained. 'Barton moved in on her; he told her there was a way she could have them. He recruited her to move clandestine funds around for the Special Operations Unit. She was ideal; she could come and go as she pleased. Who was going to suspect the wife of a British general of being a bag lady for the Pentagon?'

General Irwin got up heavily from the table and went across to the window. He stood there, hands behind his back, for perhaps a minute. Nobody spoke. Then he squared his shoulders and came back to the table.

'Hrrmph!' he said. 'Sorry, gentlemen. Please go on.'

'All right, we've got that understood,' Gottfried said. 'Now what?'

'It was easy after that. They just grafted their own operation onto the Project 23 operation. Each time Kitty left Germany to make a pickup, the proceeds of the drug sales were smuggled out to Zurich or London. They were rolling up a fortune. And then George Wood found out what they were up to.'

'He was a good soldier,' Pennyweather interceded, 'the orders-is-orders type. He would have carried the Porton consignments for as long as anyone told him to without batting an eyelid. But when he found out he was running drugs, he balked.'

'It's all in Shupe's statement,' Garret said. 'Wood wanted out, but they told him they'd fix it so he was kicked out of the army with a dishonorable discharge, no pension, nothing. Then the base was bombed, and I turned up. They couldn't chance Wood talking to me, so they decided to get rid of him quickly.

Cameron phoned the local paper and told them the Red German Army was responsible for the bombing, then used the lie to cover murdering Wood.'

'Then it was the IRA all along?' Weidemann said. 'The bombing?'

'No question,' Garrett said. 'Shupe and Cameron hoped the dodge would muddy the water enough so that no one would ever find out what had happened. They were just unlucky. They had me beaten up, hoping it would discourage me; it didn't. Then the two hunters found Wood's body. That was a shock; they had counted on a couple of weeks before it turned up. Things started moving too fast. I went to see Barton, put pressure on him. That made them even more nervous. Cameron got hold of a small-time local gangster named Zittwitz. He tried to kill me but he made a mess of it.'

'He was the one who took a shot at you?' Gottfried said. Garrett nodded, yes.

'Just as a matter of interest,' Weidemann asked mildly. 'What happened to him?'

'He had an accident,' Garrett said.

'How bad?'

'Fatal,' Garrett replied. 'Don't worry, BFV cleaned up the mess. Zittwitz just disappeared. You'll see Shupe says they thought the hit man had taken the money and done a runner.'

'BFV cleaned up the mess?' Weidemann said. 'It didn't look to me as if you hit it off that well with Gerhard Leiche.'

'I've been in this business a long time, Inspector,' Garrett said. 'And to answer your next question, no, Leiche didn't tell me about Manfred Roth, either.'

'I didn't think so,' Weidemann said sourly. 'And I don't imagine you're going to tell us who did. You know it's possible you got Roth killed?'

'It's possible,' Garrett said. 'But I don't think so.'

'Who do you think killed him — Cameron again?'

'He had a motive,' Garrett said. 'Roth was supposed to be investigating the drug trafficking, and nobody wanted that exposed. But Cameron didn't kill Manfred Roth, and neither did Paul Shupe.'

'You've lost me,' Gottfried said. 'If

neither Cameron nor Shupe killed Roth, who the hell did? Paul Barton?'

'None of the above,' Garrett said. 'It's confusing, but I'll try and explain. There were two sets of things going on simultaneously. One was Barton and his pals and their drug racket. The other was something more sinister. I didn't realize it until Roth was killed. That job was done by an expert.'

'So?'

'Think about it. Wood was shot somewhere, taken to the woods, and dumped. It kept bothering me because it was so clumsy. Then Zittwitz tried to kill me. That was even more amateurish, the work of a couple of bunglers: Shupe and Cameron. But Roth was killed by someone who could walk through walls and leave no trace. When Inspector Weidemann told me how he'd been killed, my immediate reaction was that it had all the earmarks of a pro hit.'

'You mean someone brought in a professional killer?'

'One thing always bothered me about the drug investigation, Inspector,' Garrett said. 'If USFET wanted it checked out, why didn't they bring in the Drug Enforcement Agency, or any one of a dozen other American agencies they could have called on? Why call in the BFV? That's when it dawned on me; Roth wasn't investigating the drug racket at all. That was why Gerhard Leiche tried to put a wall in front of me when I stuck my nose into the investigation. I think Roth stumbled onto Project 23, and he was taken out before he could tell anybody about it.'

'My God, Garrett, what are you telling us?' General Irwin said. 'Who did this thing?'

'General, somebody is using assassination to prevent any word of the existence of Project 23 leaking out. If the German press got confirmation that the U.S. Army is conducting genes-war experiments smack in the middle of one of the most heavily populated areas in the country, all hell would break loose.'

'I can see that,' Irwin said. 'But who is this somebody? Are you telling us the CIA killed Manfred Roth?'

'No,' Garrett replied. 'My boss in London talked to some people. The Company confirmed, and I quote, that they have effected no sanctioned terminations in this area within the specified time frame.'

'Don't you just love the way those people talk?' Gottfried said, his voice flat with anger. 'As if you could change what it is by calling it something else!'

'Spooks speak their own lingo, Klaus,' Weidemann said. 'Our boys do a good line in gobbledygook, too.'

'It looks to me that what we've got here is a very nasty can of Washington worms,' Garrett said. 'It would appear that some maverick military outfit, something like the one Colonel Oliver North was running in the basement of the White House, set up, financed, and is still supporting the genes-war experimentation at Kreuznach. When Manfred Roth got too close to Kitty Irwin, who was their paymaster, they took him out of the picture.'

'Using the same MO as the Red German Army,' Weidemann said softly.

'To bamboozle us even more. Do you have any idea who these people are, Garrett?'

'I've got some names,' Garrett told him. 'The top man is a four-star general named Wells at the Pentagon, in Washington. They've also got someone covering for them at the CIA in Langley.'

'And what about the man who killed Roth?'

'I've got a pretty good idea who he is, too,' Garrett said. 'A master sergeant in the Special Operations Unit named Leroy Jackson.'

'Just a minute,' Gottfried said slowly. 'I want to be sure I've got this straight. You're saying this Jackson killed Roth to protect the genes-war project? In that case, what about Barton and the others? Won't he go after them, too?'

'Probably,' Garrett said.

Weidemann shook his head angrily. 'What's wrong with you, Garrett? Don't you care if these people get killed?'

'Let me ask you something, Inspector,' Garrett said levelly. 'Do you think they'd ever come to trial in a German court?'

'That's not the point,' Weidemann said.

'It is to me,' Garrett replied.

Weidemann kicked back his chair and strode across to a telephone, banging the buttons down as if he could dissipate his anger by doing so. Garrett watched imperturbably. The wheels had started turning. Maybe Weidemann could still stop them. Maybe.

15

'How would you like to cut off Gerhard Leiche's balls?'

Garrett asked his friend on the telephone. Prachner burst out laughing.

'You get straight to the point, don't you, Garrett?' he said. 'The short answer is, I'd love to. With a very blunt knife.'

'I may be able to provide one,' Garrett said. 'But I need some information first.'

'What a surprise,' Prachner said dryly.

'Come on, Klaus. What's the status of BFV's USFET investigation?'

'That's easy,' Prachner said. 'Some gray-suited gentlemen with American accents called in to see us. They were from the agency that prefers not to show identification. They told us to drop the whole thing. And don't ask questions.'

'The CIA.'

'You don't sound too surprised.'

'It's been a Company take from the start, Klaus,' Garrett said. 'They used you, they used all of us.'

'Leiche's going to love that,' Prachner observed.

'Ask yourself a question: why would USFET ask BFV to investigate drug trafficking when they had the Company, the DEA, and Army G2 to choose from?'

'All right, I've asked myself. I don't know the answer.'

'The Company wanted to use the drug investigation as a cover for one of its own. They needed your people out there for exactly the same reason USFET had given you; their own agents were known to the subjects under surveillance.'

'You mean the whole drugs thing was a front?'

'No, that was genuine. The ringleaders are Barton, Gilchriese, and Rogers. Manfred Roth had it right; they were using the facilities of the Special Operations Unit to move the stuff around. That was the reason he was seeing Lucy Barton. He was getting information on Kitty Irwin from her.'

'You found out how she was involved?'

'They used Kitty to launder the money. Then Roth found out she was involved in something else, a secret operation called Project 23. I asked him if he knew anything about it. He must have told the station chief at Frankfurt. Once the Company knew I was interested in Project 23, they were interested, too. So they took over the USFET investigation.'

'What exactly is this Project 23 you're talking about?'

'It's a secret genes-war program run by an unsanctioned military unit in Washington that has diverted Pentagon funds into unauthorized experimentation. The testing ground is the closed area at Bad Kreuznach. They're prepared to go to extreme lengths to protect themselves. That's why Roth was killed: He found out Kitty Irwin wasn't just the bag lady for the drug syndicate, but for Project 23 as well.'

'Jesus,' Prachner breathed. 'I hope this damned phone is secure.'

'I'm on a land line,' Garrett assured him. 'It's as secure as anything can be. Listen carefully, Klaus. This maverick

Pentagon outfit is known as the Biogenetic Development Unit. It's commanded by a General Angus Muir Wells. And I'm about ready to blow it wide open.'

Talking slowly, choosing his words with care, Garrett took Prachner through the whole sequence of events beginning with his arrival at Rheindahlen and up to the abrupt departure of Weidemann and Gottfried.

'You mean you deliberately set Barton up as a target?' Klaus said when he had finished. 'Jesus, Charles.'

'You think we should award him a medal?' Garrett rasped. 'I want these people out in the open where I can see them. The only way to do that is to give them something to come after.'

'Maybe Weidemann and Gottfried will get to Barton first.'

'It's a possibility,' Garrett said. 'One last thing. I've got Lucy Barton locked away in a room at the Oranien Hotel in Wiesbaden. She's a material witness; she can verify Roth's interest in Kitty Irwin and the connection between Irwin and Barton. I'd like to get her out of there into protective custody.'

'Got it,' Prachner said. 'I hope you're not carrying all this around in your head, Charles.'

'I've put it all on disk. I'll get a duplicate couriered over to you.'

'This isn't going to make Gerhard Leiche's day,' Prachner observed. 'Or the Company's, come to that.'

'The next sound you hear will be my heart breaking,' Garrett said, harshly. '*Schuss*.'

★ ★ ★

When Kitty Irwin first rented the apartment on Adlerstrasse, she had done so because it made handling the money drops easier, obviating the need to rent hotel rooms or stage a rendezvous with the all requisite alibis. It had been no more than that to begin with, but then other possibilities had occurred to her. As the months passed, she turned the place into a secret hideaway. She thought of it as her love nest, her den of iniquity, her sin bin. When she knew Paul was coming to see her, she lay on the bed watching one of the dozens of pornographic video films he had brought her, drinking champagne until the lust rose in her like mercury in a thermometer. By the time he arrived at the apartment, it was all she could do to keep her hands off him. And once he was inside . . .

'You are a handsome bastard, darling,' she was saying, a chuckle deep in her throat. 'But you know that, don't you?'

She was a good-looking woman, Barton thought.

He poured some more champagne into his glass from the bottle in the ice bucket beside the bath. He was as relaxed as a clam. Two days of Kitty's brand of lovemaking had been just the kind of going-away present he needed. It was a shame it had to end, but that was how it was going to have to be.

'Hey,' Kitty said, pretending a pout. 'Where's mine?'

'Right where it always was.' He grinned, leaning over to kiss her on the right breast. She slid her hand down his belly and toyed with his penis, flaccid in the turbulent water of the Jacuzzi.

'Something I can do for you?'

'Not with that thing,' she said.

'Complaints, complaints,' he said. He climbed out of the bath and went over to the vanity table, took the top off the wide-topped airtight jar, and used the little silver spoon to lift out some cocaine. He snorted it greedily, eyes closed for the huge rush of sensation as it hit.

'Aaaah,' he said in agonized ecstasy. 'Jesus.'

'Good, darling?' Kitty asked. She stood up in the water, reaching up to touch him again, and grinned shamelessly at the immediate reaction of his body. He arched his back in an exaggerated pose.

'Wait,' she said breathily. 'Stay like that.'

She climbed out of the bath in a great slosh of water and came across to him, her skin glistening wet. She pushed him backward until he was leaning against the tiled wall. She knelt down in front of him, eyes half-closed with desire, taking his erection in her hands.

'First, I'm going to suck you, and then

I'm going to fuck you,' she said in a throaty singsong.

Barton closed his eyes and groaned with pleasure as her mouth enveloped him. The whooshing rumble of the Jacuzzi drowned the slight sound that the man in black made as he stepped noiselessly into the bathroom. Lost in lust, neither of the two naked figures in the bathroom was aware of his presence. The man was very tall, six three or four, with the flat-planed physique of an athlete. He wore a black long-sleeved sweatshirt, black slacks, and black sneakers; his face and head were encased in a black woolen ski mask. In his right hand he carried a Beretta Model 84 9mm automatic pistol with a MAC silencer.

The silenced gun in his hand gave its flat loud cough and the 9mm bullet, traveling at about seven hundred and fifty miles an hour, drove through Barton's forehead an inch to the left of the median, striking the bone of the eye socket and tearing its way into his brain. It ranged slightly left, emerging a millisecond later below the crown of the head, taking with it approximately four square centimeters of the cranium, spattering the spotless pink marble tiles with blood and brain tissue.

Half a second later, before she even realized exactly what had happened, a second bullet drove into the base of Kitty Irwin's skull, driving her facedown into the churning water, killing her as instantly as the first shot had killed Barton. The assassin watched for a moment as Kitty Irwin's long dark hair spread like some strange seaweed and the roiling water turned from pink to red. He unscrewed the silencer and put it into the pocket of his black leather jacket; the Beretta went into a shoulder holster beneath his left arm. He bent down and put a luggage label bearing the message 'Compliments of the Red German Army' around Barton's neck. Then he left as silently as he had arrived.

★　★　★

Garrett spent ten minutes at the computer declassifying the coded disks before putting them into a max-sec pack addressed to Prachner at the BFV building in Cologne's Barthelstrasse. The courier had left the room only a few moments before when Garrett's telephone rang.

'Mr. Garrett, this is Lucy Barton.'

'I told you not to use the telephone, Lucy.'

'I wouldn't have,' she said. 'Only . . . Mr. Garrett, you-know-who is here.'

'You mean our friend the gun collector?'

'That's right. I don't know how he found me, but he's here. He says he wants to give himself up.'

Garrett frowned at the phone. 'Tell him to go to the consulate. He'll be safe there.'

'He's afraid. He won't surrender to anyone in uniform. Only to you.'

'All right,' Garrett said. 'Stay there. I'll be with you as soon as I can.' He put the telephone down and stared at it thoughtfully for a few moments. Then he shrugged and looked at his watch: 3:45. If he could whistle up a plane, he could be in Wiesbaden in less than an hour. He went back to the bungalow and changed into a leather jacket, warm woolen slacks, and a pair of Timberland Ultra Light boots. When he was ready he put an absolute-priority call through to transportation, and they told him there was a plane on the runway, gassed up and ready to fly. Twelve minutes later he was in the air, checking his flight path south.

Military Air Traffic Control routed him southeast at three thousand feet, passing over the terraced vineyards of the Mosel Valley before swinging west to cross the Rhine just south of the Lorelei, approaching the U.S. Air Force landing field northwest of town from the west for a perfect, easy landing. Fifteen minutes later, a USAF jeep dropped him at the entrance of the Oranien Hotel. He went straight through the lobby without checking at the desk and ran up the stairs to the second floor. Lucy Barton opened the door of Room 211. Her face was pale and taut with strain.

'Where is he?' Garrett asked. She shook her head, and then as he stepped into the room, a man stepped from behind the door with a silenced Beretta in his right hand. He was a handsome, athletic-looking black man of about thirty, wearing a black sweatshirt and black slacks.

'Surprise, surprise,' Garrett said. 'Sergeant Leroy Jackson, isn't it?'

'Very good,' the soldier replied. 'Ve-ry good.'

'And of course, all this Barton business was a hoax.'

'Had to think of some way of getting you down here fast, Garrett.' The big man smiled. 'Seems to have done the trick.'

'Here I am. What do you want?'

'First things first,' Jackson said. 'Stand nice and still now.' He put the muzzle of the gun against the base of Garrett's spine while he expertly frisked him, removing the S&W ASP from its shoulder holster and putting it into his own pocket. When he was done, he moved smoothly away to cover Garrett from the front.

'You going to meet the Man, Garrett,' he said.

'Northrup?'

'Him too.'

Jackson picked up the phone and dialed a number, never taking his eyes off Garrett. The Beretta remained rock steady in the big black fist, its muzzle pointing unwaveringly at Garrett's belly.

'Jackson,' he said. 'Cat's in the bag.'

He waved the gun: *over there*. Garrett went across the room and sat in the chair opposite him. Lucy Barton was sitting on the edge of the bed, her eyes tearful.

'He made me call you, Mr. Garrett,' she said. 'He told me they had Paul. That they'd hurt him if I didn't do what they said.'

'That true, Sergeant? You've got Barton?'

'Ask me no questions,' Jackson said, showing perfect teeth in a wide smile, 'and I'll tell you no lies.'

'Where are you taking us?'

Jackson smiled, but did not bother to reply. He sat back comfortably in the chair, as relaxed as a tiger and just as dangerous.

'Looks like I got most of it right,' Garrett said conversationally. 'You killed Roth, didn't you?'

Lucy Barton gave him a startled look,

then stared at Jackson as if she were seeing him for the first time. Jackson returned her stare, his eyes full of amused contempt.

'What about the others, Sergeant? What about Gilchriese and Rogers? And Kitty Irwin? Where are they?'

'Save your breath, man,' Jackson said indifferently. 'I ain't *Information Please.*'

Garrett shrugged. Lucy Barton looked at him tearfully and he smiled to encourage her. She was going to need all the encouragement she could get. They waited in silence for perhaps fifteen minutes; then someone tapped at the door once, twice, then once-twice.

'Open the door, Miz Barton,' Jackson said. He didn't even bother to watch her; he kept his lambent gaze fastened on Garrett. She went across and opened the door. A tall thin man in the uniform of a colonel of the United States Army came in. He wore rimless glasses, and his gray eyes were narrow and cold. His mouth was little more than a horizontal slit in the square block of his face.

'All raght, Jackson?' he said, his voice

soft with the cadences of the Deep South.

'No sweat, Colonel,' Jackson said.

'Good,' the newcomer said. 'Real good.'

'Colonel Maximilian Northrup, I presume?' Garrett asked.

'Yoah're Garrett,' Northrup said, acknowledging the question with a brisk nod. 'You've turned aht to be a considerable nuisance. Got some impo'tant people real mad with you.'

'You know how it is,' Garrett said perkily. 'You can't please everybody.'

'Ah know you ain't stupid, Garrett,' Northrup said, 'so Ah assume yoah're trahn to annoy me. Ah don't recommend you continue doin' so.'

'Why, hush mah mouth,' Garrett said.

He didn't see the signal that passed between Northrup and Jackson. The sergeant struck out blindingly fast with the barrel of the Beretta, sideswiping Garrett above the right ear. The blow dropped him to his knees like a poleaxed steer, fighting for consciousness.

'You pay the colonel a little mind now,' Jackson said, his voice as gentle as if he were talking to a ten-year-old child. 'Or we gonna get rough.'

'On yoah feet, mistah,' Northrup said. Garrett shook his head to clear it and stood up, swaying slightly. He felt blood trickle down his cheek and wiped it away with the back of his hand.

'I'm only going to say this once, Garrett,' Jackson said. 'So listen up. Mrs. Barton and the colonel are going to walk down the stairs together. Me and you are going to be right behind them. You do anything to make me nervous, make one move I don't like, and I kill her on the spot, take my chances with you after. You got that?'

'Got it,' Garrett said. Colonel Northrup helped Lucy on with her coat, every inch the southern gentleman. He took her arm and propelled her along the corridor. Jackson prodded Garrett with the Beretta and they set off after them, along the carpeted corridor, down the curving white stone staircase that led to the foyer, and out into the street, where a tan Dodge Aries four-door sedan was parked at the curb.

'Get in the front,' Jackson said. Garrett got in alongside Colonel Northrup, who had helped Lucy Barton into the rear passenger seat. When Garrett was inside the car, Jackson slid in behind him, laying the Beretta on the back of the seat so that the muzzle rested lightly at the nape of Garrett's neck.

'Less go, Colonel,' he said.

16

'Sit down, Mr. Garrett.'

The speaker was a man of perhaps sixty, dressed in a beautifully tailored gray flannel suit. He looked powerful, in both senses of the word: broad-shouldered, tall, with bushy straight hair parted on the left, graying slightly at the temples and cut short at back and sides. His eyebrows were thick and heavy and the dark brown eyes steady and confident beneath jutting brows. The chin was square, the mouth full-lipped without being sensual.

'General Wells, isn't it?' Garrett said, sitting in the upright chair in front of the desk. 'General Angus Muir Wells.'

'You've done your homework, my boy.'

'I'm not your boy.'

Sergeant Leroy Jackson made a threatening noise in his throat and moved toward Garrett, but Wells held up a hand.

'No, no, Sergeant,' he said softly. 'I'd like to hope that sort of thing won't prove necessary. Now, then, Mr. Garrett. You've been brought here for one reason and one reason only. I imagine you know what that is.'

'To tell you what I know about Project 23,' Garrett said. 'And the Biogenetic Development Unit at the Pentagon.'

'I'm impressed,' Wells said. 'Please proceed.'

Garrett smiled. Nobody spoke. Garrett kept on smiling.

'You better not trah the gin'ral's patience, Garrett,' Northrup said softly. 'Believe me when Ah tell you, he is not a patient man.'

'I wonder if the general is aware of how badly you have fouled up, Colonel?' Garrett said. 'I wonder if any of you have the remotest idea of just how much trouble you are all in?'

Now it was Wells's turn to smile. 'Perhaps you'd care to tell us, Mr. Garrett.'

'Within the last few months, this unit has attracted the high-level scrutiny of the Central Intelligence Agency, the British and German security services, and

USFET-G2, army intelligence. You can't seriously believe all that is going to dry up and blow away.'

'I think you underestimate us, Garrett,' Wells said. 'If I were to make an analogy, I would say this organization is the military equivalent of the Mafia, a multimillion-dollar corporation whose officers hold positions of high responsibility not only on Capitol Hill but in every echelon of the military and security apparatus of the United States.'

'And you think you can fix any tickets you get, is that it?'

'That, indeed, is it,' Wells said gravely. 'And so that you do not continue to labor under any misapprehension about the, ah, delicacy of your own situation, allow me to inform you that the drug-trafficking operation has been desensitized.'

'What does that mean?'

'It means that the participants have been eliminated from the equation.'

There was no doubting the flat certainty of what he said. Garrett glanced at Lucy Barton. She clearly had no idea what Wells's chilling phrase actually meant.

'You really think you can get away with anything, don't you?' he said. 'Even murder.'

'Come, come, Mr. Garrett,' Wells said impatiently. 'You work for the British security services. You know perfectly well that salutary removal is practiced by practically every government in the world today. The CIA calls it 'maximal demotion,' the Russians call it a 'wet job,' and no doubt your people have their own euphemism for it. We are here for one reason and one reason only. Damage control, Mr. Garrett, damage control. Once we know where the damage has been done, we can take the necessary steps to effect repairs.'

'You can't fix everything, General.'

'Oh, we can, Mr. Garrett. We have been doing so for almost a decade now, and we have every intention of continuing to do so,' Wells said, his voice rising slightly. 'This work is far too important to let anyone or anything stand in the way of its completion. We must succeed, we will succeed! While I live, America will not be left defenseless!'

His words hung in the air like Roman candles, burning and falling and fading. Every eye in the room was fixed on him; the only sound that could be heard was his harsh breathing. He blinked, and sentience filled his eyes.

'You see, Mr. Garrett,' he said softly. 'You see how strongly we all feel. It would be a mistake to inconvenience us.'

'I hate to say this, General,' Garrett said. 'But you're as crazy as a bedbug.'

He heard Northrup draw in his breath sharply. Behind him, Garrett half saw and heard the movement of Jackson's arm. The callused edge of the sergeant's hand hit Garrett beneath the ear, whacking him sideways off the bentwood chair to sprawl dazed on the floor of the room.

'Pick 'im up, Leroy,' he heard Northrup say.

Jackson lifted Garrett as if he were a doll and put him back on the chair in front of Wells. Garrett's head lolled; he tried to focus his eyes. A huge throb of pain all along his jawbone matched the slow, strong beat of his heart.

'Last chance, Garrett,' Wells said patiently.

'There are too many men like you in the world, General,' Garrett told him. 'Men who think that love of country puts them above the law. They're wrong, you're wrong. You're finished, General. It's all over.'

Wells made an impatient gesture with his hand and stood up. Northrup jumped to attention. Wells put his hand on the younger man's shoulder.

'I want this taken care of, Max,' he said. 'You understand me?'

'Leave it to me, General,' Northrup said. Wells threw him a John Wayne-style movie-star salute and went out of the room. Outside, Garrett heard a car start up and move off. Across the room, Lucy Barton sat with her hands clasped tightly in her lap, her eyes wide with apprehension.

It was Garrett's first real chance to look around since they had been brought to the base. The drive up the valley along the new autobahn whose route roughly paralleled the River Nahe had taken less than half an hour. Northrup had taken the Idar-Oberstein exit and then a minor road. Garrett saw a sign, briefly lit by the headlights, for a village called Kirchenbollenbach, and then they came to a checkpoint patrolled by MPs in white pudding-basin steel helmets and gaiters, pistols in GI holsters at their sides. A floodlit sign announced:

UNITED STATES ARMY:
SPECIAL OPERATIONS UNIT
CLOSED MILITARY AREA!
NO ADMITTANCE!
LEBENSGEFAHR! DANGER OF DEATH!
INTRUDERS WILL BE SHOT ON SIGHT!

The MPs had waved the car through into the darkness, and they followed a winding road up a steep hill toward a cluster of lit buildings. The whole area was brightly floodlit and, as promised at the gateway, patrolled by armed guards carrying automatic rifles. They were taken into one of the neat, military-style buildings that formed a rectangle at the center of the enclave. Garrett thought he caught sight of what might have been a tall steel chimney, but before he could be sure Jackson had hustled him inside.

They were taken along a corridor in a building that looked like the offices of a medium-size engineering company, with prefabricated walls and hardboard doors. At the far end was what might have been, in that same company, the executive suite. It was a large room dominated by an oversize desk with a high-backed swivel chair behind it. Large windows, closed off from the outside world by venetian blinds, formed a 'U' behind the big desk. Off to one side stood a conference table, bentwood chairs ranged along it. A large map of the *Sperrgebiet* filled one wall; flags, pins, colored stickers speckled its face. Above it a battery-powered clock made a solid quartz click every second. A bookcase to one side of the room was jammed full of technical books and magazines. Northrup's office, Garrett concluded. Like its occupant, it had about as much charm as a used toothbrush.

'Okay, mister, less go,' Leroy Jackson told him, with a poke in the back to emphasize his words. 'And don't go getting any dumb idea you can jump me, or I'll break some o' your bones.'

'Yassuh,' Garrett said. If the slur annoyed the big man, he gave no sign of it.

'You too, little lady,' he said. 'This way.'

They went down the corridor and across the quadrangle outside to the building opposite. Unlike the one they had been in, this was built of cinder blocks faced with sandstone, and Garrett noted that not only were the windows barred but the glass in them was wired as well. This must be what passed for a guardhouse.

The room was bare. Nothing on the walls, nothing on the floor. A cheap wooden table stood in the center of the room, two equally cheap chairs on either side of it, and in the corner, a toilet basin with no seat.

'Welcome to the Kreuznach Hilton,' Jackson said.

He left them in the darkness and pulled the door shut, bang. They heard the jangle of keys, then the sound of his feet crossing the quadrangle. Then silence.

Lucy Barton edged closer to Garrett, found his hand, held it tight.

'What's . . . what's going to happen?' she whispered. 'What are they going to do to us?'

'Nothing's going to happen,' Garrett told her, squeezing her hand. 'Don't worry.'

His eyes were becoming accustomed to the darkness. He felt his way along the walls, seeking a light switch; there was none. A radiator on the wall next to the toilet spread a thin but even heat across the room. He stood on one of the chairs and felt across the ceiling. Nothing. They were in a stone box with a barred window of reinforced glass and — he was willing to bet from the noise it had made when Jackson closed it — a steel-lined door.

'He's dead, isn't he, Mr. Garrett?' she said tonelessly. 'Paul is dead.'

She began to cry, not loudly, just a soft, hopeless sound that went on and on. He shook his head sadly.

'Come over here,' he said. She edged over to where he was sitting, his back against the wall in the corner of the room nearest to the radiator and farthest from the door. He put his arm around her. 'Try to sleep if you can,' he said.

Shyly, she laid her head on his shoulder. Her hair smelled of shampoo. After a while she sighed; a little longer and she settled against him like a child. And later still, he slept too.

★ ★ ★

He was awakened by a metallic sound. Lucy Barton stirred as he moved. His back and body were stiff. He stood up and stretched.

'What is it?' she said, standing beside him.

'I don't know.' He frowned. Gray light came in through the unwashed window. It was nearly dawn. He looked out. The floodlights were no longer on. The quadrangle was deserted. He went to the door and listened; there was no one there. He turned to face Lucy, a finger to his lips.

'The door is open,' he said.

Her eyes widened and she drew her

354

breath in quickly. 'What does it mean?' she whispered.

It meant they were being invited to make a run for it. A simple scenario; let them escape into the gullies and hills of the *Sperrgebiet*, then sound the alarm. *Alert state black*: intruders detected. Locate and neutralize. It was a variation of the old Spanish *ley fuga*, the law that sanctioned your execution while trying to escape.

There was nothing to do but to take the chance. He stood against the wall and pushed the door so that it swung back, letting the thin cold of dawn into the room. He risked a quick look outside; there was nobody in sight. The tan Dodge Aries that had brought them stood parked outside the executive building opposite.

'Come with me,' he whispered. 'Do exactly what I tell you.'

He took Lucy's hand and eased out of the doorway, keeping his back to the wall of the building they had spent the night in. At the corner of the building a signpost indicated directions: dispensary, canteen, newsstand, laboratories. Garrett smiled like a feral wolf. Whatever choice they were expecting him to make, he would bet it was not attack. He took Lucy's hand again and ran lightly along the path toward the group of buildings at the far end.

A closed-circuit TV camera turned, its electronic eye following the movement.

17

A Klaxon blared, filling the air with its shivering blast. Crows flopped lazily out of their trees, circling and swooping, cawing furiously in anger. Out in the open, halfway between the guardhouse up the hill and the laboratory complex, which was his destination, Garrett cursed beneath his breath.

'What is it?' Lucy Barton said, her voice tight with alarm.

'It's not good news,' he told her grimly. 'Come on, no point in trying to hide.'

He grabbed her hand and ran down the hill toward a long low bank of rhododendron bushes. Somewhere up behind them he could hear the metallic whickering of a helicopter preparing to take off, the sound of vehicles roaring into life, men shouting. It was no surprise, but he still didn't like the idea of being a running target.

The layout of the base was simple: its

center was shaped like an elongated, curving 'H,' its top pointing north, the long uprights roads lined on each side by thick banks of shrubbery. The road on the west side ran from the entrance on the northern perimeter to the one on the southwestern side, at Reichenbach. The eastern upright came to an end at the laboratory complex on the northern side, about a quarter of a mile from the headquarters building; its southern arm ran southeast through the *Sperrgebiet* to the exit above Niederalben. The headquarters buildings, guardhouse, armory, motor pool building, barracks, mess, cookhouse, and recreation hall were all grouped around the center of the 'H.'

The chatter of the helicopter was louder; a moment later, he saw it rising above the buildings at the top of the hill. He pulled Lucy down to the ground, cowering under the bushes as the 'copter roared overhead, up in a long climb, turning slowly at its apex, then swooping down again toward them. He could see the young soldiers inside, rifles at the ready. The helicopter roared across the area again and then again and then swung off to the northwest.

'Run!' Garrett hissed. He led the way up the gentle slope toward the laboratory complex, and skittered to a stop between two seven-foot-high builder's dumpers standing in the area between the two main lab buildings. He looked around. There were three buildings in all: the two long rectangular units, standing parallel to each other, between which they were hiding, and a third — a glance through the windows revealed it was a computer complex — which stood along their narrower ends. At the northern end two tall slim rectifier towers rose gleaming in the morning sun. Beyond them and to the east, along a curving blacktopped path, were the generators that supplied all the base's power.

'Stay here!' he told Lucy. 'Don't worry. I'll come back for you.'

She tried for a smile, but it wouldn't stick. She was trembling, either with fear or cold. Probably both, he thought. He eased out from behind the skips and ran as fast as he could along the path leading to the generators. Behind him someone shouted and he threw himself off the path and into the bushes as a machine pistol chattered behind him. Bullets whined off the tarmac and whipped through the branches of the bushes, but Garrett was already on the far side, crouching behind the steel cowling of the steam turbine connected to the huge generator.

'Where da fuck he go?' he heard someone shout.

'Spread out, spread out!' someone else yelled.

There were at least three of them, possibly more. Garrett slid his belt out of its loops and laid it on the ground. It looked like any ordinary wide leather belt, but it was not; it had been specially made for him by the armorer at Lonsdale House. Garrett's years as a field agent had taught him a thing or two about being caught weaponless.

Inside the belt was a channel, and inside that channel was a yard-long length of piano wire with flat wooden pegs at each end. The round buckle itself split into two halves; between them was a stainless steel throwing star with wickedly sharp points. He lay on the ground and looked around the corner. The eye expected movement at its own level, not on the ground. Garrett pulled back, the scene as clear in his mind as a photograph. A young GI was standing irresolutely on the edge of the shrub-screened path, his M16 at port.

'Hey, you guys!' he shouted. 'Where da fuck ya gone?'

Garrett knew where they were: they had gone past the generator on the opposite side to the one where he was hidden, advancing warily line abreast, their M16s at the ready. He had maybe ten seconds. It was more than enough.

He stood up and threw the star. The star flickered in the weak sunlight and the young soldier saw the movement and started to turn, raising the M16. In the same millisecond, the star embedded itself in his thigh. He screeched with pain, his eyes moving automatically downward. With one bound, Garrett was on him. He hit the boy hard at the angle of the jaw, hit him again as he sank to his knees. The soldier collapsed unconscious into the shrubbery. Garrett grabbed the M16 and melted back into the shadows behind the turbine, feeling the powerful drone of the huge generator inside its massive casing. He drew in a deep breath and ran back the way he had come, heading for the laboratory complex, the soft-soled Timberland boots noiseless on the hard surface.

'Follow me!' he shouted to Lucy. He ran up the narrow corridor between the two one-story lab buildings to the steps leading to the glass doors of the computer complex, firing as he ran. The plate-glass doors sundered with a flat bang, showering glass onto the stone floor of the hall. He ran into the eerily empty complex, thrust the barrel of the M16 into a huge wastepaper bin full of tractor-feed discard, fired a burst of half a dozen shots. The paper ignited, smoke coiling. Garrett rolled it up against the huge tape cabinets, smashing the glass doors of the storage units with the butt of the gun. The burning paper ignited the tapes, which burned with a high white flame.

'This way!' Garrett yelled. Figures moved cautiously in the glass-littered hall. He emptied the machine pistol at them, heard hoarse curses. Garrett tossed the gun aside and grabbed Lucy Barton's hand, running toward the fire exit on the far side of the complex. Pillars of flame climbed high, black smoke billowing toward the ceiling behind them. Alarm bells rang dementedly. Garrett ran at the push bar and surged through the fire door, running flat out with Lucy Barton alongside him, her hair streaming behind her as she pursued him around the end of the laboratory and across the road into the bushes lining the road. They stopped, chests heaving.

'All right?'

She nodded, unable to speak. He pointed with his chin to a stand of spruce and conifers that lay about a hundred yards away. Lucy nodded again, yes, and then they ran, half expecting with every step the stutter of a machine gun. Not until they were deep inside the shadowed woods did they stop, heads hanging, struggling for breath.

'Look,' she said.

A huge cloud of smoke was drifting slowly west on the soft morning breeze. The alarm bells were still ringing. It looked like a sizable fire. That might have briefly delayed the pursuit, but it would not end it.

'We've got to try to head for the north gate,' Garrett said. 'I don't know how far it is. But we've got to try to get there.'

'I . . . under . . . stand,' she panted. 'It's . . . okay.'

'Stay close,' Garrett said. He moved off steadily into the trees, utilizing the ground-covering dogtrot they had taught him in the SAS training course at Stirling Lines in Hereford. Fifteen minutes run, five minutes walk, he thought; he hoped Lucy Barton could hack it, but he didn't think she could. She didn't have the right clothes; more especially, she didn't have the right shoes.

They came out of the woods and found themselves on the side of the hill that sloped steeply down to a chattering river running through a pebbled tree-lined gully. They slid and scrambled down the hill then followed the river for about two kilometers, moving always toward the north. When it narrowed sufficiently, they crossed over the river and climbed the hill on its far side, following faint footpaths that wound their way along its flank. Several times they dived for whatever cover they could find as they heard the whistling rattle of a helicopter. Lucy Barton was tiring; even though he slowed his pace, Garrett knew she could not keep up much longer. After they had covered perhaps four kilometers, she made a choked, despairing sound. He turned to see her sprawled on the ground, shaking her head.

'It's no use,' she said. 'I can't. I can't anymore.'

She sat up, pawing mud off her face. Her dark blue peajacket-style coat was snagged and muddy, her skirt wet, her neat leather shoes wrecked. With her scratched, mud-stained legs and her hair plastered flat on her head, she looked miserable and cold and frightened.

'Try,' he urged her. 'There's an

abandoned village just over the hill. We'll rest there.'

'You go on without me,' she groaned. 'Just leave me. I'll be all right.'

'Come on.' He grabbed her roughly by the arms, put his arm around her waist, swung her onto her feet. They labored up a long rocky slope, skirting the crest of the hill in order to avoid skylining themselves, and eased down on the far side. Below them, above five hundred meters away, was what had once been the little village of Frohnhausen. As they spotted it, they heard the distinctive roar of a Jeep engine. They flattened against the sheltering overhang under which they had stopped. The Jeep roared down the road to the village and squealed to a stop next to the four-walled stone shell of a house surrounded by a dry-stone wall.

Garrett risked a look. There was only one man in the Jeep. As he watched, the big man got out of the vehicle and stood beside it. He wore a black sweatshirt and pants and black boots; a shoulder holster nestled beneath his left arm. He stepped clear of the Jeep, looking up the hill. It was Leroy Jackson.

Garrett stood up. Jackson saw him. He pointed at Garrett and then at his own chest. *You and me.*

'What is he doing?' Lucy said. 'Why is he standing there like that?'

'He's telling me to make my move, Lucy,' Garrett told her. 'Then he'll make his.'

'What do you mean?'

'Never mind. Take my jacket. Keep as warm as you can. Stay here until I come and get you.'

He moved off along the flank of the hill, angling north away from the village. Below, Leroy Jackson set off at a steady, ground-eating jog, keeping pace parallel to and below him. Garrett stepped up his pace rate; the black man did the same, and even at this distance Garrett could see that Jackson was smiling.

Garrett moved on, thankful now for the hours he had spent poring over topographical survey maps of the area. On the far side of the hill was a wide, flat, open area, which, if he had oriented himself correctly, would lead him to a half-kilometer-wide strip of forest. Beyond that lay the perimeter of the *Sperrgebiet* and beyond that, freedom. He crested the hill and started down the far side. Off to his left, quartering across now toward him, Leroy Jackson kept coming, his legs moving in steady, muscular rhythm, arms pumping, head nicely up.

Ahead, Garrett saw the two-kilometer-wide vehicle testing area, its surface scarred and churned by countless half-tracks, Jeeps, and trucks. He picked up his pace, making as straight a line as he could for the long low line of the woods on the far side. He risked a glance over his shoulder. Jackson was coming up behind, maybe fifteen hundred meters away. Too far for a handgun, Garrett thought. He'll try to get closer. He put on as much speed as he dared, placing every footfall carefully on the treacherously soft broken ground. He could hear the sound of his own breathing, and the soft busy chatter of the birds in the trees up ahead. A hazy sun broke through the overcast.

The edge of the woods was closer now.

A quick look back; Jackson had gained on him, but not enough. Once they were among the trees it would be a totally different game. As if reading his thoughts, Leroy Jackson stopped running. He dropped to one knee and fired a wide fanned spread of shots after the running man. Garrett heard the whip of the lead nearby, the fat *plut*! of a bullet burying itself in mud. Too far for accurate shooting with a handgun, he thought, no matter how skilled the shooter. Then he was in the trees.

The watery sunlight did nothing to dispel the shadows lurking beneath the close-set, dripping branches of the sighing trees. Deep in the silent center of the whispering woods, Garrett stopped and went to the ground. Moving with infinite care, he camouflaged himself, covering his face and hands with black mud, fashioning a misshapen crown of branches and leaves for his head. He wound strands of creeper around his body and thighs, anything that would alter his silhouette. Now, when he crouched in the undergrowth, he was all but invisible. A darker shadow among the dark shadows, Garrett started moving in a long, slow, half circle that would bring him around in back of the man who was tracking him.

Moving with the unhurried caution of a practiced deer hunter, he eased through the screening trees, stopping every few paces. He forced himself to relax, slowing his breathing, concentrating on letting his peripheral vision do all the work. The trick was to keep the eyes slightly unfocused, letting each minute movement of bird or branch or woodland creature register itself in your sight.

And there he was.

Jackson was moving as slowly as he, placing each foot with equal care. He might have been alone in the forest, practicing tai chi ch'uan, that slow-motion body discipline so beloved of the Chinese. He was about four feet away. Garrett hunched motionless on his haunches at the center of a clump of tall ferns, a three-foot-long, two-inch-thick piece of wood in his hand. He picked up a pebble, balanced it on his finger ends, flipped it high and to one side. The stone made a small sound as it landed. Jackson reacted electrically, whirling around and coming down in the classic firing position, both hands around the butt of the leveled automatic, ripping off four shots that whacked and whined between the heedless trees.

Nobody there.

He whirled to face the other way.

Nobody there, either.

And then Garrett came up off the ground like Satan coming up out of hell, the wooden club moving in a long, looping arc that smashed the Beretta out of the big man's grip and pulled a yell of pain from his tight lips. The weapon spun away into the undergrowth, flashing silver blue like a jumping trout. Fast as Garrett was, the American was faster. He saw the second blow coming, parried it, and leaped forward, arching his body in a running kick so sudden that Garrett almost failed to respond. He swayed aside, but even so, Jackson's heavy boot caught him a glancing blow on the side of the head, jarring him off balance. He rolled over and away and back onto his feet in one movement. Jackson was waiting, a smile on his face like Death watching a knife fight.

'Come on, turkey,' the black man said, and as Garrett backed away, came after him fast, striking one-two, then retreating very quickly. He came in again and hit Garrett a wicked smash beneath the rib cage that completely defeated his attempt to parry it, whacking the breath out of Garrett's body. For one fraction of a second he was stock-still, and in that moment, Jackson hit him hard across the bony protuberance above his right ear, breaking open the half-healed wound he had made the night before with the barrel of the gun. Garrett went down on his knees in the muddy loam, bells ringing in his head, a roaring redness behind his eyes. Through red mist he half saw Jackson coming at him again. He kicked outward and upward in sheer desperation, catching Jackson's kneecap and spilling him in a rolling fall.

Jackson was up as fast as a cat, ready for the counterattack that Garrett had not been able to launch. He smiled ferociously, the smell of death coming off him like garlic, moving in a crablike half circle, feinting first with his right hand and then his left. Cat and mouse, Garrett thought as breath labored back into his lungs, and felt a faint feather-touch of fear. The man was too fast for him, altogether too good at this. He waited, poised, for the next attack.

It came without warning as Jackson lowered his head a little and ran at him, but Garrett knew it had to be a feint. The man would never expose his neck like that. He skipped aside, his knee moving in a strike that was as much a feint as Jackson's move, and like a flash the black man threw himself to one side, the tensed ball of his right foot striking upward at Garrett's groin in a kick that would have put him down, spasming like a gaffed fish, if it had landed. But Garrett's feint was just that, and for a fraction of a moment Jackson was committed. In that moment, Garrett's own right foot came around in a wicked arc, connecting solidly with Jackson's throat, hurling him away to land, hunched over, hacking and retching as he tried to get air into his paralyzed windpipe.

Now Garrett went after the hurt man without mercy, and again his right foot moved in that tight, killing arc. The force of the impact numbed his foot. Jackson's body humped over in agony as soft organs burst inside him. He rolled on his back and struck at Garrett's legs with a forearm like a block of mahogany, and Garrett went down on one knee, but as he did he struck with the edge of his hand on the black man's throat. Jackson's head came down, and as it did, Garrett went high over his body and then, heel rigid, stamped with all his weight and strength upon the man's defenseless belly. Jackson contorted like an obscene rubber doll, a moan of agony escaping the clenched lips, followed by a ghastly gout of bloody slime.

Garrett turned to strike again with his foot, but somehow, suffering agonies that would long since have destroyed another man, Jackson parried his blow and got to his feet. Blind with pain, he stood with both arms hanging at his sides, blood trickling from his mouth, his nose, and the corners of his eyes. Garrett watched in disbelief as this terrible bleeding thing shambled toward him. The man was as good as dead and both of them knew it, but still he was coming, like a wounded lion, intent on killing the thing that had dealt it death. Garrett bent down and picked up the length of wood he had used to club the pistol out of Jackson's hands. As Jackson lurched nearer, Garrett hit him on the side of the head. The blow made an awful sound, hard and yet soft, and Garrett knew he had crushed the man's skull. Arms outstretched, hands still reaching for his opponent, Jackson sank to his knees. Garrett swung the club to hit him again, but somehow Jackson parried the blow with his forearm. It flapped down, bone protruding from the broken flesh. Garrett reeled back, utterly spent, swaying like a tree in a high wind, his breathing as ragged as if he had run five miles. Leroy Jackson looked up with eyes that were drowning in the acid of death. Somewhere in the forest around them Garrett heard the sound of men shouting, the roar of half tracks. Jackson's battered face twisted into what might have been a smile. Somehow, using strength summoned from the last depths of his body's resources, he got to his feet again and came at Garrett.

'Quit, Jackson!' Garrett shouted. 'It's finished!'

'Kill you anyway,' Jackson said, still moving forward.

Garrett had nothing left now except the will to survive. He hit the advancing man with everything he had packed into a brutal angled hand chop on the left side of the neck. There is medical terminology for the effect of such a blow, names for the vital linkages of sinew and artery and nerve tissue that break beneath its impact. No one has ever charted that moment because no one has ever survived it. Jackson fell to his knees again, head down like a man awaiting the fall of the guillotine. Somehow, somewhere in the dying red madness of his destroyed brain, he found enough strength to lift his head once more and look at Garrett.

'Ig ug,' he said. The sound of the four

tracks was very close now. Garrett heard someone shouting his name. He had nothing left, no strength, no will, nothing. It was all he could do to stand there, staring numbly at Leroy Jackson on his knees in the middle of the gloomy glade.

'Pretty good yourself, Jackson,' he said.

Jackson's eyes blinked, and then the light went out of them. He fell to one side like an old, old tree going down. Garrett looked up to see a line of uniformed men running toward him. Klaus Prachner was in front of them, a gun in his hand. He was shouting Garrett's name. Garrett tried to lift a hand in salute but couldn't do it.

'What took you so long?' he said.

18

'When will you be leaving?' Pennyweather asked.

'Tomorrow, or Saturday,' Garrett said. 'Whenever you tell me it's okay.'

Pennyweather smiled. 'I still haven't quite got used to the idea of being in charge here. What about your Irishmen?'

'I'm leaving them to you, Clive,' Garrett said. 'You work closely with Emil Fritz over at BSSO, and you'll catch them. Sooner or later, you'll run them down.'

'I'm glad Fritz got the job.'

'He earned it.'

'What will you do now?'

Garrett grinned. 'Have a week in the hospital,' he said. 'Leroy Jackson put a lot of bruises on me.'

'That was amazing,' Pennyweather said. 'Why do you think he came after you? He must have known the jig was up.'

'I don't know,' Garrett admitted. 'Some

kind of perverted loyalty, maybe. Or maybe he thought if he could shut me up, it would help Northrup and Wells.'

'They've been shipped back to the States, I hear. What will happen to them?'

'That will tend to depend on how much pull Wells has really got. You know what they say: military justice is to justice as military music is to music. If you want my bet, I'd say Northrup will take the fall for the killings, and the old man will be retired with the maximum of speed and the minimum of fuss.'

'What about Project 23?'

Garrett shrugged.

'I'll tell you what General Harknett's office at USFET told me. They said appropriate retributive action would be taken at all relevant levels.'

'What the hell does that mean?'

'It's army doublespeak for 'go away and leave this to us.' One thing is for sure; the experimental station up at Kreuznach will be closed down.'

'What's left of it,' Pennyweather observed. 'Prachner told me you made a hell of a mess of the labs up there.'

'They're no loss,' Garrett said.

'What about the drug trafficking? You think that's finished?'

Garrett shrugged again. 'I don't want to sound too cynical, Clive, but where there's a market, there's a supplier. The people who were using Barton and his cronies as a conduit will find somebody else. If they haven't already done so.'

'It's all pretty cold-blooded, isn't it?' Pennyweather mused. 'In an odd sort of way I feel sorry for them.'

'Save your sympathy for someone who deserves it,' Garrett told him harshly.

He got up and went across to the window, looking out across the parade ground. The base looked just the same as it had that first October day. Everything had changed, but somehow, in the army, nothing changed at all.

The phone rang and Pennyweather answered it. He held it out for Garrett. 'Emil Fritz,' he said.

'Hi, Emil,' Garrett said. 'What can I do for you?'

'It's what I can do for you, Charles,' Fritz said. His voice was charged with excitement. 'We've had a break on the Irishmen.'

Garrett signaled Pennyweather to pick up the extension. 'Go on.'

'That old boy you talked to down at Schwarzenberg, remember the one?'

'Kupfer,' Garrett recalled. 'What about him?'

'He called, asked for you. Said it was about your friend, Kitson.'

Hennessy! 'And?'

'Kupfer said he didn't know at the time, but one of his women workers was having a romance with a friend of Kitson's. Young fellow called Gallagher.'

'Tony Gallagher,' Garrett said. 'We've got a dossier on him.'

'I've already pulled it,' Fritz said. 'Gallagher sent the girl a postcard. From Lauenburg.'

Garrett glanced at the map, reminding himself of the location of the little town, northeast of Lüneburg. 'What's in Lauenburg?'

'Buckinghamshire barracks. Headquarters of the British 1185th Infantry.'

'When was the card posted?'

'Six days ago. Kupfer only just heard about it.'

'All right,' Garrett said, crisply decisive. 'You know what to do. Get onto the commanding officer at Lauenburg. Tell him as of now he is to go to alert state red. Put everybody we can spare onto making a full-scale check of every hotel, inn, *gasthof*, and bed and breakfast place within ten miles of the town. There'll be at least two of them, probably more. I want them found and put under total surveillance, Emil, and I want it done yesterday.'

'I've already set things in motion,' Fritz said. 'Photographs of Sean Hennessy, Gallagher, and all other known associates. I've alerted BFV and they'll be sending surveillance units in to help us. The Federal Prosecutor's Office and the local police have been asked to cooperate. Don't worry, Charles. If they're there, we'll find them.'

'You'd better,' Garrett said. He had just looked at the calendar on the wall. It was Thursday, November 9. Two days away from Armistice Day, three from

Remembrance Sunday. *At the going down of the sun and in the morning, we will remember them. The eleventh hour of the eleventh day of the eleventh month.* 'They'll hit either Saturday or Sunday. I'd go for Sunday.'

'The same thought occurred to me,' Fritz said. 'Don't worry, Charles, everyone is giving this pinnacle priority.'

'What's the name of the commanding officer at Buckinghamshire barracks?'

'Manners,' Fritz replied. 'Colonel David Manners.'

'Get onto him,' Garrett said. 'Tell him I'll be coming in as soon as I can. We'll need mobile units up there, Emil. Something not too big, but I want them kitted out like Stealth bombers.'

'Can do,' Fritz said. 'Go on.'

'Meantime, have this Colonel Manners question all personnel, anyone who's been on that base during the last two weeks, and no exceptions. We want details and descriptions of anyone — *anyone* — who's been asking questions about procedures at the camp, security, troop dispositions, anything at all.'

'I'll see to it.'

Garrett put the phone down, his mind racing. Clive Pennyweather was already on the other telephone, instructing the officer in charge of transportation to ready a helicopter to take them north. The whirlybird would be ready to fly in ten minutes, he reported.

'I need a sidearm,' Garrett said. 'What have you got?'

'Name it.'

'An ASP,' Garrett told him. Armament Systems and Procedures of Appleton, Wisconsin, produced a 9mm combat version of the Smith & Wesson M39 pistol that was his favorite weapon, a seven-shot automatic with a Guttersnipe sight that combined high reliability with good first-shot accuracy. It was slightly less than nineteen centimeters long and weighed a little over half a kilo loaded. 'Have we got THV ammunition?'

'We use Equaloy for handguns,' Pennyweather replied. 'Is that okay?'

Equaloy was a nylon-coated-aluminum lightweight bullet that traveled three times faster, and had a wounding capacity up to ten times greater, than conventional lead bullets.

'That'll do nicely,' Garrett said grimly.

★ ★ ★

About twelve kilometers south of Lauenburg, between the villages of Scharnebeck and Erbstorf, the main road used regularly by the British army convoys crosses the Elbe-Seiten canal. The bridge that crosses the canal is a single solid span of massive steel girders with a concrete base carrying two lanes of traffic, with hard shoulders on both sides wide enough to accommodate any vehicle that might break down and impede the traffic flow.

Hennessy had examined and photographed the site from every possible angle. It took him only a short while to realize that the bridge's construction itself was far too massive to blow up; they simply did not have enough plastic explosive to be sure of a sufficiently destructive blast. That being the case, the only remaining option was a car bomb.

'We'll steal two cars on Saturday and change the license plates,' he told his team. 'You'll drive one down to Scharnebeck and leave it there overnight,' he told Davy McGinnis. 'Tony will take the other one to Erbstorf and stash it. I'll pick you both up in the Merc and bring you back here. All clear so far?'

'A doddle,' Tony Gallagher said.

Hennessy glared at him. 'There's no such thing as a doddle in this business, lad,' he snapped, 'and don't ever forget it! Now, then, the convoy will leave Buckinghamshire barracks at ten A.M. on Sunday morning. We leave here at eight-thirty, drive down to Scharnebeck with the PE. We drop Davy and Pat off there. They get into their car, drive to the exit sign outside town, and wait.'

'Got it,' McGinnis said.

'Tony and me will drive back to Lauenburg in the Mercedes,' Hennessy went on. 'When the convoy moves out, we'll run on two minutes ahead of it. Now comes the important part. Get this firmly fixed in your heads, because there'll be no room for mistakes. The convoy will take approximately half an hour to get to the bridge. They'll reach Scharnebeck at about ten-twenty-four, give or take a minute or two. So at ten-twenty precisely, Davy and Pat move out.'

'It's damned tight, Sean,' Davy McGinnis said.

'You've got all the time in the world,' Hennessy told him. 'You can cover the distance from the exit sign to the bridge in one and a half minutes or less.'

'All right,' McGinnis said. 'What then?'

'You drive onto the bridge. When you get to the far end, you have your 'breakdown.' Pull over, get out, lift the hood, do the business. There shouldn't be any police about, but if there are, give them the no-speak-German act.'

'It's not an act.' McGinnis grinned.

'Keep the stopwatch running,' Hennessy told him. 'Watch every second. The timing is critical.'

He was conscious of the tension building up inside him, but made no attempt to stop it. Tension was a necessary adjunct of a thing like this. It made you jumpy and nervous and very aware of everything that was going on around you, and that was the way you needed to be.

'All right, you're 'broken down' on the bridge. Tony and me will be on the road, two minutes ahead of the convoy. We'll stop on the bridge to pick you up. If anybody asks, we're giving you a lift to a garage in Erbstorf. We drive off. One minute later the convoy rolls onto the bridge and Pat pushes the button.'

'Beautiful,' Gallagher said, grinning. 'Beautiful, Sean.'

'Right,' Hennessy said. 'The minute the bomb goes off, we split up. Tony and I will drop Davy and Pat in Erbstorf, then head for Lüneburg. You two will pick up your car, drive to Hamburg Airport, and dump it there. I've got tickets for you both on BA737 to Manchester, leaving at six-fifteen. When you get to Manchester, go to Ryan's in Wythenshawe and wait for me there. Any questions?'

'Aye,' Pat Mullan said. 'I've a question, Sean.'

'Go on.'

'Is there any chance of a bloody beer?'

'All right,' Garrett said. 'What have we got?'

'Hennessy and Gallagher here,' Penny-weather said, tapping the large-scale map of the town with a wooden pointer. 'Safe house on Elbestrasse. We're checking that out now. Mullan and McGinnis here, at the White Swan.'

'What about wheels?'

'They've got three vehicles. A tan Opel Manta, a green Volkswagen Passat, and a dark blue Mercedes CLK, taken from a car park near the Palace of Justice in Hannover ten days ago.'

'Locations?'

'The Merc is at the White Swan. McGinnis took the Opel to a little place called Scharnebeck. That's here on the map. Gallagher took the Volkswagen to Erbstorf, here, on the other side of the canal.'

'And in the middle is the Elbe-brücke,' Garrett said. 'The bridge across the canal.'

'You think that's the target?' The

speaker was Colonel David Manners, commanding Buckinghamshire barracks. It was in his neat, well-appointed office that the conference was taking place. Garrett had set up a field headquarters there as soon as he and Pennyweather arrived in the big Westland helicopter. Manners was a tall, slender, trim man in his late forties, with shrewd blue eyes and a luxuriant cavalryman's mustache.

'No,' Garrett said slowly. 'The bridge is the location. Your troop convoy to Lüneburg is the target.'

'Great God!' Manners said. 'I'd better give orders for it to be rerouted immediately.'

'Don't worry, Colonel,' Garrett said. 'None of your people will get hurt. What time is the convoy scheduled to leave here?'

'Ten A.M. precisely.' Garrett looked at his watch. It was now 8:35 A.M. They had been up all night.

'How far is it to Scharnebeck?'

'A little more than fifteen kilometers,' Manners supplied.

'The speed?'

'Fifty kph. Thirty in built-up areas.'

'So it takes about eighteen minutes to get there.'

'More like twenty-five or thirty,' Manners said. 'They have to go through Lauenburg, don't forget.'

'We've got a movement, sir,' the BSSO surveillance controller reported. As Garrett strode across the room the controller switched on the loudspeaker. The voice of a 'footman' watching the Elbestrasse house Hennessy was using filled the room.

'Subjects Alpha and Beta leaving house . . . waiting on sidewalk outside. A blue Mercedes CLK pulling over. Registration Henry-Apple one four five two four Henry-King. Driver is subject Gamma. Handing over to mobile surveillance. Out.'

'Mobile One, I have them. Proceeding west on Elbestrasse. Turning onto Elbe Bridge and south on Bundesstrasse 209.'

'Mobile Two, subject vehicle is a dark blue Mercedes 200, registration Henry-Apple one four five two four Henry-King. Any visual contact?'

'Mobile Two, I have him.'

'Mobile Three, report your position.'

'Mobile Three. Opposite target Opel Manta in Schulstrasse, Scharnebeck.'

'Your subject arriving imminently. Are footmen in place?'

'Affirmative.'

'Stand by.'

The loudspeakers hissed emptily. The controller looked at Garrett as if expecting instructions. Garrett shook his head.

'Mobile Two, subject entering Scharnebeck. Slowing . . . stopping on Schulstrasse.'

'Mobile Three, we have him.'

'Mobile Two, continue without stopping,' the controller said. 'Disengage and return to base.'

'Mobile Two, affirmative.'

The immobile men in the office on the second floor of the headquarters building listened tensely as the watchers reported in, one by one, on the movements of Hennessy and his men. A package heavy enough to require two men to move it was transferred from the trunk of the Mercedes to that of the Opel Manta. Hennessy and Gallagher, coded Alpha and Beta, turned the Mercedes around and headed back toward Lauenburg. The surveillance teams noted their every move and fixed their location at the south end of the long straight road that led into the town from Buckinghamshire barracks.

Garrett's fingers tingled; he tried to imagine Sean Hennessy sitting in the car, just a few kilometers away. Hennessy would be as tense as he himself was, as anxious to ensure that his plans did not go awry.

'What's happening, Mobile Three?' the controller inquired.

'Subjects are sitting in the car, smoking,' the watcher replied. Garrett looked at his watch. Nearly nine-thirty. The convoy would be leaving in half an hour. He went across to the window. Squads of uniformed men were lined up outside the hangars where the army trucks had been stored overnight. Sergeants with clipboards were checking names.

He picked up a hand mike. 'Mobile Three, this is Team Leader,' he said. 'Can one of your footmen get near enough to the car to see inside of it?'

'Affirmative, Team Leader.'

'Listen carefully. I want one walk-past only. If he can't see anything, take him off the street, then try again with someone else. Nobody to pass the car more than once, understood?'

'Affirmative. What are we looking for?'

'A walkie-talkie.'

'Understood. And if there's one there?'

'I need to know what make it is.'

'Understood. Mobile Three out.'

The loudspeakers resumed their empty hiss. Garrett jumped when another voice broke in abruptly.

'Team Leader, this is Footman Three. Unable to fulfill your request. Footman Four will attempt. Over and out.'

Hiss. Crackle. Garrett tried to visualize the Sunday morning street, the parked car, the watchers making their choreographed moves. There would not be many people about at this time of day, which made their job that much harder. The only thing they had going for them was that Hennessy's people had no idea they were being watched.

'Team Leader, this is Footman Four, I have what you want.'

'Go ahead.'

'The unit is an Icom IC2, repeat I-Idaho, C-Charlie, O-Orange, M-Mother, I-Idaho, C-Charlie, two, figure two.'

'Understood, Five, well done. Disengage immediately. Out.'

Garrett put down the microphone and turned to Colonel Manners. 'Colonel, have you got any Icom IC2s on the base?'

'How many do you need?'

Garrett grinned. 'One will do.'

Manners snapped an order and one of his men left on the double to fetch the walkie-talkie Garrett had requested. He was back within two minutes, breathing heavily.

'All right, listen to me,' Garrett said. 'We know the bridge is clean, because Colonel Manners's engineers checked it out and our pigeons haven't been near it. That and the fact they've got a walkie-talkie in the car can only mean one thing: the car is the bomb.'

'Come in, Central.'

Garrett grabbed the microphone. 'Team

Leader receiving you loud and clear.'

'This is Mobile Three. Gamma and Delta are on the move.'

'Heading south?'

'Out of town. Wait. They're pulling over. Parking in a lay-by at roadside. Going by . . . now.'

'Keep going, and disengage,' Garrett said. 'Mobile Four come in.'

'Mobile Four.'

'Check subjects still in position, then return.'

'Affirmative.' There was a short pause as the surveillance vehicle covered the distance from the town to the place where McGinnis and Mullan were sitting in their car.

'Mobile Four. Confirm, repeat, confirm vehicle is parked as reported by Mobile Three.'

'That's it,' Garrett said, putting down the mike. 'Hennessy checks the convoy out, drives ahead of it to Scharnebeck. They'll have it timed down to the minute. The two in the Opel will go to the bridge and abandon the car. Hennessy comes along, picks them up. They clear off, then when the convoy is on the bridge, they detonate the bomb.'

'Then we'd better move in now,' Pennyweather said.

'You're right,' Garrett said. 'Let's go.'

★   ★   ★

'Nine-forty-five,' Tony Gallagher said. 'They'll be on the move directly.'

He was thirty-one years old, a good-looking fellow with clear blue eyes and a boyish grin. He looked a good five years younger without the beard he had sported when he first joined Hennessy's team as a driver the preceding year. He was no intellectual, but he was one of the best fast-wheel men in the business.

Gallagher had parked the blue Mercedes 200 at the side of the divided highway about five hundred meters south of, and pointing away from, the army barracks on the opposite side of the road. At the gates were controlled traffic lights that were used to enable convoys to cross from one side of the highway to the other.

Hennessy wiped the inside of the

windshield, which had misted up. There were only a few cars on the move this early on a Sunday morning. The trees lining the road were all but bare of leaves now; their branches shone like bones in the thin sunshine. Two gray squirrels capered on the grass beside the road. A silver-gray Audi 100 came out of Buckinghamshire barracks and crossed the highway and came toward them. Hennessy hunched down in his seat, watching as it went past. Four men inside, all in uniform. The Audi turned right at the T-junction ahead, taking the road into town.

A few minutes later, Hennessy thought he saw the same car cross the junction ahead of them in the opposite direction; he frowned. At the same moment a VW Kombi panel truck came out of the gates of the barracks, crossed to their side of the highway, and came to a stop about fifty meters behind them. Two men got out. One was wearing a short casual jacket and blue jeans, running shoes, no hat. The other wore a thick sweater and dark pants; he, too, had on running shoes.

They slouched along the sidewalk toward the Mercedes, shoulders hunched, heads down, fists thrust into their pockets.

'Start the car,' Hennessy said tensely. Gallagher looked at him in puzzlement, but did as he was bid. Hennessy watched the two men. They picked up their pace slightly as the engine fired. At the same moment, Hennessy saw the silver-gray Audi moving across the junction ahead of them and easing to a stop at the corner.

'Go!' he screamed at Gallagher. 'Left at the junction, go go go!'

Gallagher burned rubber putting the big car into motion, fishtailing slightly on the compacted dead leaves at the side of the road as he roared away. The two men on the sidewalk were running after them flat out, guns in their hands. Shots starred the rear window and smacked metallically into the body work. Gallagher screeched around the corner and headed east along the road leading out of town. The gray Audi swung around behind them, moving too fast for the turn. The car sideswiped one of the traffic signs on the central reservation, straightened up and came after them fast.

'Get off this road!' Hennessy said tersely.

Gallagher swung the car right and then left, hurtling down a narrow street, horn blaring to scatter astonished Sunday morning churchgoers. He swung right again and they were on the road flanking the river, the big Elbe Bridge ahead of them. A police car swung out of a side street and fastened on to their tail, siren screaming, lights flashing.

'Hold tight!' Gallagher shouted. He yanked on the emergency brake and swung the wheel hard over to the left, spinning the speeding car through a shrieking, dizzying hundred-and-eighty-degree turn. The police car swerved and wavered, skidding to a stop as Gallagher rammed down the accelerator, powering the Mercedes back toward town against the flow of the oncoming traffic. The gray Audi was directly ahead of them, coming fast. Hennessy braced himself; there was no way they could avoid a crash now. At the very last moment, Gallagher swung the wheel. The Audi hit the Mercedes's front wheel on the driver's side, smashing it sideways against the stanchions of the bridge. Hennessy thrust open the passenger door, rolling out of the car as the uniformed men in the Audi spilled out, guns in their hands.

Garrett! There was no mistaking the rangy figure, the craggy face. *It was Garrett!*

'Halt, armed officers!' Garrett shouted, but Hennessy kept going. He heard the sharp spiteful crack of pistol fire as he ran the four or five meters to the rail of the bridge. He leaped onto the rail, and in that quarter of a second Garrett fired three shots in a tight burst. Hennessy felt the awful smash of a bullet, and knew he was hit.

'Fuck you, Garrett!' he shouted, and jumped, over and down and down and down into the dark turning waters of the river.

19

Garrett still couldn't believe it. That close, he thought. That close, and still the bastard got away. He didn't know how he could have missed the Irishman at that range, but it looked as if he had.

'We've got police launches all over the river looking for him, Charles,' Pennyweather said. 'If he survived the jump, they'll pick him up.'

'Maybe,' Garrett said, but he knew he didn't believe it. Hennessy was a survivor, and survivors gave no thought to friendship or loyalty. In Hennessy's rulebook it wasn't important who got killed, who got hurt, who went to prison for life, as long as it was not him. He was possessed by a consuming particularism common to terrorists, the belief that he was more important than anyone else. He knew when he jumped off that bridge that he was not only abandoning his entire operation but cold-bloodedly jettisoning

402

every member of his team, and he had done so without hesitation or compunction.

When they left Lauenburg, Tony Gallagher was already under maximum security guard in the military hospital at the barracks, his right leg shattered from the two bullets he had taken when he tried to run for it on the bridge. Now Pennyweather drove fast and expertly south, the powerful Mercedes 350SEL Manners had put at their disposal eating up the short distance between Lauenburg and Scharnebeck.

'How are we going to play this?' Pennyweather said.

'Let's see what the police have got in mind,' Garrett told him. 'I don't want any of our people trying to take them.'

They came around a long bend and crossed the bridge over the Neetze canal.

'Here we are,' Pennyweather said. 'Scharnebeck.'

At the end of the street Pennyweather came to a stop behind the surveillance team's VW Kombi. Garrett got out of the Mercedes and followed him over as

Pennyweather tapped on the sliding panel door. It slid open, and a round, bespectacled face appeared.

'I'm Garrett,' he said, holding up the ID. 'Our pigeons still in place?'

'Yes, sir,' the technician said. 'You want us to stay on this?'

'No, you can disengage,' Garrett said. 'The police will take it from here.'

'The head honcho's over there,' the technician said. 'Inspector Weidemann, State Prosecutor's Office.'

He nodded at a dark green Volvo 780 parked across the street. Weidemann was sitting in the driver's seat. Next to him was Gottfried, drinking coffee from a thermos-bottle top. Neither of them so much as lifted a hand in greeting. Garrett checked the street; there were a lot more cars parked at the curb than might have been expected on a Sunday morning. Once he heard the interrupted crackle of a police radio. Subtle as hell, he thought. He went over to the Volvo and Weidemann wound down the window.

'Don't get involved with this, Garrett,' Weidemann warned him. 'You have no power of arrest, no jurisdiction.'

'I know that,' Garrett said. 'How are you going to play it?'

'I've got a special squad ready. Blue van outside the garage.'

Garrett checked his watch: 10:15. 'The convoy will be here in fifteen minutes.'

'We're just getting ready to move,' Weidemann said. 'We'll wait for them on the bridge. The minute they get out of the car, we'll take them.'

'Could be iffy,' Garrett told him. 'They're heavily armed, Inspector. And they've probably got a couple of hundred pounds of C4 on board.'

'We know all that,' Weidemann said impatiently. 'What would you suggest?'

'You just told me to stay out of it.'

The policeman made an angry sound. 'Excuse me,' he said. 'I have things to do.'

'Me too,' Garrett said. He went over to the Mercedes and got in. Pennyweather was up the street somewhere, dispersing the surveillance teams that had shadowed Davy McGinnis and Pat Mullan. Garrett slid the car into gear and eased away from the curb, heading out of town. The tan

Opel Manta was parked just off the road about two hundred meters on the right, its windows slightly misted. As he drew level with the car, he saw the driver lean forward to start the engine prior to moving off. That left him with absolutely no options at all. If McGinnis and Mullan got to the bridge . . . He reached into the glove compartment and took out the Icom IC2 walkie-talkie. As the Opel signaled left, pulling out onto the road, Garrett pushed the send button on the transmitter.

Three hundred meters behind him he heard a huge roar, and a pale yellow ball of fire mushroomed upward. A moment later he felt the blast hit the rear of his car, moving it on the road. Transformed in microseconds into a blazing hulk of twisted metal, what was left of the Opel was hurled fifty feet into the air, landing upside down thirty meters off the road in a plowed field. Garrett drove on until he came to the bridge over the canal. He stopped the car and dropped the walkie-talkie into the water, then turned the Mercedes around. By the time he got back to where the explosion had taken place, the road was packed with police cars and uniformed men. A *schupo* waved him down.

'Go back, get away from here!' the policeman snapped. Garrett got out of the car and let the man see his ID. He went across the road, stepping carefully around the edges of the smoking four-foot-deep crater where the explosion had taken place. Through the great scorched gap in the hedgerow he could see what was left of the Opel out in the middle of the field, still burning furiously. Inspector Weidemann and his assistant came back toward the road, stepping from furrow to furrow. The policeman's face was twisted with anger and disgust.

'What happened, Inspector?' Garrett asked innocently.

Weidemann looked at him sharply. 'Where the hell did you disappear to, Garrett?' he ground out. 'I told you to keep your damned nose out of this thing!'

'I was doing just that, Inspector,' Garrett said disarmingly. 'I was on my way to Lüneburg when I heard the explosion.'

'You drove right past the target vehicle!' Gottfried snapped. 'They might have recognized you!'

'Mullan and McGinnis didn't know me by sight,' Garrett said. He looked across at the burning wreck in the field.

'Go and look in his car,' Weidemann told Gottfried. 'If there's any kind of a transmitter in there, Garrett, I am going to see to it that you go to jail for a very long time.'

'Save yourself the trouble,' Garrett told him. 'There's nothing in the car. They must have set their own bomb off accidentally. What we in England call an 'own goal'.'

'Go and look anyway,' Weidemann growled. Gottfried went over to the Mercedes, checked around inside, then shut the door. He looked at Weidemann and shook his head.

Weidemann regarded Garrett with narrowed eyes. 'I know you did it, Garrett,' he said softly. 'That's your job, isn't it, killing terrorists?'

'Somebody's got to do it,' Garrett said.

Everyone in London was talking about the glorious weather. The Thames sparkled like a wide silver ribbon sprinkled with diamonds. It was good to be back.

Garrett turned away from the window. Jessica was lying on the floor in front of the fireplace, newspapers strewn all around her. She frowned furiously as she read, then rolled on one side and held up a page.

'Was this your operation?' she asked.

'Let me see.'

VICTIMS OF BOMB
HIGH ON RUC WANTED LIST

One of the two IRA men who blew themselves up with their own bomb in Scharnebeck, a small German town near Lüneburg, was wanted in Northern Ireland for at least twelve killings, security sources said last night.

Patrick Mullan, 28, was rated 'most highly sought' by the Royal

Ulster Constabulary, and his death is believed to have prevented a major IRA attack. Mullan and David McGinnis, 24, died when their bomb — believed to have contained two hundred pounds of explosive — exploded in the car they were using.

The IRA said the two men died 'on active service' and as the result of an accident.

★   ★   ★

'Yes,' Garrett said. 'That was my operation.'

'It wasn't Hennessy, then?'

'He was there,' Garrett said. 'But he ditched his people and got away.'

'What an awful way to die,' Jessica said, and shuddered.

'They were going to use the bomb to blow up unarmed soldiers going back to barracks, Jess,' he told her. 'God alone knows how many men they would have killed if they had succeeded.'

'I know,' she said, quietly, and he knew

what she was thinking. They had discussed it many times.

You see it all in black and white, don't you? she had said on one occasion. Does that make it easier?

Nothing ever makes it easier, Jess.

You're not interested in their causes, their reasons for doing what they are doing?

I'm not a psychologist, Jess. My job is fighting terrorism.

Killing.

If necessary, yes. That's part of it.

Why, Charles? Why do you do it?

Someone has to. Someone has to make the stand, someone has to say, 'No, you will not.'

He believed that. There had been a time when he had his doubts about the rights and wrongs of it, but that had been before he saw the bright bloody flayed strips of meat hanging on the trees at the site of a crashed airplane brought down by a terrorist bomb, the charred remnants of what had been children in the wreckage of a torched church, the jibbering wrecks of women tortured with cattle prods and broken bottles, the jellied bodies of babies used to shield assassins from return fire. No cause, no belief justified inflicting such suffering.

You have to believe that. You have to believe it, or you couldn't do what you do.

She was right. He had to carry inside himself the conviction that what he was doing was for the greater good. He understood, of course, that many terrorists believed implicitly that what they were doing was also for the greater good, but he knew that they were wrong. If history had taught men anything, it was that nobody ever won wars, that killing — one man or a million — did not make your cause more just, your claims more believable, your demands more persuasive.

Ordinary people had a right to expect to live a decent life, to watch their kids grow up and get married and have kids of their own, to succeed or fail or win or lose. The madman who wanted to take that away from them with guns or bombs forfeited his own rights. This was

Garrett's credo; he had to live by it and maybe one day he would die by it. That fact alone freed him from the need to justify or apologize. In his jungle all the animals were feral.

'Listen,' he said. 'We've got the whole day to ourselves. Let's not waste it.'

She looked up at him from beneath her eyebrows. 'I entirely agree,' she said. 'So let's start by having some of that smoked salmon you bought at Harrods. Thinly sliced brown bread, lemon juice, black pepper. A bottle of Krug.'

'Your wish is my command,' he said. 'And then?'

The dark devil was dancing in her eyes again. 'Oh,' she said airily. 'We'll think of something.'

THE END

We do hope that you have enjoyed reading this large print book.

Did you know that all of our titles are available for purchase?

We publish a wide range of high quality large print books including:
Romances, Mysteries, Classics
General Fiction
Non Fiction and Westerns

Special interest titles available in large print are:
The Little Oxford Dictionary
Music Book, Song Book
Hymn Book, Service Book

Also available from us courtesy of Oxford University Press:
Young Readers' Dictionary
(large print edition)
Young Readers' Thesaurus
(large print edition)

For further information or a free brochure, please contact us at:
Ulverscroft Large Print Books Ltd.,
The Green, Bradgate Road, Anstey,
Leicester, LE7 7FU, England.
Tel: (00 44) **0116 236 4325**
Fax: (00 44) **0116 234 0205**

SHERLOCK HOLMES AND THE GIANT'S HAND

Matthew Book

Three of the great detective's most singular cases, mentioned tantalisingly briefly in the original narratives, are now presented here in full. The curious disappearance of Mr Stanislaus Addleton leads Holmes and Watson ultimately to the mysterious 'Giant's Hand'. What peculiar brand of madness drives Colonel Warburton to repeatedly attack an amiable village vicar? Then there is the murderous tragedy of the Abernetty family, the solving of which hinges on the depth to which the parsley had sunk into the butter on a hot day . . .